Praise for *Breathe Into Me*

"Compelling and engrossing. The romance was fabulous, and I loved the sweet, slow-burn feel."   —*The Book Pushers*

"Intriguing, gripping, romantic, and suspenseful! *Breathe into Me* is a fast read, and it never has a dull moment!"
                                                                                —*A Bookish Escape*

"Wow. This story was captivating and enthralling and had me on edge throughout the entire thing. Sara Fawkes's writing style blew me away and kept me intrigued until the very end with mystery, drama, and heartbreak all in one book."
                                                                                —*Bout-A-Book Blog*

"An amazing story. *Breathe into Me* makes you look at your own life and truly be thankful for what you have, and to value the mistakes that you've made because they've made you into who you are today."   —*Bits of Books*

"*Breathe into Me* is an intriguing story full of secrets, heartbreak, drama, passion, learning to forgive, and believing in yourself. A beautiful, emotional story that will warm your heart and leave you with a crush on Everett."
                                                                                —*Book Crush*

Also by Sara Fawkes

Anything He Wants
Castaway

Breathe into Me

Sara Fawkes

St. Martin's Griffin ☕ New York

BREATHE INTO ME. Copyright © 2014 by Sara Fawkes. All rights reserved. Printed in the United States of America. For information, address St. Martin's Press, 175 Fifth Avenue, New York, N.Y. 10010.

www.stmartins.com

The Library of Congress Cataloging-in-Publication Data is available upon request.

ISBN 978-1-250-04851-6 (trade paperback)
ISBN 978-1-4668-4953-2 (e-book)

First published in e-original format in April 2014 by St. Martin's Griffin

St. Martin's Griffin books may be purchased for educational, business, or promotional use. For information on bulk purchases, please contact Macmillan Corporate and Premium Sales Department at 1-800-221-7945, extension 5442, or write specialmarkets@macmillan.com.

First St. Martin's Griffin Paperback Edition: August 2014

10 9 8 7 6 5 4 3 2 1

acknowledgments

Books are often community efforts, and this one is no exception. A BIG thank-you goes out to my editor, Rose Hilliard, for having the courage to fix the messiest first draft in the world; Lauren Hawkeye-Jameson, for listening to me rant about what a hack I was, then calling BS; and my Street Team of Awesome for being, well, awesome. I heart you all SO BIG!!!

Breathe into Me

chapter ONE ❦

A handsome boy was lying in bed behind me, but the condescending leer on his face made me want to run away.

Too bad he was my boyfriend.

"Why are you getting all dressed up? It's barely eight o'clock."

I ignored him and hooked the bra behind my back, picking up my clothes from the floor before ducking into the bathroom. I wanted to lock the door, but Macon hated that. I didn't want him to get mad or break down the door, not tonight. I should have been out the door half an hour ago but I had to clean up after sex with him—he liked it dirty and rough. Nothing a washcloth and some foundation couldn't fix, but the memory was an oily stain on my mind.

I played with my blond hair, contemplating what quick style would work for going out, then grabbed a hair tie and put it back into a ponytail. As I looked through my makeup, the door slid open and Macon squeezed into the small bathroom behind me. I braced myself against the sink when his hands grabbed my hips, his flaccid groin thrusting against my backside. One hand crept up to my neck, pulling me back against him and squeezing enough to restrict the blood flow. "What's your rush, Lacey?" he murmured in my ear.

"I promised Ashley I'd drive tonight."

The hand around my throat squeezed harder, and I started to tremble as my airway was blocked. Macon thought playing rough like this was somehow sexy—that women liked a man who took control—but I had a feeling he just got off on my fear.

I swallowed, or at least tried to, around the tight grip on my windpipe. "Ashley needs a designated driver," I rasped, putting my hand on his in what I hoped he'd see as an appeasing gesture. "I don't want her to get hurt."

My evident altruism finally won a smile from him. "You're a good girl," he said, letting go of my neck and patting my cheek. "You promise to think on what we talked about?"

Angry words at his condescending manner rose like bile, but all I felt was relief when he stepped away. I nodded silently, not trusting myself to speak. Coughing would only make him angry, so I held my breath until he closed the bathroom door behind him. Only then did I sit down on the toilet, trying to take slow breaths through my bruised throat.

At times like this, I had to tell myself over and over that being with him was better than being at home, but it no longer felt like the truth. The way he acted sometimes sickened me, made me afraid, but I stayed silent. At least with him I had some measure of respect, and people didn't bother me.

Much.

My makeup was mostly done, but I put an extra layer on my neck in case the skin showed signs of bruising. I'd grown very adept at hiding the bruises and scratches; he'd certainly given me more than enough practice. Macon was lying on the couch as I hunted around for my shoes. Outside, someone honked, and, peeking out the blinds, I saw Ashley's car.

Shit. She wasn't going to be happy about having to pick me up.

"Looking for these?"

Macon held up my heels with one hand, and I forced myself not to snatch them from him. Trying to put them on while walking, I opened the door and was barely through the entryway when hands grabbed me and pulled me back inside. Slamming me back against the wall beside the door, Macon lowered his head and kissed me brutally. He was all tongue and teeth, his hands grabbing my breasts and twisting painfully.

"Should I tell her to leave without you?"

I shook my head, trying to keep the sudden panic off my face. "I'm her DD, remember? I'd feel terrible if she got hurt driving home."

The darkening of his gorgeous blue eyes made me tense in preparation for his answer, but he finally let me go. "I'll see you later, then," he said, the words more a dark promise than a farewell.

My legs were shaking as I got into the small car. Ashley had the music blaring, a sure sign that she was pissed, but she gave me a cheerful smile that didn't reach her eyes. "Looks like the boy toy can't keep his hands off you."

"Yeah. Look, Ashley, I'm sorry I didn't get to your house. Macon wouldn't let me leave and ripped my other top when he—"

"Meh. Bored now."

I knew Ashley was a fair-weather friend, the kind you

went clubbing with but didn't talk to much besides that, but her casual brush-off of my problems hurt. I'd been there for her when her last boyfriend beat her enough to draw blood, but she couldn't be bothered to do the same for me. She started chatting about one of her other friends who'd gotten pregnant without knowing who the daddy was, and I kept my mouth shut, letting her ramble and pretending interest.

"Ready for a night of fun?"

I shrugged, not caring either way. Lately, barhopping and clubbing had ceased being fun and turned into an excuse to get out of whichever house I was staying in at the time. I didn't answer and Ashley didn't seem to care, continuing to prattle on as we headed toward the bar.

I couldn't remember ever being sober at this bar before, which was probably on account of how lame it was without the haze of alcohol.

Ashley had worked up a buzz right out of the gate, hitting on a few of the older gentlemen and getting shots for both of us. She'd taken four, including the two bought for me, saying I was the designated driver for the night. One of the men, a forty-something with a gold band on his left hand, had tried to pull me down onto his lap. I'd deftly maneuvered my way out of it, laughing and patting his cheek while giving him an easy view down my shirt. That had seemed to be enough for him, and thankfully he'd let me go.

The hotel bar was packed. Summer had hit, and people had returned from college or come to take advantage of the area's beaches. The romantic prospects were much more abundant, but I couldn't make myself care. The thought of any more relationships didn't interest me in the slightest.

"Ooh, who's that delicious piece of ass over there?"

I looked over at Ashley, who was fiddling with her beer bottle label, and then followed her gaze across the room. I zeroed in on the blond boy at the table. "Is that Trent Maverick?"

"Who?"

I'd forgotten that Ashley had gone to a different high school than me. It was easy to forget our age difference. At twenty-two, the brunette was three years older than me, but with her petite frame she looked fresh out of high school. "I went to high school with him," I said over the band's music.

"Did he play any sports?"

He hadn't been on my radar in school. I shrugged. "Probably."

"I'd fuck him in a heartbeat."

The crude way she said it made me wince. Ashley's brain-to-mouth filter was always MIA, but it grew worse when she was drunk. She'd gotten us into trouble more than once by saying the wrong thing at the wrong time. The girl had been constantly moving since we'd arrived at the bar, and I felt like a babysitter trying to keep her out of trouble.

A predatory smile crossed Ashley's lips. "Oh yeah, he's so mine."

I fought the urge to roll my eyes. I was too tired to argue or play games tonight. I hadn't had anything to drink, and I just wanted to find somewhere to lie down. I needed sleep; my two jobs had me running ragged lately, but Ashley had insisted I come with her tonight.

Ashley grabbed my arm, tugging me around the dance floor toward the occupied table. I went along willingly enough but wasn't in the mood to do anything more than sit.

"Quit being such a spoilsport, just take the other one."

Other one?

I hadn't seen the other boy from across the room, but as I drew closer I realized Trent may not have been who Ashley was talking about. Whereas the blond boy I knew was leaning forward, eagerly watching two girls dancing nearby, the dark-haired boy beside him was lounging back in his seat. The tabletop was filled with beer bottles, but it was impossible to tell who had drunk what.

"Hi," Ashley said loudly, still managing to sound sultry even when nearly yelling. "Is this seat taken?"

Trent looked at her, and he seemed to appreciate what he saw, but Ashley only had eyes for the boy beside him. She did what I called her power pose, arching her back to better display her assets. The dark-haired boy ignored her, however, his gaze instead moving to me. Something sparked in his eyes, and I felt goose bumps break out over my skin.

Butterflies fluttered in my belly. Suddenly nervous, I looked away to the dance floor, hoping he would stop staring. My own reaction bothered me; I didn't like how the other boy made me feel. Ashley slanted me a dark look but kept her smile in place to keep up appearances. Without waiting for an answer, she took the seat next to her target. She had no qualms moving in for the kill and leaving me to fend for myself. Reining in my annoyance, I pulled up a chair across the table beside the familiar blond boy, who finally seemed to notice me.

"Didn't I go to high school with you?"

I nodded mutely. Trent was staring at me, a slightly confused look on his face as he tried to place me, then he snapped his fingers. "You're Lacey, right? What happened to you? I know you didn't graduate with us."

"I dropped out before Christmas."

I kept waiting for him to recall me, my body tense and waiting for his reaction, but he just cocked his head to one side. "You dropped out in the middle of senior year?"

"It wasn't the greatest decision in the world," I hedged, uncomfortable at being called out. Even two years later, the decision still haunted me. So close, and I'd just given up.

"Well, it's cool to see you again."

I blinked several times as he turned his attention toward Ashley. His words seemed sincere enough, and I looked away, surprised by how that fact shocked me. Our school had been small, but apparently he really didn't remember much about me except my name. Maybe it was a blessing in disguise.

Across from me, Ashley was trying to entice the other boy into dancing, with no luck. I could feel his eyes on me, but I didn't look back at him, hoping he would eventually ignore me. I didn't miss Ashley's glare, however. She didn't seem to like the fact that I'd managed to attract the attention of both guys, and as usual it was all my fault.

Typical.

Abandoning the dark-haired boy, she pasted a big smile on her face and held her hand out to Trent. "Wanna dance?" It was obvious she was trying to steal him away from me, make me jealous maybe, but I didn't care and Trent didn't seem to mind. He jumped up, eager to get close to the perky brunette, and followed her out on the dance floor.

Once they left, silence reigned at the table. I felt rude ignoring the other boy, but for some reason he made me jittery. The band continued to loudly butcher Johnny Cash, and conversation throughout the room only added to the raucous din.

"Are the bands always this bad?"

I bit my lip at his question. He had a deep voice that sent shivers through me, and I didn't like my reaction to him. "Only if we're lucky." I glanced at him and then looked away again. He was leaning toward me, obviously interested. I'd tried to ignore him, not wanting to rile Ashley, but he really was handsome. There was a ruggedness about him that was totally unlike Macon's pretty-boy good looks, and I could feel my attraction building. That only made ignoring him more imperative, but I hated being rude. "At least this time the singer isn't completely tone deaf. The keyboardist can't keep the tempo to save his life, though."

"Do you play?"

I nodded. "Piano."

"Really." The news perked his interest. "What kind of music do you play?"

"Classical." It had been a handful of years since my fingers had touched ivory, but, despite my tension, I smiled at the memory. "I was really good at it, too."

"Was? You don't play anymore?"

The smile slipped from my lips, and I gave a jerky shake of my head. Eager to change the subject, I continued hastily, "You're not from around here, are you?"

He shook his head. "I'm house-sitting down here with

Trent for the summer," he said, and then held out his hand. "I'm Everett Ward."

His hand was soft but thick and heavy; the touch made the butterflies in my stomach dance faster. "Lacey St. James." I cleared my throat, trying to act like his proximity wasn't getting to me. "What house are y'all watching?"

"It's down by the ocean. Really big, too, there's a guest-house and boat storage behind the house."

"Are y'all staying in the Pass? The Cove?" At his blank look, I added, "You know, Oyster Cove, or Bay St. Louis, or Pass Christian, or . . . ?"

Understanding entered his eyes as I named the area's coastal towns. "Oyster Cove. Trent is friends with the family. It's a big white mansion off the coast highway."

I blinked. "You talking about the Plymouth plantation house?" I asked.

"Didn't know it was named."

"Do you know y'all are house-sitting for one of the richest families in the county?"

He shrugged, looking back to the dance floor. "Far as I can tell, they haven't lived there for a while."

I might not have originally been from this little corner of southern Mississippi, but I'd learned a thing or two over the last few years. I'd only ever seen the large white antebellum house from the highway, nestled back on the massive prop-erty amid regal trees far older than me. I looked back out over the dance floor, a little amazed. "Nice place." *An under-statement.*

Everett shrugged again, but I saw a smile play at the

corners of his mouth. For some reason, that made me warm up inside. I got the feeling he didn't smile much, and the lop-sided tilt of his lips made him even more handsome. A lock of dark hair fell across his forehead, and I had to resist the in-sane urge to push it back so I could see his face. He had on a black button-up, long-sleeved shirt with expensive-looking jeans. While he didn't really look out of place in the bar, something still managed to set him apart.

"Unfortunately," he continued, "they don't have a piano, or I'd ask you to come play."

I'm sure you would. Reality crashed in, and I flushed. Boys had been inviting me over for years now with similar lines, and some that weren't as subtle. A bitter gall worked its way up my throat and I swallowed it back. Regardless of what my heart wanted to believe, experience told me I couldn't trust him.

My mood soured by my own thoughts, I stood up. "I need to use the bathroom," I mumbled. Not caring if he heard me, I walked away into the crowd. My view of him was immedi-ately swallowed up and I let out a relieved sigh, ignoring my disappointment. The boy made me nervous, and I couldn't quite explain why. Maybe it was because part of me wanted to trust him, which was a ridiculous idea. I didn't know the boy at all, other than that he was a friend of Trent's.

The bathroom was just inside the corridor leading to the back, but as I reached the end of the hallway an arm snapped into view, blocking my path. "Where've you been all my life, beautiful?"

I whirled to see Macon standing beside me. He was wear-ing slacks and a tight blue shirt that showed off his muscles.

His golden hair was slicked back, and the grin he gave me had a decidedly wicked gleam. Suddenly jittery, I tried to hide my anxiety as he stepped close. If he'd seen me sitting with the other boy . . .

"You look good enough to eat tonight," he murmured, running my ponytail through his fingers. I fought back a flinch, but he didn't grab my hair like I thought he would. His hand slid down my shoulder and around my forearm. "Why don't we go talk outside?"

"Macon, I gotta pee." Sometimes being blunt disarmed him enough that I could get away, but the tactic didn't work tonight.

"Come on, I need your help."

Briefly, I thought about fighting myself free—I was in public, there wasn't much he could do to me here—but ultimately decided against making a scene. In my experience, it was easier to just get things over with quickly and go back inside. When our path took us past the storage areas toward the back entrance, however, I started getting nervous again. There was no breaking his hold now; as he drew me farther away from the crowds, his grip on my arm tightened painfully.

It's hard to dig in your heels when you're wearing three-inch stilettos, but I tried anyway. I didn't know what was going on, but I knew for sure I wasn't going to like it.

Whistles and catcalls preceded us as we stepped outside into the Mississippi night. The back of the bar let out into a dark area that housed the bar's Dumpsters and sat adjacent to the connecting hotel. A single light beside the rear door lit the scene enough for me to recognize three men standing nearby. Two of them were familiar, Macon's friends, although

I didn't know their names. They were passing around a small glass pipe, but the third boy pocketed it when Macon closed the heavy door behind us.

"Damn man, she's even hotter in person!"

Macon just laughed, a nasty sound in the darkness. "I only keep the very best."

"I watched what you did to them other boys." The shortest of the bunch stepped forward, his smile crooked from the chew wedged beneath his lower lip. I tried to pull away but Macon held me firm. "Been wantin' to meet you ever since."

"These are my good friends," Macon murmured as I began to tremble. "Won't you at least say hello?"

Panic welled up and I pried at his fingers on my arm, but he only dug in deeper. The pain increased my feeling of helplessness as the short boy reached down and blatantly rubbed himself through his low-slung pants. His clothes seemed less a fashion statement and more a consequence of how thin he was, but his eyes gleamed eagerly in the dim light. "How's she with givin' head?" he asked.

"Pretty good, actually." Macon jerked my arm down and, unbalanced, I stumbled to my knees with a cry. "Now, baby," he all but crooned, "I'd hate for you to prove me wrong. What do you say we show them how good you really are?"

Sobbing, I tried to get up but was pushed back down by Macon. This time, he did grab my hair, holding me in place while the short guy fumbled with his pants. "She ain't gonna bite me, is she?"

This isn't happening, tell me this isn't happening. I moaned, panic-stricken, and grabbed at Macon's wrist. He just jerked my head back, throwing me off balance again, as the other boy positioned himself in front of me. "God, I wanna come all over her ti—"

The door beside us burst open, and someone came stumbling out. Startled, everyone froze as the stranger staggered drunkenly to the wall and pulled down his zipper. There was the sizzling sound of urine splashing against the hotel stucco, and only then did he seem to notice us. "Hey," he slurred, giving us a small wave. "Don't mind me."

"Get the *fuck* out of here," Macon hollered, releasing my hair and pointing at the door.

I took the only chance I knew I'd get and stumbled across the uneven ground, half-crawling to the door. Barely managing to evade Macon's grab for me again, I hurried inside the corridor, rushing as fast as I could for the safety of the bar. I heard him call out my name, and then the swell of music surrounded me.

chapter two ❧

The restrooms were at the back of the building, butting up against the hotel lobby, and I slipped inside and into one of the few empty stalls. My chest felt like it was about to explode and I sat down hard on the toilet seat. Staring at the metal door, I squeezed my eyes shut and covered my mouth to muffle my sobs.

How did it get this bad? My life wasn't roses, but nothing like this had ever happened to me. I'd known that Macon was trouble, but I never thought he'd go this far. As long as I gave him what he wanted, things were usually okay. He'd offered to let me live with him, an escape from my own wretched home life. I'd actually been seriously thinking of taking him up on it.

Was this what I had to look forward to, being whored out to all his friends?

The bathroom door banged open, and a couple girls spilled inside. "Oh my god, I want to have his babies!"

I recognized Ashley's voice, but stayed quiet. Right now I didn't want to deal with the girl; hell, I didn't want to deal with my life. To keep from being discovered, I lifted my feet up onto the toilet bowl, hugging my knees to my chest.

"Oh yeah, he's hot! I wanna dance with him next."

I hadn't seen Samantha come into the bar. She was an-other one of Ashley's cronies, an older girl who liked to pick up younger guys. I wasn't sure how old she was, but I would have guessed close to thirty. Either that, or smoking had aged her like it did my grandma.

"No, he's just cute. I'm talking about Macon. Did you see him all hot and bothered just now?"

"I thought you were talking about the blond one."

"Meh, he's not my type. I sicced Lacey on him, but she's fuck-all as a wingman. Bitch cockblocked me on the other guy."

My throat closed at her words, and I had to fight not to make a sound. The noise of the club right outside the door allowed me some measure of anonymity, but I suddenly found it difficult to breathe.

"The blond one's cute enough, but I wanted that other boy, the one who came with whatever-his-name-is I danced with. *Gawd*, he's sexy!"

"Ooh, you totally gotta point him out." Samantha giggled. "Why do you even pretend to be friends with Lacey anyway? She's so boring."

"I know, right? Plus she's a total skank."

I couldn't breathe. Hands flattened to the walls beside me, I dipped my head down between my knees, struggling to get air into my quaking lungs. My whole body trembled with hu-miliation, small breaths tearing from my mouth. They were quiet enough to be covered by the music in the bar, and I cov-ered my mouth to hold them inside.

Ashley had been a constant in my life for nearly a year.

I was her chauffeur and party buddy, but we rarely had mingled outside the club scene. The last time she'd called needing my help, I'd come running, only to have her so-called emergency be that a boy wouldn't go out with her unless she found someone for his father. Namely, me. She hadn't spoken to me for nearly a month when I'd walked away from that "opportunity."

Dry heaves wracked my body as the two girls left, giggling like loons, but I swallowed them back, taking quick short breaths. I had to get out of there. My life was nothing but a huge lie, one big hellhole that never ended. I was tired of perpetuating it, allowing it to control me and my decisions.

When I'd steadied myself, I pulled open the stall door and checked myself in the mirror. Wetting my fingers, I cleaned up the smudged mascara under my eyes and then exited the bathroom. The cacophony around me added to the pounding in my head as I made a beeline for our table.

Everett was still sitting back in his chair, just taking in the surroundings, but when he saw my face he sat up straight. "What's wrong?"

Everything is wrong, that's the problem.

"I have to go."

"Did something happen?"

Telling him anything about my pathetic life would only make me feel worse. I grabbed my purse off the table, eager to get out of there as fast as possible, but a nagging suspicion made me pause and check my wallet. I cursed and, ignoring the dark-haired boy, stomped over to the bar across the room. The place was packed and the bartender busy, but something must have shown in my face because she came up to me immediately. "Oh baby, I'm not gonna like this one, am I?"

I'd only seen Cherise in the bar, and I really liked her. She had a way of getting straight to the point that I appreciated. You always knew where you stood with her, and she didn't tolerate bullshit. "I think Ashley used my card to start her tab."

Cherise gave a low whistle. "Hold on, let me check."

The man beside me vacated his seat, and Everett slid over into his place. "Is everything all right?" he asked again.

I swallowed and shook my head, unable to meet his eyes. At that moment, I was barely holding myself together; I couldn't bear to talk about it now. I wanted to ignore him and leave the bar, but he didn't seem to get the hint. I was still reeling from everything that had happened in too short a time, and I couldn't take much more tonight.

Cherise appeared a few seconds later and handed me a card. Sure enough, it was mine. "Goddammit," I muttered, stuffing it blindly back into my purse. "How much was she up to?"

"Baby girl, you don't want to know."

I felt like crying. She must have seen it in my face because she leaned over the bar, waving a hand to grab my attention. "Look, this time it's on the house. But try to keep your stuff safer, and tell your friend she's cut off for the rest of the night."

Considering it wasn't even midnight yet, I knew Ashley wouldn't like that news. And I didn't fucking care. "She's not my friend." *Not anymore.* She'd once told me she did this kind of things to girls she pretended to be friends with, stealing their cards and starting up her own bar tabs. She'd sworn that I'd *never* fall into that category.

The joke was once again on me.

Everett was still there, silently watching my humiliation. I couldn't take his staring anymore and pushed away from the bar. "I'm not drunk enough for this shit," I muttered darkly, my fingernails digging into the faux leather purse. Alcohol always made things easier, even if I regretted my decisions in the morning.

"Think a few shots will loosen your knees a bit?"

The vulgar statement made me freeze. Thick arms wrapped themselves around my shoulders, and Macon pressed his groin into my backside. My hands clenched around the strap of my purse, my whole body tensing with dread. Macon laid a kiss on the top of my head, and I flinched, the trembling beginning anew. Where once I'd found comfort in the beautiful man's arms, now I couldn't get his words out of my head. *What do you say we show them how good you really are.*

Was I really that blind?

"You ran off on me, baby. A man gets worried."

His arms were like an iron prison, pinning me to the bar. I tried to shrug him off, too petrified to say a word, but he only held me tighter. "Macon, I was just . . ."

He ignored me, dipping his head close beside my ear. I could smell the alcohol on his breath as he murmured, "Why don't we go for a ride and talk about some things?"

He wasn't asking a question; Macon expected me to meekly get into that jacked-up truck of his like I always did. He'd insinuated himself into my life right as I was trying to change myself, trying to turn away from the dark path I was on. He'd whispered about love and escape, promising me a safe haven with him. That promise of security had blinded me to so much. I'd known that I couldn't trust him, but my need for a fresh start had convinced me I could make it work.

When did my life get so fucked up?

"I'm going home," I mumbled, twisting and trying to duck out of his arms, but Macon pushed me back against the bar.

"No, I'm going to buy you a drink. Then we're going to take a ride."

His hand clamped around my upper arm, thumb digging cruelly between the muscles. He smiled again at my gasp, the expression a direct contrast to the tightening hand around my arm. "You can sleep afterward. C'mon, baby, just one drink."

I struggled against his grip. "Macon, no."

Terror bloomed in my heart as his face twisted. It was like he was trying to smile, but the expression warred with how he really felt. "What do you mean, no?"

I cringed away as another voice spoke up. "Are you illiterate as well as stupid? The lady said no."

The dark-haired boy I'd been trying to ignore all night was staring at Macon, eyes narrowed. Macon's lip curled in distaste. "Fuck off, loser."

Everett moved in close, narrowly insinuating himself between us until he was face-to-face with Macon. Macon was taller by an inch or two, but Everett had more muscle. Everett's face was motionless and chillingly blank, but Macon turned red with fury. "Who the *fuck* is he?"

"Hey. HEY!" Glass shattered behind the bar, and all our gazes swiveled toward Cherise. The bartender held the top of an empty beer bottle, jagged glass points still dripping with the remains of the liquid inside. "You two," she said, indicating Macon and Everett with the jagged weapon, "can take that outside, but *she* stays here."

Macon let me go and I stumbled back to the wood bar. The crash had drawn unwanted attention; our disagreement had been lost in the roar of the club noise until then. Mortified, I couldn't do anything more than cling to the wood, wishing this were just some bad dream.

I cringed as Macon reached for me, but he just smoothed a strand of hair behind my ear. "C'mon, baby, I'm not mad. Why don't you stop making a scene and just come with me. You don't want to disappoint me, do you?"

Disappoint me. He said that to me a lot. That line, I realized, always made me go back to him. Even now, I could feel what the words were doing, eating at my soul and begging me to apologize for whatever I'd done. But I still felt my lips form my response, even if it was too low for anyone else to hear. "No."

I knew what was about to happen the instant I saw Macon's face twist. I flinched away, waiting for a blow that never came. Macon's hand was wrenched from my arm, and there was a popping noise of flesh on flesh. I turned back just in time to see Macon fall flat on the floor. Everett, his face still cool, stood in front of me, fists at his side as he stared down at the blond man. He was so still now, I wouldn't have known he'd knocked Macon to the floor if I hadn't seen it. His motions had been a blur, and he stared coldly down as if daring Macon to get back up.

"The lady's spoken," Cherise said behind me as two big men in dark shirts appeared. "And you can go to hell if you think you're ever coming back in this bar again."

"I don't see any *ladies* here," Macon snarled at her, wiping at his mouth.

Cherise's lips thinned, the hand around the broken bottle tightening. "Take this piece of shit out of here before I do something I *won't* regret."

One man picked up Macon from the floor while another reached for Everett. I laid my hand on the bouncer's arm and looked at Cherise. "He's with me," I said, not wanting to see him tossed out.

The bouncer looked over at Cherise, who nodded. The second man took Macon's other arm and the two dragged him out of the bar.

"You little *bitch*," I heard Macon shout over the din of the bar before he was ejected.

Once they were out, everyone around us turned back to whatever they'd been doing before the spectacle. My legs were too shaky to walk in the narrow heels I'd worn to the club. At the edge of the crowd I saw Ashley watching me, distaste written all over her face.

"Do you need a ride home?"

I looked up into Everett's face, then back down. His voice was soft, even in the loud bar, and the kindness was almost too much to take. Close to tears, I nodded and fished through my purse for the keys. I was supposed to be Ashley's designated driver, but I didn't care what happened to her now. I turned to Cherise. "See to it that my ex-friend gets these, please."

Cherise nodded. "Will do."

I stared at the floor, wishing it would swallow me whole. Eyes around the room burned into my back, and I knew my name would be on the rumor mill by morning. Maybe I should have been used to that by now, but the thought made my heart hurt.

"We can go through the hotel. I'm parked around the side."

The thought of going out the back entrance again made me nervous, but I knew it was the right choice. There was no doubt in my mind that Macon was waiting outside the front door for us to leave that way. This bar could be rough, and while the bouncers inside wouldn't let anyone fight, the parking lot wasn't safe. Issues were frequently resolved out there, usually violently, and I didn't want to take that risk tonight.

Everett laid his hand on my elbow and I flinched away, moving quickly to the hotel door. I could feel eyes from all sides silently judging me. *There goes that tramp.* Even if I couldn't hear them, I knew what they were thinking.

Once we got outside Everett took the lead as we made a beeline for his vehicle. I saw no sign of Macon but didn't breathe a sigh of relief until I was inside the car. It was a ratty old thing, not quite what I'd expected, but the interior was nice and the engine started up smoothly.

"Where do you live?"

My distrust reared up again, but I tamped it down. He needed to know where to drop me off at least. "Closer to the coast. I'll show you when we get there." Street signs were impossible to read in the dark anyway.

He nodded and pulled out of the parking lot. As we pulled past the entrance to the bar, I saw Macon outside the door, craning his head to see inside. Bitterness churned in my gut at the thought of having to face him again, and I crouched low in my seat until we were past.

"You okay?"

I spared a quick glance at Everett and then shook my head. "I just want to go home."

He nodded and stayed silent as we headed south. The clock told me it wasn't yet midnight. I couldn't remember the last time I'd gone home so early on a Saturday night. I was beat, though; between a long day and a night from hell, I wasn't sure I wanted to wake up the next morning.

There was no conversation other than directions, and for that I was grateful. Everett was little more than a stranger, but I desperately wanted to trust him and that scared me. It was so much easier to do things like get into a stranger's car when I was drunk. Tonight, however, I was as sober and clear-eyed as I'd been in years, and I was tired of making poor choices.

My grandmother lived in a mobile home, and we'd been there since I was fifteen. Even after four years, I was still embarrassed to be living in a trailer park, so I had Everett stop at the entrance instead of driving to the house itself. As I opened the door and got out, I heard him ask, "Are you going to be okay?"

I almost nodded, then took a deep breath and leaned down to face him. "Thanks for the ride."

He smiled, and in the light of his car I saw dimples that I'd missed in the bar. "Maybe I'll see you around."

Oyster Cove was a small town, making it difficult to keep away from folks. I wasn't even sure if I wanted to see him again and relive the night's events, but I still gave him a wan smile before closing the door. He didn't drive off until I'd already gone a few yards, as if waiting for me to turn around and ask for help.

It amazed me that the thought to do so actually crossed my mind.

My grandmother's narrow trailer was at the first bend in the road, and I saw with some dismay that the light was still on inside. Sighing, I walked up the steps, unlocked the door, and entered.

"So, where have you been off gallivanting tonight?" My grandmother Diana sat at the dining room table, glaring up at me as I set my purse on a small end table.

"Work went late, then somebody asked me to be the DD tonight." I wasn't going to apologize to this woman.

She sniffed, looking down her nose at me. "I can smell the alcohol on you. So irresponsible, you could have killed somebody driving like that."

I bristled at her lie. I hadn't had a drop of drink all night, and there was no way I smelled of alcohol.

"I could have used your help tonight," she continued, "but, no, you had to go and spend your money on booze and parties."

It was an old argument, and one I didn't feel like having again. "I'm going to bed. You can yell at me in the morning."

"Don't you sass me, girl! This is my roof you live under; I pay your bills."

A sharp retort rose and died on my lips. Diana had long since paid off the mobile home. In fact, the "rent" I paid to her exceeded any expenses for the small plot of land in the park. There was always something I had to pay, some bill she'd wave in my face for something that my mother or little brother needed. If I didn't help, then I was a bad daughter or sister.

There was never enough, at the end of the month, for me to afford my own place. Rent in this part of Mississippi was absurdly cheap, yet despite holding down two jobs I never had more than two nickels to rub together.

"Good night, Diana."

My grandmother made an angry noise when I used her given name. "You are so . . . so . . ." She couldn't seem to find the right word, and I didn't care. Hurrying to my room, I shut the door on her and picked up my headphones and old iPod.

Flopping onto the twin bed, I picked out my "Catharsis" playlist and turned the volume up loud enough to drown out everything. Even as Skrillex blared through the tiny earbuds, my eyelids grew heavy and I lay back against the pillow. I dabbed at one eye, picking up the excess fluid there before it could turn into a tear, then pulled the comforter over me and fell into a fitful slumber.

chapter three ❧

My job as a grocery bagger sucked, but at least the constant action made time go by quicker.

"Paper or plastic?" I asked automatically as I began organizing the groceries coming down the line. I was on my last pull for the day, only an hour before I got done, and I was itching to leave. When I didn't get an answer to my question, I looked up to get the customer's attention, only to see Everett standing in front of me. I froze for a second, shocked to see him, and then managed to come to my senses. "Paper or plastic?" I repeated, albeit in a less forceful voice.

"Paper, please."

Swallowing, I bent my head to the task at hand, piling groceries into the paper bags. *You knew you couldn't keep away from him forever, not in a town this tiny.* As far as I could tell, this was a simple grocery run, and, judging by the selection, he ate pretty healthy.

"Told you I'd see you around."

I looked up to gauge his expression and found him studying me. His words didn't sound like a threat, but after the incident in the bar I'd been on hyperalert. "Yes, you did," I agreed cautiously, still a bit mortified. In the daylight, he was even cuter than I'd thought. He'd seen me at my lowest, and I waited nervously for him to mention it.

"What are you doing after work?"

I stared at him, surprised by the question. Something about him was different from the other boys around here, although I couldn't quite put my finger on it. He dressed well, his dark, shaggy hair hung almost to his shoulders, and that dimple was prominently back on his cheek. It pained me to turn down someone this cute, but I shook my head. "I have another job."

"Oh." He paused as I loaded the cart. "What about after that?"

"Sleep, hopefully."

"What about tomorrow?"

"More work."

He shrugged. I was trying to let him down gently, but he was persistent. "What's there to do around here?"

"Not much."

"If I gave you my number, would you let me know if you remember anything fun to do?"

I frowned at him, trying to figure out whether he was serious. That I hadn't scared him away after the incident in the bar boggled my mind. Yet here he was, wanting to give me his number. Unsure how to answer, I kept my mouth shut and finished bagging his groceries.

Everett paid for the food before turning back to me. "Can I get help with my bags?"

Car-side service was standard for the store, but most men didn't ask for it. Rolling my eyes, I turned the cart toward the door, but he tried to cut in.

"I can do that for you."

"Do you want my help or not?"

He held up his hands, a smile tipping one side of his mouth. "Whoa there, I was trying to be nice."

Shaking my head, I pushed the cart toward the exit, not waiting to see if he was following. "What do you want?" I snapped once we got outside.

"To talk."

"What else do you want?"

"To get to know you."

"Why?"

"Because you're the most interesting person I've met since coming here."

Interesting. That was one way to put it. "Clearly you don't get around much."

He pointed his car out in the parking lot and cringed. In the light of day, it looked even worse than I'd remembered. A large crack split the windshield, with several more fanning out from some impact point. Rust was already starting to eat away at his fenders, and the antenna was broken off halfway up. It was a wonder the whole thing didn't fall apart on the spot. "Did you drive this all the way from college?"

"No, I bought it here." He regarded the vehicle fondly, leaning one hip against the rear. "I like it; fits me better than what I have at home." He opened the hatchback and watched me quickly unload the groceries. "You seem eager to get rid of me."

"Maybe." There was no conviction in the word. It had been a long time since I'd just talked to a boy like this, and it was nicer than I cared to admit. Most were after only one thing, which made the game old and depressing. Everett had come to my rescue in the bar, however, something that deserved more than the cold shoulder.

Unfortunately, old habits died hard.

"Why?" He lifted one arm and took a dramatic sniff. "Do I smell?"

The action brought out a surprised laugh from me. He grinned at my response, twin dimples creasing his cheeks again, and I couldn't look away. He really was handsome; I totally understood why Ashley was ready to fight me for him. *Rugged* was probably the best word to describe him. His shoulders were broad like a football player's, but he didn't act like any jock I'd ever met. I remembered the cold look he'd given Ashley and the blank hardness when he'd stared down Macon, but I saw none of that now.

"So what's your other job?"

"Why, so you can stalk me there, too?" The words came out almost flirty, and I blinked. Everett just kept smiling at me, and I rolled my eyes. "See you around," I echoed, turning the cart around toward the store . . . and paused. My hands worked the handle of the cart nervously. Finally, I turned back around. "Fine, give me your number."

Everett leaned inside an open window and pulled out a receipt and pen. He scrawled a few numbers, and then handed it back to me. "You're a tough nut to crack."

I gave him a bemused stare. *Pot, meet kettle.* I glanced at the writing, and then stuffed the paper into my pocket. "I gotta get back to work."

Walking the cart back toward the supermarket, I resisted

the urge to look back. I added a few more carts scattered through the empty spaces to my stack, resolutely refusing to peer in his direction. I wasn't going to play this game, I wasn't.

Then, just as I got to the door of the store, I hazarded a glance back just to see if he'd left yet.

He waved to me, still leaning back against that ratty hatchback.

Dammit.

I used my mother's car to pick up my little brother that afternoon before changing and riding my bike to the sandwich shop, my second job. It was already dark by the time I got home to find my grandmother in the middle of a shouting match with my mother. I almost walked back out the door, but the eagle eye of my grandmother singled me out before I could make my escape. "And where have you been?"

"Working."

"You were supposed to watch your brother this afternoon."

I glared at my grandmother. "I told you before, I was scheduled to work tonight . . ."

"Family should come first, family *always* comes first."

"Oh that's rich, coming from you." I could count on one hand the number of times I'd either seen or spoken to my grandmother before I was fifteen. We'd lived on the opposite sides of the country, but my grandma Diana had not been a part of our lives. She'd never even come to visit until one tragic accident had taken everything away from me.

"What the hell is that supposed to mean?"

This time I kept my mouth shut, looking over at my mother and silently begging her to help me in this argument. She, however, simply looked relieved to no longer be the brunt of her mother's ire.

Resentment built up inside my heart. I still remembered when Gretchen St. James had been one of the strongest women I knew, a great mother. Now, she got herself drunk at every opportunity so she wouldn't have to deal with reality. She rolled with the punches life threw at her, not even bothering to try and fight for anything. When I was being honest with myself, we weren't so dissimilar, she and I, and that part pissed me off.

"I'm going to bed," I muttered, and ignoring my grandmother I moved around the couch and toward my room. She came after me, her strident voice bellowing, "Don't you turn your back on me!" Her words fell on deaf ears. I beat her down the hall and managed to lock my bedroom door on her.

Despite being the type that criticized neighbors for vocally airing their dirty laundry around the park, my grandmother had no problem making a scene all on her own. She screeched and banged on my door, and I knew the thin walls and windows of the mobile home let all the neighbors know what was happening. It was humiliating living like this; there was no privacy except for those times when I didn't bother to come home.

Those nights, though, depending on whose bed I slept in, were often worse in their own way.

My grandmother beat and hollered outside my room, eventually resorting to kicking the wood. The whole trailer shook under her wrath, but the cheap door held firm. Finally she left me alone, and as I slipped my earbuds into my ears I heard her take up again with my mother. Both women went back to yelling at the top of their lungs as Rammstein's "Du Hast" drowned out their voices.

My mother woke up hungover the next morning and asked me if I could drive my little brother to school. I got him ready for classes and made breakfast for both him and my mother. My grandmother had left earlier for her own job, so I didn't have to face her barbs, which was a relief. Mornings like this, I could almost pretend we were a normal family again . . . almost.

But it was my baby brother's innocent question in the car that turned my world upside down yet again: "Sissy, what's a 'whore'?"

I'd almost swerved off the road before gaining control of myself. Still, I waited a few breaths before answering his question. "Where'd you hear that word, Goober?"

"Gamma called you that a few times," he answered in his high, piping voice. He met my eyes in the rearview mirror, and his face was perfectly solemn. "What is it?"

I didn't know what to tell him at first. Finally, after several more breaths, I said, "Honey, it's a word that grandmas and little brothers shouldn't use."

"Why?"

I couldn't help the mirthless laugh that escaped. "Because it's mean. Do you like to be called stupid?"

"No."

"Exactly, because you're not stupid. You're smart, very

smart." And he was. Even at four years old, Davy St. James was arguably the smartest one in the entire house. He was also the kindest and most loving child I'd ever met, and I wanted to shelter him from the cruelties of the world for as long as I could.

Apparently, the rest of my family didn't share the same inclination.

"But if Gamma said you were one, then it can't be bad, right?"

Tears sprang to my eyes. God, how I loved my little brother. It tore at me that he was in this position. "I'm sorry, baby, but it's a bad word. Not something I want you to repeat."

He digested my answer silently. "So I shouldn't tell anyone?"

I shook my head emphatically. "No, that'll get your mouth washed out with soap and Mama would get called. Teachers don't like that."

He'd immediately switched the subject after that, but the conversation wouldn't leave my mind all day. In only a few years he'd be old enough to know what the word meant, and I couldn't bear it if he in any way connected the word to me. I felt as trapped in my situation as a bird in a cage; there had to be a way out, and I was desperate enough to consider all my options.

I did a quick Google search on my phone at lunch for local places where I could take my GED test. I'd been thinking about doing that for a long time, but since the weekend's fiasco it was foremost in my mind. Because I didn't have a diploma, there were some things I couldn't do, some jobs I would never qualify for. It wasn't the perfect choice, but a GED would be a step in the right direction.

I hadn't seen either Macon or Ashley since I'd left the bar, although both had blown up my phone the last several days with texts. I tried to ignore them, but the flood had left me uneasy. I couldn't remember if I'd told Macon where I worked, but he definitely knew where I lived. His messages alternated between cursing me out for not returning his calls and saying he wanted me to move in with him.

It bothered me that, after what happened at the bar, he still thought it was a viable option.

Based on some of his messages, it would have been a good idea to stay somewhere with a friend. By separating myself from Ashley, however, I'd cut off the one tie to anyone I could have called "friend." When I wouldn't reply to requests for a ride or money, her texts had turned nasty. I didn't listen to the voice-mail messages anymore, just deleting them as they arrived, but I couldn't miss her texts. She called me every name under the sun and promised to make my life hell—like it wasn't already.

I pulled out the crumpled receipt from my pocket and stared at the number Everett had given to me. Grabbing my phone, I brought up the Web browser and typed in the area code.

New York City. *Huh.* What was an East Coast boy doing down in Mississippi? I briefly toyed with saving the numbers on my phone, then erased them and pocketed the receipt again.

Heading back out to the front after break was over, I saw Clare didn't have a bagger so I moved in to help her. The new checker was about my age and had transferred here only a couple weeks earlier. The redhead seemed nice, although we hadn't had much chance to talk away from the line. We worked in amicable silence for the next few customers, and then when we had a free moment she sidled toward me. "Lacey, watch out for Mrs. Holloway."

I peered in confusion at the other girl. She had a concerned look on her face that worried me. "Why? Did I do something wrong?"

"I don't know." She looked around, and then leaned in toward me. "But she asked Rob about you and didn't seem happy when he said you were doing well."

Rob Hines was the supervisor in charge of both the checkers and the baggers. We got along well enough; he left you alone for the most part unless you did something wrong. But Mrs. Holloway was a friend of my grandmother's. My grandmother had once insinuated that she'd "pulled strings" to get me this job. I'd almost quit when she'd told me that, but I needed the work and nobody else was hiring. It was also something my grandmother would say just to prove I was indebted to her, but now it had me worried.

"Just be careful," Clare murmured, then pasted on a smile as the next customer came through the line. Chills snaked through my body, my brain turning over what could possibly be the problem as I automatically loaded up the bags. I knew my grandmother and the store manager went to the same church; perhaps my grandmother had bent her ear on my reputation?

The remainder of my shift was difficult. I didn't see Mrs. Holloway, but I couldn't shake Clare's warning from my head. It was silly to think there was some kind of conspiracy against me, yet that's what it felt like. I needed this job; the sandwich shop had crappy hours, usually fewer than twenty a week, and barely paid minimum wage.

I was ready to get out of there when my shift was over, and I punched out as soon as I could. Changing quickly out of my work clothes, I slung my purse over one shoulder and headed out of the employee area. I'd barely gotten a few steps outside the marked door, only to stop up short when I saw Samantha walk into the store.

Her eyes widened in recognition when she saw me but otherwise there was little reaction as she walked past me. The chills from earlier spread through me as I realized that Samantha would probably tell Ashley, who might tell Macon I was working here. In fact, it occurred to me that the attacks from both of them had started simultaneously.

As desperately as I wanted to believe that we were over and I was finally moving on, I couldn't shake the fear that my life was about to get much worse.

< So I'm taking the GED test. >

I stared at the text message for a long time before pressing Send. The receipt in my hand was ready to fall apart by now; it hadn't left my pocket for the last week. The digits had almost completely disappeared; if I hadn't already unconsciously memorized the number, I wouldn't be able to read them anymore.

My hours at the sandwich shop had been cut again, so I was free for the entire afternoon. I definitely wasn't ready to deal with home right now, so, pocketing my phone, I unlocked my bike and headed south toward the beach. Of all the things in this town, the beaches were my favorite. If I could live there permanently, I would be happy. My grandmother's trailer park wasn't too far from the Gulf, and I visited the water as much as I could.

Summer was in full swing down along the water. Oyster Cove would never be as big as Daytona or Panama Beach in terms of drawing the crowds, but that didn't mean the town didn't try. The beaches were full of pale sand, trucked in from elsewhere and kept well groomed for locals and visitors alike.

A volleyball tournament was being held by one of the piers, and I locked my bike back up around a nearby pole. Pulling my phone out of my pocket, I saw I'd received a text message.

< I'm assuming this is the blonde who thinks I smell? >

I smiled but didn't reply immediately, instead walking toward the water. There wasn't a cloud in the sky and the sand was hot around my sandals. Slipping my shoes off, I moved close to the water, then sat down on the damp sand. My shorts would be wet when I stood but I didn't care.

Only then did I take out my phone and answer the text.

< It feels like forever since I've been in school. What happens if I fail
the test? >

I wasn't sure why I was telling him this. I guess texting seemed so much safer than seeing him in person, or even talking on the phone. This was like asking a stranger online a question, not a boy I'd met in real life. When you thought about it, he was still a stranger to me anyway.

My phone buzzed.

< So then you take it again until you pass. >

< Yeah. >

I glanced over toward the volleyball players, but they were ignoring me. I was alone on the beach, and that's how I liked it.

< What are you up to? >

< Started working for Trent's dad this week. I'm stuck with the heavy lifting. >

I smiled.

< So those muscles I saw are just for show? >

< You wound me, these muscles are the real deal! >

It felt nice to just talk to someone without them expecting something from me.

< What kind of business is it? >

< Construction. We're putting up the framework for a new house today. >

< What time do you get done? >

Now, why had I asked that?

< Dunno. I stink, don't want you running for the hills like last
time. When's the next GED test? >

I relaxed again at his subject change.

< Next month. >

< Need help studying? >

The question jolted me, and suddenly I couldn't sit still
anymore. I strolled down the beach, carrying my sandals in
one hand. The wind was whipping up, telling me that a storm
would probably blow in soon, but there was already one going
on inside me.

On the one hand, I could use the help. I'd left high school
almost two years before, but I'd checked out mentally long
before that. I knew there were books I could buy to study,
so it was conceivable to do this all on my own. But I really
wanted to do it right and not fail.

I wasn't sure what I'd do if I failed at anything again.

My mind kept going round and round with the question,
so I didn't answer his text until I finally reached my bike.

< Maybe. >

It was all I could commit to at this point. While I could
talk to him via text, I couldn't bring myself to trust anyone
just yet.

Especially a boy.

The reply came almost immediately.

< Just tell me when and where, and I'll be there. >

I read the text several times, trying to see what the ulterior motive could be with this boy. Was he being nice just to get close to me? And if so, why? There was only one reason in my mind why a boy like that would want to get close to a girl like me, and I was tired of that.

"*Because you're the most interesting person I've met since coming here.*"

I wanted to believe him but couldn't afford to be wrong again.

chapter four 🦋

I changed my cell phone number three days later.

Macon's calls and texts were getting more frequent and increasingly nasty. I made the mistake of listening to one of his messages, and that one voice mail left me shivering. *"I know where you live, bitch. If you don't call me, maybe I'll swing by for a visit. You've missed me, haven't you?"*

I deleted the voice mail, along with the seven others he'd left, and immediately went to get a new number and the cheapest phone I could find. No longer feeling safe with my smartphone, I traded it in for the most basic model they had in stock. The salesman assured me there was no way this one could be tracked as it didn't have GPS, unlike the higher-tech phone.

I'd lost a few amenities but gained a little peace of mind. But the message still left me a nervous wreck.

The first person I texted with the new number was Everett. It took me several minutes to figure out how to work the letters; I'd grown so used to the touch screen on my smartphone.

< Hey this is Lacey, I got a new number today. >

< What happened with the old one? >

Telling him that I thought I was being stalked sounded overly dramatic.

< Phone fell into the toilet. >

It was an outright lie, and I felt bad, but I kept going.

< Getting the new number was easier. >

It was early afternoon, and the summer heat was beating down on me. My bike felt a little wobbly, like the tires were low, and I stopped at a gas station to get some air. My shift at the grocery store was later today than usual, which threw off my regular schedule. Thankfully, my other job had cut my hours down enough that I didn't even work there today, but it felt weird sleeping in so late on a weekday. It also made the ride into work much warmer.

I stowed my bike and quickly clocked in, moving toward the checking aisles. There were several open lines for me to choose from, but I saw Clare wave me over to hers. The normally happy girl wasn't smiling today, and as I came up to her she said, "Someone was looking for you earlier. A blond boy, do you know him?"

My horrified stare must have confirmed her suspicions, because she frowned. "I knew it was suspicious! He asked Rob about you first and then tried flirting with me. We weren't busy at the time so I didn't know how to get him to leave without being rude. He wanted to know if you came in today."

"What did you tell him?"

"I said you were off for most of this week. He seemed to accept that but still tried to get my number until I got customers. Even then, he stuck around for a long time like he was waiting for me to notice him, but he finally left when we got busy."

Considering most people were easily taken in by Macon's charm and looks, Clare's reaction surprised me. My stomach roiled with the knowledge that he had tracked me down at work. I knew he wouldn't give up right away, but coupled with his threats I was freaked out now. "Clare," I murmured when the customers were out of earshot again, "don't get involved with him. Please."

"I wouldn't dream of it, but what's wrong? Is he your boyfriend?"

"I think he's stalking me."

The words sounded pretentious on my tongue, overly dramatic and strange. I worried Clare would shrug it off but she gave me a horrified look that spoke volumes. Whatever she was going to say had to wait until after she rang up the people in her line. My gut churned, and I felt like I was going to be sick.

"Have you told anyone?" she murmured when the line finally disappeared.

I shook my head. "Just you." Even though I'd said the words, I didn't believe it. Why would anyone do that to *me*?

"How bad is it?"

"Not good." The voice mails echoed through my mind. "Really not good."

"At least tell Rob. He didn't seem to appreciate that guy hanging around."

I swallowed. Was Macon going to get me fired from my job? "He wouldn't understand."

"He has to, they have laws against these kinds of things!"

We grew quiet again as more customers came into the line. One thing I was coming to like about Clare was she understood boundaries and discretion. So many of my coworkers wouldn't have kept the news to themselves. Gossip was rampant, made worse by this being such a small community. Clare was new to the area so either she wasn't like that or hadn't yet tapped into the rumor mill.

"Ms. St. James? Can I speak with you for a moment?"

Rob motioned me away from earshot. I shared a worried look with Clare before following him toward the exit. He waited until we were alone before speaking. "There was a gentleman looking for you earlier."

"Yes, Clare told me." I felt suddenly breathless. *Please don't fire me, please don't fire me.*

"We have rules about keeping personal business free from work. Did you know this man?"

I nodded mutely. Rob peered closely at me. "Is there anything I should know about?"

My mouth opened and shut. Glancing over at Clare, I saw her watching us, and she pointed emphatically toward Rob. When he turned to see what I was looking at, she quickly turned back to her register.

Rob wasn't a bad supervisor. As long as someone didn't screw up big-time or need attention, he generally left us alone. I couldn't be sure how close he was with Mrs. Holloway, however, or how he would react to my news. It seemed too unreal that this was happening to me; if I couldn't believe it myself, why would anyone else?

"Ms. St. James?"

Unable to speak, I just shook my head. He frowned at me, and then sighed. "Please tell your friend to limit his time with you to when you're not working. I don't see the point in telling Mrs. Holloway, but consider this a first warning."

I let out a breath I hadn't realized I was holding. "Thank you, sir."

"Well?" Clare asked when I rejoined her line. "Did you tell him?" When I shook my head, she gave me a disbelieving look. "Fine, then I'll tell him."

"Clare, *no*." While I appreciated her trying to defend me, I couldn't let her do it. "I'll be okay."

"Well, what if you're not?" she hissed, obviously irritated. When I drew back, she let out a breath. "I'm not mad at you, I just . . ."

She couldn't seem to figure out how to finish her sentence, and then we had customers. I busied myself with my job, and Clare didn't ask me any more about it. When she quit her shift an hour later, I watched to make sure she didn't go talk to Rob, but she walked right out the door without even looking at me.

It felt weird to have someone try and stick up for me. I used to think I could handle myself, but lately life had spun out of my control. There was no support from home; strangers had my back more than my own family.

I tried to hang on for my full shift, but two hours later I was a nervous wreck. I kept watching for any sign of Macon and couldn't keep my mind on the job. When a large jar of pickled eggs slipped out of my hands and shattered on the floor, I knew I was done. After cleaning up the mess, I told Rob that I wasn't feeling well, and since we weren't busy he let me go for the evening.

It was still light out when I left, and I had no desire to go home yet. I also desperately wanted not to be alone. If I'd had Clare's phone number, I might have called her, but we weren't that close yet. I had a handful of numbers in my new phone, but only one belonged to someone I actually wanted to talk to.

< What are you up to? >

There was a moment's wait for the reply.

< Just got off work. Why? >

< You want to hang out? >

There was a longer pause this time, and I instantly regretted even asking. God, I didn't even know this boy; he was a total stranger, not even from around here. Everything told me that this was silly, that I shouldn't be trusting anyone I didn't—

The phone buzzed in my hand.

< Where should I pick you up? >

I debated what to tell him. *Never mind, I was just kidding. Haha, fooled you.* I clicked the Reply button, and then slowly typed out my location before pressing Send.

His answer was immediate.

< I'll be there in ten. >

He was there in six.

Standing up from the curb, I stared at his car for a few seconds, then opened the door and climbed inside. "Hi," I murmured, staring straight ahead.

"Hi."

There was an awkwardness now that had never been there in texts, as if being together physically had put up a wall of some kind. I almost wished I could whip out my phone and have us talk that way now in the car, but that would be silly.

"Where to?"

I looked over to see him studying me, his face placid. It made me nervous, so I turned and stared straight ahead. "I'm hungry."

"You like ice cream?" When I nodded, Everett shifted the car into gear and we pulled away from the store. I stared straight ahead the whole way, but we didn't go far, probably less than a mile before pulling off into another strip mall. Everett stepped out of the car, and after a brief pause I followed suit.

Johnson's Dairy had been in this town, in one way or another, for longer than I'd been alive. After Katrina came through, it had downsized a bit, moving into the strip mall farther inland, but it was still considered a local hot spot. "How'd you learn about this place?" I asked.

"Trent likes coming here for lunch. When you're working

outside all day in the middle of summer, ice cream sounds like manna from heaven."

The place was as packed as usual, but the line was quick. Johnson's mixed up whatever combination of ice cream and sides that you wanted, as long as it all fit inside the cone or cup. Everett paid for our ice cream—I got chocolate with a brownie and caramel while Everett had a cone of plain vanilla and almonds—and we found a small table inside. "So how long have you lived here?"

"Since I was fifteen." I spooned the soft edges of the ice cream and let the coolness melt against my tongue.

"Where did you live before this?"

"Oregon."

He gave me a bemused look. "So what brought you down to Mississippi?"

I didn't answer, lifting a big bite of ice cream and caramel topping into my mouth. It was a delaying tactic as I tried to figure out what to say. "My stepdad died."

"I'm sorry."

The chocolate turned to ash in my mouth, and I forced myself to swallow. "Yeah," I murmured, and then waved my spoon around. "It was a surprise when I found out, at his funeral no less, that he wasn't even my real father."

"Damn."

I looked up to gauge his reaction but couldn't read anything in his face. "My grandma was the one who told me," I continued, bitterness lacing my words. "I hadn't even seen her since I was really little, but for some reason she came up for the funeral. Right after she told me this, she let me know my mom was selling the house I grew up in and that we'd be moving into a trailer park down here with her."

"Harsh."

Everett's attention was on his ice cream, and I couldn't tell if he was being sarcastic or not. *Why was I even telling him this stuff?* I stuffed another bite of ice cream into my mouth, annoyance burning inside my gut. These were things I hadn't told anybody, because nobody had ever cared to ask.

So why would he be any different?

"What was your dad like?"

"You mean my stepdad."

Everett shrugged. "He was the man who raised you, is there a difference?"

Yes, there was a big difference. "He wasn't my blood." I didn't want to go any deeper with the boy in front of me. I'd laid out enough of my past for one night.

When Everett said nothing, I thought back to his previous question. I hadn't wanted to think about Ben St. James for a long time; the memories hurt too much. "My stepdad ran his own machine shop. People would come inside and ask him to make something and he'd whip it up on the lathe or mill."

A reluctant smile came to my face as I remembered his perpetually dirty shop. "We had one guy, Jared Jackson, who used to race motorcycles. He always brought burned-up engines to my dad and had him rebuild them, at least two motors per season."

I stopped when I realized what I'd said. *My dad.* For a moment, my eyes burned, and I ducked my head, pretending to wipe my mouth as I blinked furiously. "Anyway, yeah. My life story in a nutshell."

"Well, you're tough. I like that."

The compliment made me smile. "What about you?"

Everett shrugged. "I'm boring. My parents have been married forever. Dad's in business, Mom teaches. Like I said, boring."

"But you're from New York."

The moment the words left my lips I wanted to call them back, but Everett seemed to find my statement amusing. "Trust me, I like it down here a whole lot better. You always know exactly where you stand with a Southerner."

He had a point. Down here, you were who you were for everyone to see, for good or for ill. It would be nice to get lost in a crowd, though, a courtesy I was rarely afforded.

My ice cream was long gone, and I stared forlornly at the cup. The sun was starting to set, and like it or not I needed to get home.

"How's the GED thing going?"

"Meh." I didn't know where to start, but felt silly saying that.

"The offer for help is still open."

I sighed and finally met his beautiful blue eyes. They were the color of a warm summer sky; I could easily get lost in them. He was watching me, patiently awaiting my answer. Nothing in his gaze told me what he wanted in return, and I found it difficult to believe he'd give me help just *because*. But I needed it. I'd taken a practice test online and had barely scored enough to pass; the thought of the test itself scared me to death.

"What could you teach me?"

"Whatever you need to pass. And if it makes you feel any better, you can always pay me for tutoring you."

Surprisingly, that did make me feel better. If I paid, I didn't owe him anything else. The more I thought about it, the more I liked the idea. "How much?"

"Ten bucks a lesson."

I gazed at him shrewdly. "Five bucks, and you've got a deal."

Everett gave me a lopsided grin. "The lady drives a hard bargain," he said, but held out his hand. "Deal."

We shook hands, and I tried to ignore the electric zing that his touch sent coursing through my body. A small smile worked its way across my lips. "What should I bring?"

"I'll take care of it. You hired me; I'll bring the supplies."

I felt a sudden weight lift off my shoulders. If he hadn't been a boy, I probably would have hugged him. "I need to get back to my bike."

"You'll be okay riding home in the dark?"

I nodded. "Do it all the time." He gave me a dubious look, and I wondered what sort of neighborhood he lived in. "Seriously, we're not in New York. I'll be fine."

The sun had already passed the horizon and twilight was settling in when he dropped me off back at the grocery store. I hadn't realized just how late it actually was, but still paused and turned back to the open window. "Thanks for the ice cream."

"No problem. Sorry I don't have any air-conditioning."

"Well, I'm used to it on the bike." I didn't know what else to say but really didn't want to leave just yet. "When do you want to meet up for the GED stuff?"

"How about tomorrow? We've got the day off since Trent's dad is heading into Biloxi. Are you working?"

I shook my head. "It's one of my days off."

"Cool, then maybe I can pick you up?"

The idea of him seeing the ratty trailer where I lived didn't sit well. "Can I meet you somewhere instead?"

"Sure, maybe another ice cream?"

Nodding, I gave him another smile. "Thanks again."

"Heh, wait until I start drilling you. I tend to go overboard with studying."

Somehow, I couldn't see the laid-back boy before me as a nerd. "As long as I can pass." I winked at him, then pushed away from the car, waving as he drove off.

The lock on my bike was stuck, and it took me a minute to get it to let go. When it finally broke free, I wrapped it around the frame and turned the bike around, only to come face-to-face with Mrs. Holloway. The large woman glared at me, and my breath caught in my throat. "Didn't you leave sick, Ms. St. James?"

"Yes, ma'am," I murmured, uneasy about being questioned. "A friend picked me up, but I need my bike."

Her expression told me quite clearly that she didn't believe me. Swallowing, I gave her a small wave that she didn't reciprocate, then pushed off the curb and headed straight home.

My mother was slumped on the couch watching news when I came through the door. A half-empty bottle of whiskey sat on the table before her, along with two cans of Coke. I could tell from the way she sat that she was already toasted; she didn't even say hello to me when I came inside.

Beside the television, my little brother was playing quietly with his toys. When he saw me a big smile crossed his face and he ran over to hug me.

"Hey, Goober," I said fondly, picking him up in my arms. He was getting far too big for this, but I'd carry him in my arms until I broke my back. "Ready for bed?"

He shook his head, and then yawned. I smiled. "Mom, I'm putting him down for the night."

All I got in reply was a grunt and a wave. I stared at the slug that used to be my mother and then wordlessly took my brother to his room.

"Where's Gamma?" he murmured as I rummaged around for clean pajamas.

"She's working late tonight, sugar. She'll be in later to kiss you good night." My throat closed up after that. It helped that he really was as angelic as she proclaimed to everyone in town. Heaven help us if he'd been a natural brat, given how much she spoiled him, but the little boy was perfect. He came from good stock, she always told people. His father, rest his soul, had been the salt of the earth.

It all came down to parentage. His biological father was a good man. Mine wasn't. And to her, that made me just as evil.

I slipped his shirt off, and then frowned. "Baby, where'd you get these?" I asked, holding out his arm. He had twin bruises on his right bicep that I didn't remember seeing before.

"I dunno." His eyes kept closing as he swayed in place. Taking pity, I pulled the pajama shirt over his head and lifted him into bed, pulling the sheets up around his body.

Once I was sure he was tucked in, I turned on his night-light and watched the shapes circle the walls. The revolving light had been mine as a kid, a gift from my father. *My stepfather*. Music notes danced around the small room, and I swallowed as I remembered how much bigger my room had been when I was younger. My brother deserved so much more than this.

I closed the door quietly behind me and looked over at my mother. Her head was lying back on the couch, and I could tell from the snores that she was passed out. For a long moment, I stared at the woman from across the trailer, then went and locked myself inside my bedroom.

chapter five ❧

W hat's all this?"
"Study aids."

The bag of books in front of me was more than a little daunting. Books also took up almost all the space on the table. "Where'd you get these?"

"Bookstore. There were more, but I figured these would be a good start."

More? These were bad enough in my opinion. I hadn't done homework in years, and the small mountain of material was a tad overwhelming.

"I also think we should head someplace a little more private."

He was right on that score. The ice cream shop was already packed with the summer crowd and not likely to get any better. Still, I eyed him suspiciously. "Like where?"

"Is there a public library around here?"

There was, in fact, although I'd never been inside. I relaxed again, realizing I'd tensed up the minute he suggested we go someplace alone. So far he'd proven reliable; maybe I could give him some benefit of the doubt. "Sure, I'll show you where it is."

Oyster Cove's library was not far from the ice cream shop, near the water. Honestly, the town was small enough that nothing was too far away from the Gulf shores. We parked his small car outside, and Everett looked up at the old building. "Nice."

I'd driven past so many times that I'd forgotten how pretty the library actually was. While not as majestic as some of the older buildings still standing around the county, long columns lined the front façade in typical Southern style. Time and a life next to a hurricane-prone ocean had given it a weathered look, but it still bore the stamp of history. It wasn't all that large, but it definitely had a regal air. "I don't even notice it anymore," I said as we walked inside.

"That's too bad." He peered around the inside, too, and I tried to see it through his eyes. The interior, while updated, still had an old-world aesthetic. The second floor had a big skylight in the center where sun shone down from a domed window. The stairways were lined with ornate wrought iron handrails, although I saw they'd become loose with age as we climbed the steps.

The upstairs was well lit but crowded. After Hurricane Katrina had brought in super high tides that washed away large swaths of town, the library had moved most of its wares to the top floor. Bookshelves hemmed us in from all sides, but we soon found an empty nook with two medium tables.

"So what do you want to start on first?" he asked, pulling up a chair and setting the books on the table.

I shrugged. For some reason, it was strange to see him so eager to help me. Boys this handsome usually had something better to do than help some girl they barely knew study for a test. Yet he'd bought me books and supplies and gave me his day off expecting . . . what? I didn't know what to make of the boy before me, and that was both intriguing and scary.

I sat down next to him and started sorting the various books by subject. Sitting this close, I caught the scent of him. Like soap and aftershave and something distinctly Everett. It filled my senses like a drug, and I felt a rush of heat shoot straight through me.

Whoa, simmer down, Lacey. Time to put on the brakes.

I turned to Everett, who was watching me curiously. "Everything okay?"

"Yup, never better," I said too quickly, my voice too high.

I pushed my chair away from his, pretending to reach for a book. I shuffled through the stack, happy for a distraction.

"How were you at science?" Everett asked.

"Decent," I said, feeling my pulse start to go back to normal.

"Social studies?"

"Slightly better."

"Math?"

My mouth tipped up. "Lousy."

"Ding-ding-ding, we have a winner!" He pulled a book out from the stack and handed me a packet of pencils. I took them from him, careful not to let our skin touch. "It's pretty straightforward: you take a few practice tests and they explain the answers. Then you take more tests."

I glanced at my phone. Ten o'clock in the morning. Sighing, I resigned myself to a long day.

Surprisingly, I didn't start out too badly. By noon, I'd

already done two tests and seemed to remember more from school than I thought. Everett thought he could make my mediocre scores better, but still switched me over to some of the English tests, which were a breeze.

My stomach was rumbling by one o'clock. At one thirty, I leaned back in my chair. "God, I'd give my right eye for an oyster po'boy."

"A what?"

I snapped my head around to look at Everett. "You've never heard of a po'boy sandwich?"

He blinked. "Is it like a hoagie?"

What the hell is a "hoagie"? "Come on, lunch is on me."

We stuffed the books back inside the paper sack and headed out to the car. "You're either gonna love or hate this place, but it has the *best* po'boys in the area."

The deli wasn't actually in Oyster Cove but a few miles north, closer to the freeway. We were almost to the interstate when I pointed out a lone gas station. "Here?" he asked, giving me an odd look but still pulling inside.

"Yup." I understood his confusion. The gas station, as far as I knew, had no real name except Gas Station. It was in the middle of nowhere, out of view of both the main roads and the highway. It had been built about half a century ago and, from the outside, didn't look like it'd been updated anytime in between.

"Trust me," I said as we walked inside, "you'll love it. Hey, Meg."

Meg was at the counter, and when she saw me come inside she gave me a gap-toothed grin. "Hey, gorgeous, haven't seen you in a while."

I'd always liked Meg, ever since I found this place. She was a little older than my grandmother but not nearly as up-tight. Her hair was a bright maroon, as if she'd gotten her hair dye at Hot Topic, but it fit her personality. She always had a smile for me, which I appreciated.

That, and she made the best fried food I'd ever eaten.

Pointing to Everett beside me, I said, "This Yank's never had a po'boy. Think you can fix him up?"

"I got just the thing. Gimme a few minutes, doll."

Everett was looking around, a bemused smile on his face. While the booths lining the windows were fairly new, the rest of the store looked like it'd just survived a hurricane. Barely. The walls had a dingy tint from decades of grease fryers and cigarette smoke, but the countertops were clean.

"Don't mean to be alarmist," Everett murmured, "but I'm not going to get food poisoning, am I?"

His question made me grin. "You probably don't want to see the condition of the kitchen, but I've eaten here probably too many times and never got sick. You'll be fine." I made my way to one of the colorful booths, and Everett sat down across from me. "So, tell me about you," I said.

"Like I said before, I'm boring."

"Well, you're a boring person with a New York area code. So spill: what's it like on the East Coast?"

Everett sat back, staring out the window at the old gas pumps. I wasn't even sure they worked anymore; I'd never seen anyone actually buying gas here. The place usually had a few more people, especially this close to lunch, but today was bare except for Meg in the back and her son sweeping.

Finally, he spoke. "Everyone is on the go in New York

City. There's always something that has to be done now or, better yet, two days ago. When people *do* stop, it's usually to refuel for the next activity, not to appreciate what they already have.

"There's also a lot of masks, although I never noticed that until I came here." He frowned, as if struggling how to explain it. "You never really know who a person is, even if you live or work around them every day. There's a need to portray a certain image, to be a certain way. Fashion plays a big part, but it's more than that. Even in conversations, if you're not talking about the right things, then you're insignificant in certain situations. If you don't want the right things, then you're nobody."

That didn't sound all that fun to me. I peered at him, realizing there was something deeper in his words than just my answer. "So what do you want?" I finally asked when the silence stretched on too long.

My question woke him out of his thoughts, and he gave me a sheepish smile. "To try new things, not be forced down roads I'd rather not take." He cocked his head to one side. "What about you? What do you want to be when you grow up?"

He said it with a smile, but the question resonated in me for some reason. I thought for a moment. "I don't know," I said finally, staring at my nails. "Once I wanted to be a veterinarian, then when my piano lessons took off I wanted to be a concert pianist."

"Well, why don't you go for one of those?"

I shook my head. "It's been years since I've so much as looked at a piano, and I know I wouldn't make it through all the schooling to become a vet." I sighed and blew out a breath. "I don't even know what I want anymore."

"Well, if you could do anything, go anyplace, what would it be?"

"Get out of here." I didn't even have to think about that one. "Be anyplace but this little town."

He looked like he wanted to say more, when Meg appeared with two baskets in her hand. "Here's yours, darlin'," she said to me, handing me the smaller sandwich, "and here's yours, babycakes. Enjoy."

Everett stared at the sandwich before him. My mouth was watering from the smells alone. "You ever eaten fried oysters before?" I asked, gathering together the thick sandwich. "Well, whatever you do, don't look at them. Just enjoy the taste."

"You know that's not very comforting," he said drolly as I bit into my sandwich, but I was too hungry to answer him. He picked up half his sandwich gamely and took a bite. His eyebrows shot up as he chewed, and for a few minutes we ate in companionable silence.

"Good, huh?" I said as I ate.

"Amazing," he said through a full mouth, then grinned. "Just like the view."

He was looking at me when he said it, and the comment caught me off guard. I couldn't think of a response just then so I took another bite of my sandwich.

"So what's the plan for the rest of the day?" he asked between bites.

"I need to go pick up my little brother from day care at three o'clock, so I should probably head home to pick up my mom's car."

"Why don't you have a car? Wouldn't it be easier?"

"Well," I hedged, and then looked at his ratty mode of transportation. He'd probably understand better than most. "Right now my vehicle isn't working all that well."

"Vehicle? Way to be cryptic."

I just grinned. "She's my pride and joy, but right now she's up on blocks."

"Is there anything I can help with?"

"Dunno, you ever rebuild a transmission?"

"No, but Trent can."

I mulled that information over. Riding the bike was getting old; I could only go so far, and being stuck in such a small area as Oyster Cove was beginning to chafe. "Yeah, see how much he'll charge," I said finally, sliding out of the booth. "It's an old automatic Ford, shouldn't be too hard."

"I'll ask. So, tomorrow then?"

"Four o'clock tomorrow sound okay?"

"Cool. I'll pick you up."

"No, I'd rather—"

Everett held up a hand. "You can at least meet me at the end of the lane where I dropped you off before, can't you?"

He had a point. "All right, then I'll see you tomorrow."

We waved good-bye to Meg and walked out of the Gas Station. Everett held open the door for me like a gentleman. Being treated nicely felt good, and I fought to keep a silly grin off my face.

"So, what's a boy from New York City doing in Mississippi working construction?" I asked as we pulled out and headed back south toward town.

"I needed a change is all. Trent's a friend and promised me a job with his dad's company, made it sound fun."

"And you came all the way down here?" I teased. "Are you running away from something?"

He smirked but kept his eyes on the road. "You're not going to go looking me up online, are you?"

I shook my head, my smile fading. "I'm not a big fan of the Internet," I said, looking out the window.

"Neither am I, to be honest."

It felt strange to meet somebody else who wasn't online twenty-four/seven. I wanted to ask for the story behind his choice but feared he would ask the same of me. "How long are you staying down here?"

"The original plan was just for the summer, but I like it here. Don't know if I'll stay in construction, but it's peaceful here." He looked over at me, winking. "And there are other perks to staying."

I clamped my lips together, fighting to keep the stupid grin off my face. Warmth spread through me, and I stared out the window as we pulled up to my bike. Being appreciated again felt good, especially after feeling like a burden to everyone for so long. A quick glance at my watch told me I had to hurry, but I paused and covered his hand with mine. "Thank you for helping me with all this."

He brought my hand up to kiss the knuckles, his eyes not leaving mine. A tingle spread through my body, and between my thighs an ache of longing started. "I'll help you however I can," he murmured.

Leaving that car was difficult, but I forced myself to get

out and unlock my bike. Everett stayed in the car, waving as I took off, and pleasure coursed through me. Maybe there were a few good men still left in this world. With all the bad luck in my life to this point, maybe I was finally getting a break.

That happy feeling lasted the whole way home, right up until I realized my mom's car wasn't at the house. Leaning my bike against the side of the stairway, I hurried up the steps and checked to see if anyone was home, but nobody was inside, either. I got home at twenty minutes to three, still more than early enough to go pick up my little brother.

But I had no car.

I tried to call her cell but she had it turned off. The thought of calling my grandmother didn't sit well; I'd automatically be made to blame. I thought perhaps my mother was just out running errands and had forgotten the time. Annoyed at my own helplessness, I passed the time by picking up beer bottles strewn across the living room as I waited for her to get home.

At ten minutes after three, I called the day-care office. The lady who answered was kind enough to go check to see if my little brother was still there.

"No, his teacher said his mother picked him up," she said when she finally got on the phone.

I thanked her profusely and paced the length of the trailer, continually checking the clock. I finally heard the car pull into the driveway and moved outside to help. "I thought I was supposed to pick him up," I said as my mother unbuckled Davy from his car seat.

"You weren't here," she said, a belligerent note in her voice. "I tried calling you and kept getting some error message."

I hadn't given her my new number yet. *Shit.* "I'm sorry, Mama, I changed it two days ago."

She gave me a dirty look. "Goddamn, irresponsible . . . I didn't raise you to be this fucking lazy, Lacey May."

God, I hated it when she was drunk. She never would have talked like that to me before Ben died; I'd never once heard her cuss, in fact, until we moved back down here. Resentment burned in my gut. "I was here ten minutes beforehand," I persisted as I followed her into the house. "Where did you go?"

"Had to get cigarettes."

"Mama." I gave an exasperated sigh. "You know you shouldn't drive when you've been drinking."

"You made me do it," she muttered darkly, setting my brother on the ground. "If you had been here when you were supposed to . . ."

"Mama, you just said you went to get cigarettes. You were driving drunk even though I—"

Crack!

My head whipped around and I stumbled sideways. I turned to look at my mother, shocked to my core. No matter how bad things had been, Gretchen St. James had *never* laid her hand on me before.

I stood there stunned, holding my cheek, as my mother stared back at me. To her credit, she looked as astonished as I was, but I didn't care. Part of me wanted desperately to hit her back, make her feel the pain that was tearing me apart.

"Sissy?"

Davy was watching us, his blue eyes as round as saucer plates. Tears sprang to my eyes as I realized he'd witnessed the whole thing, but I had no idea what to say. Rage and impotence enveloped me, but I couldn't make myself move.

My mother looked between us, her eyes still wide, then she turned to my brother. "What do you want for dinner, honey?" she said in a shaky voice, ignoring me completely.

That was the final straw.

I knew where my mother kept her stash of liquor. She wasn't very creative with hiding it, and I'd raided it before. Sure enough, she had several bottles in various sizes of tequila and vodka in the small cabinet under the kitchen sink.

"What the hell are you doing?"

Grabbing the smaller bottle of vodka, I ignored her and checked the contents. It didn't appear to have been opened.

"Lacey May!"

I rounded on her. "Fuck you," I whispered, and was pleased by the shock I saw in her eyes. I'd never said those words to her before, never cursed at my mama. She'd been the one person I thought I could rely on in this house.

No more.

Without another word, I turned and stomped out of the trailer, slamming the door behind me. I picked up my bike and, stuffing the thin bottle in the back of my shorts, I took off down the street.

I had no idea where I was going, but when I got to the beach, I threw down my bike on the edge of the sand and walked out to the water. Plopping my butt next to the pier, I unscrewed the top to the bottle and tipped it back, letting the burning liquid make its way down my throat.

* * *

By five o'clock, I was drunk as a skunk and horny as hell.

Vodka had always done that to me. Maybe that was why it was my drink of choice when I went out; any given night's outcome could be blamed on the liquor. It wasn't my fault, the alcohol made me do it. I could almost believe it.

Almost.

Macon's number sprang immediately to mind, even though I didn't have him in my new phone. He was the one I used to call at times like these; invariably, he would come and pick me up wherever I was. The price was always sex, but he'd keep me drunk enough that I wouldn't mind, until morning came around and I'd sobered up.

I punched his familiar numbers into my phone, then a sane part of my mind made me close the clamshell, deleting them again. The small vodka bottle was empty, and I tossed it toward a nearby trash can. When it bounced off the side and plopped in the sand, I stumbled over and picked it up, putting it carefully through the hole.

For some reason, this struck me as hilarious.

Sitting down with my back to the trash, I opened my phone again and scrolled through my messages. A slight smile tipped the corner of my mouth as I reread Everett's conversation. As I tried to hit Reply to text him something new, however, the unfamiliar phone began dialing his number instead.

Oh well. I put the cheap phone to my ear and listened to it ring.

"Hey, I didn't think you'd ever actually call me."

"Hey," I drawled, grinning widely. "What are you doing tonight?"

"Not much. I'm watching TV with Trent. What about you?"

"I'm drunk." It seemed really important to make sure he understood my words, so I spoke slowly. "My mother slapped the shit out of me, in front of my brother no less, so I stole her vodka and went to the beach."

There was a long pause from his end. "Where are you now?"

I looked around. "On the beach," I said, smiling at my joke.

"No seriously, Lacey. What's around you right now?"

I huffed and rolled my eyes. *Pushy, ain't he?* "Um, I'm next to the long pier right on highway ninety."

"Okay, stay there, I'm coming to get you."

"Aww! You are such a sweetheart." My mood changed, however, when I realized he'd hung up on me. Groaning in frustration, I poked at the sand, and then glanced at my feet. *Hey, where did my shoes go?*

By the time Everett's car pulled up beside the beach, I'd managed to find one shoe but the other remained hidden. "Hi," I said as a couple walked by, giving them a small wave and a smile before going back to my task. At that point I was a little steadier on my feet, but still stumbling over the soft sand.

When I saw the dark-haired boy coming toward me, I grinned widely. "Hi," I said, throwing my arms in the air like I'd scored a touchdown. Before he could say anything I enveloped him in a big hug. My head came right about to his jawline, and I cuddled up against his neck. "Where've you been all my life, gorgeous?"

A bemused smile tipped one corner of his gorgeous mouth. "Lacey, do you need me to take you home?"

"Nah," I purred, pushing myself against him. "I like it fine right here."

Everett stiffened, his Adam's apple bobbing as he swallowed, then he tugged gently at my arms around his neck. "Lacey, you're drunk."

"So?" I leaned in for a kiss but Everett twisted his face away, so I set my lips to his neck. Hot damn, but he tasted good. His body went rigid beneath me, the fingers around my waist digging into the soft flesh. I dragged my teeth along the hollow of his throat, enjoying the soft prickle of his five-o'clock shadow.

When I lifted my head, his lips were parted, and I knew for sure that he was about to kiss me. His hands tightened on my waist, however, and he took a step away. "I want to kiss you, Lacey, but not when you're drunk."

"Why do you have to be such a gentleman?" I asked, pouting.

"Come on, let me take you home."

"Wait." I held up a finger; there was something I was forgetting. After a short pause while my brain caught up, I remembered and lifted up my shoe. "I lost one of these."

Everett looked between the shoe and my face. Another bemused smile touched his lips. "I think the other one's by the road," he said.

"Really?" Letting him go, I turned toward where I remembered my bike being, then frowned when I didn't see it. "Didn't I ride my bike here?"

"How about we get your other shoe, and I take you home?"

"No," I said again, this time planting myself in place. The alcohol haze was wearing off, taking my good mood with it, and I frowned. "My mom's mad at me, and by now my grand-ma's probably home, too." That meant double the trouble, and I was drunk to boot. It was like winning the damned trifecta . . . except I was sobering up enough to know what I'd won wasn't worth shit.

"How about we get you some food?"

It took a few seconds for the words to sink in, and then I smiled. "Yeah, I'm hungry." My stomach chose that moment to twist, further underscoring the fact that I was right. Bile crept up my throat.

Oh, that's not good.

"Come on, there's a Waffle House just down the road here, maybe we can—"

And that was the moment I decided to hurl all over his feet.

chapter six ❧

An hour later, all I wanted to do was crawl under the table and die.

"I'm so sorry I threw up on you," I moaned for the hundredth time. "And for saying such stupid things."

"It's all right, can't be worse than some of the stuff I step through every day on the job site. And nothing you said was stupid, so stop beating yourself up. Everyone's been there."

But all I could do was sit there, miserable, going over every detail of the last half hour. Already I wanted to apologize again, but this time I kept my lips closed.

"Drink some water. It might help; you were probably dehydrated."

I'd already had two glasses of water, but dutifully took another sip anyway. "I'm sorry I drunk-dialed you," I murmured. I was apologizing for something different, so it was okay this time. My head was still buzzing from the alcohol, but shame and mortification at my behavior had dampened the effects.

"Yeah, I was pretty surprised to see you call. You usually just text."

My mood sank further south until he dipped his head so our eyes met. "It was a good surprise, I promise."

"Yeah." I poked again at my rapidly cooling grits and then took a small bite. The oyster po'boy I'd enjoyed only hours earlier was spread out over the beach and Everett's shoes. My stomach rumbled for more food, but I was reluctant to listen this time.

"So what happened with your mom?"

It was the first real question about my day he'd asked. "We had a fight. She slapped me." I ducked my head so he wouldn't see the sudden tears that sprang to my eyes. Apparently I was still buzzed enough not to have any control over my emotions. "She's never done that before; I didn't even get spanked as a kid. My grandmother's used her belt on me before, but my mother never hit me."

"I'm sorry, Lacey."

I shrugged one shoulder, taking another bite of the grits. Despair welled up suddenly. "I hate my life here."

"Then why don't you leave?"

"And go where?" I looked up at him, then back down at my bowl. "The only family I have is down here."

"What about your stepdad's family? Can't you call them?"

The memory of my grandma Jean flashed through my mind. "No," I said miserably, "they don't care about me. I'm not their blood."

"What do you mean?"

"I'm not really their family. My stepfather adopted me because he had to, but I'm not really his kid."

"Who told you that? No man *has* to adopt the child of someone he marries, it's a choice."

I just shrugged, not wanting to talk about it. The memories hurt too much, and I wasn't up for dealing with more emotion right then.

We stayed quiet for a couple minutes, and then Everett sighed. "Look, I might know someplace you can stay the night."

That old familiar suspicion rose up inside me again. "Where?"

"There are guest quarters or something behind our house, an entire building all by itself. It doesn't have a kitchen, but it has at least one bathroom, probably more. To be honest, I haven't explored it much, but there has to be a bed or couch in there."

I thought about it for a moment. "What about Trent?" I asked, wondering why I was looking this gift horse in the mouth. It was a bed for the night, and not in the trailer park—a step in the right direction, if you asked me.

"He should be okay with it, but I'll text him anyway."

The thought of one night where I didn't have to face my grandmother's barbs and my mother's unbearable silence sounded heavenly. I deliberated for a moment, and then sighed. "Can you text him now?"

Everett quickly typed out a message as I stared at my own phone. I realized I should probably let my mother know that I was okay, but I just couldn't do it. The blow to my face had long since stopped stinging, but the jolt to my heart was a raw, seeping wound.

A phone chimed, and I saw Everett turn his over. "He says it's fine, and wants to know if you like pizza?"

Slowly, a smile crept across my face. "I love it."

It was one thing to drive past a dream house for years, but another thing entirely to actually go inside.

The grounds were immaculate, the flowers and green grass perfectly trimmed and maintained. White columns rose up from the entrance, as tall in person as I'd imagined when I'd seen it from the road. Whoever had built this cut no corners with the house; it looked straight out of a Civil War documentary.

When I stepped through the front door, it was like walking onto the set of *Gone with the Wind*. The furniture in the entryway was almost delicate, ornately carved and filigreed. I was afraid to touch anything, for fear I'd break it. The house opened up immediately once you entered, with high ceilings and a staircase on the far right wall. A great crystal chandelier hung above us in the entryway, all gold and brass and sparkling facets.

"This place is incredible," I murmured, awed by the over-abundance of splendor.

"Yeah, a little posh for my tastes," Everett said in a dry voice. "Watching over a place like this definitely makes you paranoid. My entire summer's salary couldn't replace some of these antiques."

The smell of pizza wafted to my nose, and I heard noise farther in the house. I followed Everett into the kitchen to see Trent with a large pizza box on the counter. He was pulling several slices onto a paper plate and didn't bother to look up as we walked in.

"Save us some, will you?" Everett said as Trent piled the wedges high on his plate.

"There's more than enough. I gotta eat and run, though. Got a date."

"Seriously? Who is it this time?"

"No idea, but Cole called saying he needed a second guy for a double date. I guess the threesome he'd been gunning for was a miscommunication, so he's doing damage control." His eyes swung over to me. "Hey, Lacey."

I didn't say anything, just gave a small wave. My insides clenched nervously, realizing with him leaving I was going to be alone with Everett. On the best of days, the boy alternately confused and aroused me, and now I was still tipsy. Mixing alcohol with the situation all but guaranteed I'd make a bigger mess of things.

"I figured his little story sounded too good to be true." Everett shouldered his way into the kitchen, checking out the refrigerator. "You drank the last of the beer?"

"Yeah, I was gonna leave you a note to get more."

"Asshole."

They bickered like a pair of old friends, and I wondered how exactly they'd met. I didn't know where Trent had gone off to college, but was fairly certain it wasn't New York. They acted like I wasn't even there, and I preferred it that way.

"Hey, before you leave, think you can take a look at an old transmission?"

"What, that rat trap of yours finally dive off the deep end?"

"No, this is for a friend. Just want to see how much it'll cost."

Trent's eyes darted over to me, and then he hitched a shoulder. "Can do. Just tell me when, where, and what. See you lovebirds later."

I flinched at his words, and watched out of the corner of my eye as he walked out the door, still carrying his paper plate and pizza. The silence that fell was uncomfortable, at least on my part. I took a moment to survey the living room, which was much more modern and livable. In typical male fashion, clothing was strewn across random pieces of furniture and beer bottles dotted the tabletops, but it looked more homey and less like a movie set.

"Want to see the back?"

I looked over at Everett and, tamping down my sudden nervousness, smiled. "Sure."

The house sat on a huge plot of land, at least two acres by my estimation. I'd never been able to see the rear of the house; it butted up against the back of another smaller house that hid everything from view. Thick oak trees dotted the open area at the back, but it was the large two-story white building that captured my attention. I had always wondered what exactly was inside; it looked like servants' quarters, or a guesthouse, something along the lines of a mini hotel.

I heard the pop as the old door unstuck itself from the doorjamb, and knew this place hadn't been used in a while. The interior was nice, although not quite as ostentatious as the main house. The main area was a big open room with sparse furniture in comparison to the house. A pool table sat against the side wall, and a covered couch in front of a big flat-screen TV sat across from it.

"Trent said the first floor of this place was razed by Hurricane Katrina, so everything down here is fairly new." He pulled off a sheet covering some of the chairs. "There's water and electricity out here as well as cable, but if you're hungry you'd have to come to the house for food."

My eyes moved to the far end of the room, toward a large piece of covered furniture in the corner. Lips parting, I stepped lightly over the tile floor and pulled at the thin cloth. It slid easily off the smooth surface, piling to the floor around my feet.

Everett moved in beside me. "Well, damn, I didn't know that was here or I would've invited you sooner."

I ran my fingertips over the smooth wood surface of the baby grand piano, moving around to the front. My lessons as a child had been on an instrument just like this; a different make, but the exact same size. The brocade bench seat wobbled when my knee brushed it, and I left it alone as I lifted the lid for the keys.

Unfortunately, I knew the instant I hit middle C that the tuning was off. Disappointed, I ran a quick scale and listened to the discordant notes fill the air. Sighing, I put the lid back down. "Oh well, that would have been too much luck for my life lately."

"I *will* hear you play one of these days."

The conviction in Everett's voice made me look at him. He stared back, and I could see my own disappointment mirrored in his eyes. Despite my frustration, I smiled at him. "I know exactly what I'd play for you, too."

I could see it in his eyes that I'd sparked his interest, but before he could reply I held up my hand. "Find me a piano first."

He grinned. "Deal. Now let's see if we can find you some-place to sleep."

Two more sheets later we came across an old maroon couch that didn't quite match the decor, along with some pillows and an old quilt. "This'll be great," I said, arranging things on the couch. There were a few lumps in the cushions but I'd slept on worse.

"Are you sure you don't want to stay in the house? We've got more rooms than we know what to do with."

I shook my head. Everett didn't seem to like my answer. "Is it that you don't trust me?" he asked in a curiously hesitant voice.

"No," I said quickly, and to my surprise I realized it was the truth. I looked away. "I don't trust myself."

I didn't see what he thought about that information, and honestly I didn't want to. "Thank you for the bed," I said, sit-ting down on the couch.

"If you need anything, just come up to the house. I'll leave the back door open for you."

I nodded mutely, still staring straight ahead. All this talk of beds and sleeping arrangements felt too intimate, some-how, and I knew if I looked at Everett, the *awareness* I felt for him would be painfully clear. After another awkward mo-ment, he said, "Good night."

"G'night." And then I was alone. I let out a pent-up breath I hadn't even realized I was holding.

The sun still hadn't gone down yet, but my body was

slowly succumbing to drowsiness. Pulling the quilt over my shoulders, I stared at the far wall before lying sideways on the pillows. I needed to be up early again in the morning for work and would have to budget extra time to call a taxi. Despite a cursory search of the beach after we cleaned up Everett's shoes from my lunch, my bike was nowhere to be found. I hadn't been particularly attached to it, but that meant one less freedom in my life. I was running low on options.

But for now, at least I had a place to sleep. I curled inside the thick quilt around me and closed my eyes, praying sleep would come quickly.

I made it to my shift on time the next morning, glad I left an extra change of clothes at work for days such as this. Six in the morning was an ungodly shift, but I'd slept surprisingly well on that lumpy couch and was actually feeling good for once.

Work was normal right up until after lunch. My only clue that something bad was about to happen was Clare's anxious look from two aisles over at something behind me. I turned to see Macon approaching me, and there was nothing I could do to get away.

"Why didn't you tell me that you were having an abortion?"

At first his words didn't register. "I . . . what?"

"You should have told me you were pregnant. I would have taken care of you!"

I stared at him, his words a sudden blow to the gut. "Macon," I murmured, struggling to formulate an answer to a conversation I *never* thought I'd have, "I'm not . . . I wasn't . . ."

"You had an abortion?"

I looked up at Dolly, the checker I was helping. The appalled look on her face drove the entire situation home, and it was like a blow to the gut. "*No*," I said emphatically. "I would never do that!"

I knew from the expression on her face that she didn't believe me.

"Why didn't you call me?" Macon said, and I rounded on him.

I stared at him, openmouthed, unable to speak. This had to be a sick joke. "Macon, I wasn't pregnant, I never had an abortion."

"What kind of person are you to kill an unborn baby?"

I was the center of attention for the entire front of the store, all eyes on me, and suddenly I couldn't breathe. My lungs seized, unable to pull air into my body; nothing could get past my throat. I hadn't had an asthma attack since I was a little girl. Long ago I'd thrown away my inhaler, not thinking I'd ever need it again. The familiar sensation of a fist squeezing my heart and lungs threw me into a panic, and I fought against the feeling as I struggled to get air.

"Out of the way!" I heard a familiar voice ring through the air, and then Clare was there. "Come on, girl, nice and slow. Just breathe in and out."

Rob appeared beside us. "What happened? Is Lacey all right?"

"I think she's having an asthma attack." Clare's arm moved

around me as she guided me toward the shelves along the front wall. "Lean down and focus on breathing, sweetie."

"Baby?" Macon crouched down across from me, face filled with false concern. "Are you all right?"

"Get *back*," Clare snarled next to me, and stepped in front of him. "Come on, nobody's going to hurt you, just breathe."

It took several choking gasps for air before I felt my lungs begin to unclench. By now tears were streaming down my face, and I swiped at them with the back of my hand.

"What's going on here?"

Mrs. Holloway's voice almost made me go into another asthma attack, and I kept my eyes on the floor.

"Lacey was having an asthma attack."

"I can see that."

I looked up to see the store manager staring down at me, her lip curled with disdain. Her frosty gaze moved over to Macon, then Clare, and back to Rob. "Is she better now?"

By now, air was flowing once more. I still wasn't one hundred percent, but I nodded and answered anyway. "Yes, ma'am," I croaked, my voice all but gone.

"Very well. Ms. St. James, if you would follow me."

My gut shriveled into a hard knot. I couldn't even look at the woman as I straightened up, knowing exactly what was about to happen. My gaze fell on Macon, who'd melted into the background to watch the proceedings. There was a savage glint in his eyes as he watched everyone's reactions. A small wrinkle at the corner of his mouth told me he was holding back a smile.

Oh, God. The whole ordeal *had* been a cruel joke, and I was stuck on the butt end of it.

Nearby, Clare spoke up. "Mrs. Holloway, it wasn't her fault . . ."

"Ms. Bishop," our manager said in tones that brooked no argument, "please return to your customers."

I couldn't bear to look at Clare or anyone else in that storefront. As I walked past the cash register I heard someone ask a question in a low voice, then Dolly answered back in a loud whisper. "Bless her heart, she had an abortion."

"No, I didn't," I snapped as I walked by, but it was too late. By the time I was out of the manager's office, the whole store would know. The truth didn't matter; this gossip was too juicy to bother with the details.

I followed the large woman through the aisles and into the manager's offices in the back of the building. It wasn't large, but there was enough room for a desk and chairs. Mrs. Holloway closed the door behind me. "Do you know why I've asked you in here?"

Because you've never liked me? Whatever my grandmother had said in Glenda Holloway's ear had poisoned the store manager against me since the day I was hired. I'd worked hard, been on time nearly every day, but nothing I could do ever seemed enough.

"You've already been warned once about allowing personal problems to affect work performance," she continued, not bothering to wait for my answer. She sat down and pulled out a drawer. "Please sit down, Ms. St. James."

I sat, too tired to argue. So Rob had told her about Macon's previous visit.

"I don't appreciate having a liar among my workforce," she continued, thumbing through her files until she pulled mine out. "You've made a habit of falsifying your timecard, clocking in either too early or too late."

I listened mutely as she ticked off a myriad of offenses that were either overblown or blatant lies. I just stared blankly at her, not giving her a chance to see how my heart was breaking. She was thorough, I had to give her that. She showed me every instance I'd gone outside the lines, proving that what was coming was inevitable and all my doing. Rob's warning was a single-line statement, but it was also included in her laundry list.

"I took a chance hiring you, Lacey, because your grandmother was a friend. Unfortunately, based on your performance, I'm afraid I'm going to have to terminate your employment. You will be escorted to your locker to make sure you only take what is yours and not what is company property."

Behind the desk, my hands clenched into fists but I didn't allow any emotion to show on my face. I was going to be escorted out of the building as if I had stolen something or wasn't trusted enough to be left unguarded. As much as I wanted to rant and rave about how unfair this was, there was nothing I could do. Such a reaction would only validate Glenda Holloway's opinion of me, and I had enough pride not to let the bitch win.

She studied me, as if eager for my reaction. Seconds ticked by before she frowned. "Well? Do you have anything to say for yourself?"

When I didn't reply, she seemed annoyed by my silence.

"Your conduct here will be kept permanently in your file. Any potential employers will be given a full rundown as to why you were dismissed."

I just stared at her, keeping my gaze blank. The door behind me opened, and Elton, the old security guard, came inside the room. I cringed inwardly at having someone else witness this but didn't allow my frustration to show. Tears of frustration were threatening, and my lungs still burned from the asthma attack, but I held everything in. I wasn't going to give her the satisfaction of seeing me beg or show any emotion that she could gloat over.

Finally, Glenda gave an annoyed grunt and motioned for Elton. "Please escort her out, and make sure she doesn't steal anything." To me, she added, "Your grandmother will be so ashamed that you killed her great-grandchild so callously."

Elton accompanied me silently to the employee area while I packed up my things into a plastic grocery bag. Then I was escorted from the building, left alone only once I'd exited the front doors. Macon was nowhere in sight but I couldn't care less at this point. I kept on going, walking straight through the large parking lot.

"Lacey!"

Clare's voice sounded behind me but I didn't turn, continuing forward toward the main street. Tears stung my eyes but I didn't stop, even when she called my name a second time. I couldn't let her see me cry, couldn't bear for anyone to see my tears.

Beside the shopping center was a six-foot cinderblock wall separating it from the nearby neighborhood. Nothing was on the other side except an alley nobody ever used. I turned up that narrow road, continuing down the dirt path until I was halfway between the two streets at either end and nobody could see me.

Then I leaned back against that gray wall and slid to the ground, bawling my eyes out.

"You seem distracted."

"Mmm." It was true I had a lot on my mind. I hadn't told anyone about my being fired. It was a conversation I was dreading, and I had hoped to replace the job quickly, but my plans on that front weren't working out so well. The fight with my mother still weighed heavily on me as well. We hadn't spoken of it, and the unresolved feelings made me edgy.

I stared at the math problems before me, but my eyes were already starting to cross. Sighing, I leaned back in my chair. "Math has never been my strong suit."

"Well, you're doing better than before. That's a start at least."

Snorting, I turned to look at Everett. He was leaning over my latest test, his hair partially obscuring his face. I stared at his profile, the slightly-too-large-for-his-face nose that still fit, the square jaw that on anyone else might have been too much. The T-shirt he wore stretched across his hunched shoulders, setting off the thickness of his arms.

I'd always been a chest-and-arm-muscles kind of girl, and Everett had those to spare. I would catch myself staring and have to look away sometimes, struggling to focus on whatever we were studying. It'd been a long time since someone, a stranger to boot, had been this nice to me without expecting anything in return.

Didn't hurt that he was cute.

"Oh, by the way, I've got some good news and bad news about the transmission. Trent said he's too busy right now to rebuild another one, but he'd be willing to swap yours out with one he's already got."

"That's awesome! So what's the bad news?"

"Well, it's only potentially bad. He needs to know what kind of vehicle you have to know whether it'll work."

"Admit it, you just want to know what I drive."

He grinned. "The question has crossed my mind," he teased, bumping my ribs with an elbow good-naturedly.

Well, it wasn't like it was a national secret. "It's a 1973 Ford Bronco, stock manual transmission."

Everett blinked, and then gave a long whistle. "Now I feel woefully inadequate. Hang on, let me text Trent and see what he says."

The answer came almost immediately. "He says it'll work, and he's free tomorrow."

Tomorrow was another day off from the sandwich shop. "That could work," I said carefully. "I need to call my uncle Jake first to let him know not to shoot us when we go pick it up."

My uncle Jake lived up in the northern part of the county amid the pine forests. We weren't exactly close relations, but he'd been friends with my grandmother for years and when I'd expressed an interest in cars, we'd bonded.

"How about we move the transmission to wherever you're storing the truck? Trent can use his dad's flatbed, so it shouldn't take much work to get it up there. Probably cheaper than towing the Bronco down here."

I thought about it for a minute. "All right, see if he can set it up. Now, chop-chop, I'm paying you to tutor me, not to sit here playing on your phone."

"Yes, ma'am!"

The entire swap went without a hitch.

I was surprised by how quickly Trent installed the heavy piece of equipment. The wiry boy still manhandled the large transmission better than men twice his size.

"That boy's got the knack for them machines," my uncle Jake said as we watched Trent and Everett work under the truck.

I grinned. "Which one?"

"Not yer boy, doubt he knows a socket wrench from an Allen. That blond boy, though, he's got the touch."

Coming from Jake, that was quite the compliment. My uncle probably would have fixed my truck himself if I didn't have too much pride to ask. As it was, he helped them out, keeping on his feet since both his knees were messed up from an old motorcycle injury.

Trent rolled out from under the truck, wiping his hands on his jeans. "All right, start it up."

I climbed up into the cab and stuck the key in the ignition. It felt so good to be back inside the big Ford. The view was much higher now due to the jack stands, but I'd missed being surrounded by the huge cab. "Hang on," I called, then turned the key.

The old Bronco coughed, attempting to start. She'd been sitting for a good while and didn't like being made to work again. I babied the gas pedal and tried again, and this time it only took three tries for the starter to get her going.

Everett poked his head around my open door. "All right, put it in reverse."

Crossing my fingers, I slipped the stick sideways on the floor. It shifted much easier than I ever remembered before, and I could tell from my uncle's whoop that the tires were moving.

"Try cycling through the gears."

Keeping the clutch pressed, I put it in each gear, my smile growing bigger with each one. By the last gear, I was grinning like a loon: I had my baby back! I hit the gas, glorying in the rough sound of the exhaust, before finally letting it idle in neutral. "That was awesome," I exclaimed, sliding out of the cab.

"Son, lemme talk to you a sec." Jake swooped in and pulled Trent aside, leaving Everett and me alone.

I stared at the Bronco, biting my lip to contain my smile before it overwhelmed me. God, I hadn't been this happy in so long.

"And you called my car ratty?"

"Hey," I said in mock affront, "she's a diamond in the rough. Give her some credit." Truthfully, I enjoyed what Jake called *patina*; the rust didn't bother me, only made me identify more with the old girl. "Anyway, don't judge a book by its cover. Want to see the engine?"

He whistled in appreciation when I finally levered up the hood. "I may not know what half this stuff does," he said, "but it looks good."

There had been a time when nearly every dollar I had went into my truck. Call it a phase, but I'd had great plans for her. Reality set in, however, when my transmission went out just as I'd lost my previous job.

"I'm curious, though, why not ask Jake to take you in?"

His question dimmed some of my excitement. "His wife doesn't like me much."

"Ah." I guess there wasn't much more for him to say. Emmaline Dupre was only a few years older than me and made it no secret that she didn't want me anywhere near her husband. The fact that Jake didn't seem to care only made her hate me more. Jake had been a whole-hearted supporter of my plans for the Bronco, letting me use his yard to do my modifications and eventually store it. Given the fact that Emmaline was closer to my age than Jake's, she probably thought of me as competition.

I bit my lip again, then turned and threw my arms around Everett's neck in a tight hug. "Thank you *so* much, this is awesome!"

It wasn't until he put his arms around me that I realized I'd thrown myself at him again, just like that day on the beach. But without the haze of alcohol, this seemed more intensely *real*. Something in him filled me with a fierce sense of wanting, though I didn't even know what it was I wanted so badly. I froze, waiting for him to see my need and for the groping to start, but his hands stayed in the safe zones. Uncomfortable about my reaction, I pulled away only to be brought up short by his hands locked behind my back. He was watching me, head cocked sideways, an assessing look in his eyes.

My gaze fell to his lips, and a yearning desire to see what they felt like had me leaning forward. I checked myself just in time, disappointment lashing through me. It didn't matter that his arms felt good, or that I wanted to hug him again for being, well, *him*. I knew he'd seen some of my life in the bar and when he'd picked me up from the beach drunk, and I felt ashamed.

I was better than that, and yet, it was all he'd seen of me and my life.

Jake and Trent walked back toward us, and I ducked out from Everett's arms. He seemed reluctant to let me go, his hand sliding down my arm and leaving behind a trail of goose bumps.

Beside us, Trent had a star-struck expression in his eyes, and Jake was grinning from ear to ear. "Now don't you forget, I need your papa's approval before you can do anything on my cars."

"He races," Trent said to Everett in an excited voice. "Wants me to be part of his pit crew."

Jake clapped the boy on the back. "Maybe even a driver, if you know anything 'bout being behind a wheel."

It didn't surprise me that Jake would try to scoop up the young mechanic. My uncle Jake had always liked speed, even if it came with a fair number of crashes. His racing days were the reason why he had two bum knees and a bevy of back problems, as well as a barn full of vehicles to make any racing fan jealous. It also probably explained why he liked robbing the cradle.

Or so my grandmother said.

"You think it's safe to drive home?" I asked.

Trent shrugged. "Everything looked fine, I guess you won't really know until you take it out."

"It's a shame to see this beast so clean." Jake peered at me from over the hood. "Especially given how wet it's been up here lately."

A slow smile crept over my lips. "Uncle Jake, you still have that mud hole on the other end of your property?"

By the time we got back to Oyster Cove, every inch of the Bronco was covered in red clay and Everett had only just managed to pry his hands off the Oh Shit bar. "I see now why you broke a transmission," he said.

I gave him a smug smile as we pulled through town. The look on his face when I'd revved that new transmission and driven straight into what looked like a large lake had been priceless. "Well, now you can tell everyone that you've been mudding down in Mississippi."

"Down in Mississippi and up to no good?"

"Well, look at that: city-boy knows his country music!"

His laugh made my heart dance. I hadn't had a day this fine since, well, a very long time.

"I had fun today."

I looked over at him when he spoke. His blue eyes were dancing, and I could tell the truth from the small smile on his normally placid face. "Yeah, me, too."

We drove along in amicable silence for a while. When I pulled up in front of the white mansion, he didn't immediately get out. It was already getting darker, the overcast skies making the sunlight dimmer than usual.

"I've never been around a girl who knows her way around cars like that." He waggled his eyebrows. "It's kinda hot."

His words made me simultaneously want to laugh and cry. Friendship with a boy wasn't something I had much experience with. There was no use denying that I was attracted to him, although I tried to suppress the feeling. I was so used to rushing in too fast that trying to take it slow was proving difficult, and I wasn't ready to give up our friendship.

At my silence, Everett sighed and stared outside the window. "Look, I know you have issues you're dealing with, and I'm trying to be a friend. But you should probably know that I like you. A lot."

Part of me knew I should be happy—he liked me!—and yet I could feel only fear. Fear that it would end up like every other "relationship," that he'd get whatever he wanted and be done with me. I knew I needed to say something, but didn't know what. *Was being "normal" so difficult?*

When I didn't say anything, he sighed again. "I'll see you tomorrow then."

Panic threatened to overwhelm me as he opened my door and stepped out. "I got fired from my job."

I don't know why I said that right then, but it definitely got Everett's attention. "Why?" he asked, frowning.

"I . . . Someone came in and accused me of something I didn't do, and the manager fired me over the ensuing ruckus."

Macon's accusation still stung, and there was a lot about my life I'd never told Everett.

His brow lowered even more, and concern lit his eyes. "You going to be all right?"

I gave a jerky nod, swallowing down the sudden emotion. He hadn't even cared to know what people had said, only about my well-being. For some reason, this made me want to cry. "I told my other job and they promised me more hours."

He nodded and then leaned back into the truck. "Don't you think about canceling the GED tutoring sessions. I'll take a rain check before a cancellation. And don't play hooky. I know where you live, remember."

The playful threat made me want to smile, and I bit the inside of my cheek to keep my lips from moving.

"And Lacey?" I looked over at him. "If you need anything, just call."

The wind was picking up off the water, a sure sign we were in for a summer storm. Oak trees rained down leaves and debris along the road ahead of me, but I didn't want to leave just yet. Everything in me wanted to stay with this boy, spend more time talking and getting to know him. But going down that road would lead to too much temptation, too much worry that I'd fall into old habits and expectations, which was why I had to get out of there.

Nodding to his statement, I started up the old Bronco as he stepped back and shut the door. My heart was heavy as I pressed down on the gas, heading away from all I wanted right that moment for the place I hated.

chapter eight ✿

I stood in the pharmacy aisle, staring at the boxes. It had been a while since I'd gone looking for do-it-yourself hair color, and I didn't remember there being so many different shades and brand names.

Absently, I twisted my blond hair around my finger. This morning I'd looked at myself in the bathroom mirror and found I hated my reflection. That had been a weird feeling. It wasn't so much that I thought myself ugly, or that my hair was a mess. I just woke up hating the image I portrayed, so here I was trying to do something about it.

Pulling one of the boxes down, I stared at the model on the front before turning it around to check what the various colors looked like. Ordinarily I would have gone to a beauty shop for this, but because I'd lost my job, funds were tight. As much as I wanted a change, I had to prioritize my spending. Right now, drugstore hair dye was cheap, and I was willing to do it myself to save money.

"Hey, girl, haven't seen you in a while."

Surprised by the familiar voice, I looked sideways to see Cherise leaning on a shopping cart, smirking over at me.

Hastily, I put the box of hair dye back on the shelf and heard her chuckle.

I'd only ever seen the bartender in the bar, and under those dim lights I had mistakenly assumed from her self-assurance that she was older. In the light of day, however, she didn't look much older than me. Like a true Southern girl, she rocked the cutoff shorts and halter top, with the cowboy boots being a nice added touch. She seemed far more comfortable in her body than I was with mine. Her dark hair was pulled back in a loose ponytail beneath an Ole Miss red cap.

Right now she was waiting for my response, one eyebrow quirked. "Yeah, I'm sorry," I started, and then trailed off as she waved her hand.

"Don't be. From the look of things, it seemed you needed to take a break anyway." She tilted her head sideways. "Looking to do a makeover?"

"Um . . ."

A knowing smile crossed her lips. "Change can be fun." She studied me for a moment, tilting her head to the side, and then plucked a box of color from the shelf and tossed it to me. "Here, bet you'll like this one."

I turned it over to see a cover model with flowing chestnut hair staring at me. "Thanks," I said tentatively, fidgeting with the box in my hands.

"If it's any consolation," Cherise continued as if we were having a conversation, "I quit that place, too. Got a bit rowdier than I prefer. Looks like I'm taking over at the Calamity Jane here in town."

"You're bartending there?"

"Nope, own the joint. Well, technically the *bank* owns it, but it's mine to run. You should come by some night. I promise to keep better tabs on who's allowed inside."

The bar Calamity Jane had been an Oyster Cove tradition far longer than I'd been around. The club was less than a block from the ocean and had lain barren due to hurricane damage until a couple years ago. I hadn't yet been there but always meant to go.

"I'll see," I said cautiously. "I'm trying to get away from that life; it's . . . not me."

"Good girl." At my bemused stare, she grinned. "Never be ashamed to go your own path. Sure as hell ain't easy, I'll tell you that, but it makes life worth living."

A slow smile crept over my lips, and Cherise winked at me. "See you around, girl," she said, slipping past me and around the corner. I stared after her for a second, then at the box of hair dye in my hands, before moving up to the counter.

While the cashier rang up my purchase, I pulled out my phone to text Everett.

< Where are y'all working today? >

< Down off 90, by the water. Why? >

My smile grew into a grin as an idea formed in my head.

< No reason. >

Half an hour later, I was cruising down the coastal highway looking for construction. In the seat beside me was a large cooler full of flavored snowballs. I was glad I'd brought the cooler because it took me longer to find the site than I'd expected. Eventually I saw men at work on the frontage road and pulled off.

I recognized Trent first. He wore a black tank that was already dusty from the day's work. He noticed me and called to somebody behind a wall as I pulled the cooler from the passenger seat. Indecision hit me suddenly. *This is such a stupid idea.* What was I trying to do anyway?

Then another figure appeared beside Trent, and I swallowed. The shaggy dark hair and broad shoulders identified Everett, but it wasn't his hair I was looking at. Unlike Trent, Everett had opted to shed his shirt entirely; even from a distance, I could see the outline of muscles on his torso. His hands were in large work gloves, which he pulled off and tucked under one arm, staring at me from across the site.

I realized I had been staring with my mouth ajar, and shut it with a snap. Weakly, I gave a small wave, rooted to the ground, the cooler dangling beside me. When he started my way, I almost bolted back into the Bronco but held my ground by a thread. Up close I could see the sweat and dirt coating his entire body. Gray smudges of what I guessed was concrete ran up his arms. All I wanted to do was reach out and see if he felt as good as he looked.

"My eyes are up here."

I jerked my gaze up, face flaming. Then the absurdity of his words hit and I laughed. That seemed to break the tension, at least on my end, and I lifted up the ice chest in my hands. "I brought snowballs."

At his blank look, I opened up the cooler and picked out

one of the colorful balls of ice in paper cones. "Here," I said, handing him a blue one and a spoon.

He took the cup from my hands, staring at it. "We call these snow cones where I'm from," he said, spooning a bite into his mouth.

The ice treats were a summer tradition down here. Already the sun was beating down; I could feel perspiration prickle my scalp just from standing there. I'd lived here for several years and still had trouble with the humidity in summer. "I figured y'all would probably be needing something like this about now," I said, finally finding my voice.

"I hope you brought enough to share."

I hadn't seen Trent come up and turned a startled look at him when I realized he stood just behind Everett. "Um, yeah, actually," I replied, lifting up the cooler. "I couldn't fit more than eight in here, though, but I can run and get more if you want."

"No shit." Trent's cocky smile broadened as I showed him the rest. "My dad left with a few guys to pick up supplies, so this is perfect. Bet they stopped to get something cold anyway; doubt they'll bring anything back." He took the cooler and then slapped Everett on the back. "Dude, your girlfriend's awesome."

My jaw dropped at the other boy's declaration, but I couldn't get any words out correcting him before he hurried away back to the work site. Several other boys in various states of undress had appeared to see what the commotion was about. They swarmed around Trent as he set the cooler down on a pile of cinderblocks, each pulling out their own treat.

"I think you just gained several new fans."

I cringed at Everett's words, and pointed awkwardly between us and Trent. "About what he said . . ."

Everett waved his hand. "Don't worry about it. You want to meet them?"

"Meet who?"

"The crew. Your fans await, m'lady."

I gave an awkward laugh but followed hesitantly after him toward the group. There weren't as many as I'd thought, barely a handful, and they all seemed about the same age. They turned at my approach and the sudden attention was hard to bear; I gave a small nervous wave.

"You already know Trent. His dad runs the company." Everett pointed at each boy in turn. "This is Cole, Jake, Daniel, and Vance. This is Lacey St. James."

One of the boys with a small ponytail, Cole, stepped forward, studying me. He was definitely the handsomest of the lot, but there was a hardness about him I found disconcerting as he studied me. "I know you, don't I?"

Come to think of it, he did seem familiar, and then I realized where I'd seen him. "You're the bass player for Twisted Melody." The band was a regular institution in bars around the county. I remembered Ashley telling me she'd slept with the band members, although I never wanted the dirty details. "I've seen y'all play a few times around here."

"Ignore my gorgeous friend over here." Vance, the lone black boy of the group, bumped Cole aside with his shoulder and extended his hand to me. "Nice to meet you. If you keep bringing treats by, then you're welcome to come here anytime."

Daniel was staring at me, a goofy smile on his face. He

seemed to be the youngest of the group, barely out of high school if even that old. His eyes traveled down my body, then back up, and his grin widened. "I've seen you too somewhere, haven't I?"

Chills spread through me even in the hot sun, and I tried to shake off my apprehension by shrugging. "It's a small town." I didn't like the way he was looking at me. Too many other boys had given me the same look, and I wished the summer temperatures let me comfortably wear more clothing.

Trent must have sensed something was amiss because he cuffed the younger boy upside the head. "Oy," he said in a sharp voice, "back to work." As the others drifted away, he gave me a small salute. "You feel free to visit my roommate at work anytime you want," he said, giving me a wink before turning away, slurping down the rest of the flavored ice.

Daniel's weird reaction to me had dimmed my mood, but I still gave Everett a small smile. He was studying me again, head cocked to one side. Finally, his lips turned up in a lopsided smile. "Thanks for the snow cones."

"Snowballs."

His smile widened into a grin. "Whatever."

There was an awkward pause, and I bit my lip and backed away. "So, um, I guess I'll be going. . . ."

"Do you want to see Cole play?"

I paused. "I've seen him in a few places before."

Everett shook his head. "The lead singer of his band quit, decided to go pro or whatever, so Cole's stepping up to lead. His debut concert is tomorrow night and we're all going to be there to watch him play. You game?"

I was all ready to say no once again when I paused. My

interactions with Everett were disjointed and careful because I felt like I needed to hold so much back. Being with a bunch of strange boys, especially in a bar setting, was asking for the exact trouble I was trying to get away from. And yet, it sounded like fun, and I had to wonder why I was holding myself back. There hadn't been much fun in my life lately, as if I was punishing myself.

Maybe it was time to try relaxing the reins a bit.

I must have paused for too long, because Everett ducked his head down so he met my eyes. "You don't have to if you don't want to."

I wished desperately that it were easier for me to just say yes. The invitation sounded safe, but I'd already made a fool of myself once in front of Everett. Thinking straight with him this close was also very difficult. My hand itched to touch his bare chest, and I dug my fingernails into my palm. "Can I think about it?" It was the best I could do, despite my heart wanting me to scream *Yes*.

"Sure, no problem." He leaned in close. "But let me know if you aren't up to it, maybe we can do something together."

I searched his eyes, trying to find anything that said he was picking me up for sex. That was how his words sounded, but the teasing look in his eye and his casual tone gave me conflicting signals. "Okay," I said after a moment, realizing I needed to reply.

Everett grinned suddenly. "I'll see you around," he said.

He turned and walked back to the construction site, and I stared after his retreating figure. Tearing myself away from that spot was difficult. All I wanted to do was stay there, spend more time with the boy who actually seemed interested in *me*, not in what I could do for him. I saw it in Everett's eyes: I wasn't a toy to be used and tossed aside. There was respect in his eyes when he looked at me, more so than even my family bothered to show.

It was enough to make a girl want more, and that desire, the neediness inside my heart, terrified me. That same feeling had, for too long, chained me to Macon's side. I was only now finally finding my own independence, struggling to discover who I wanted to be. Why would I give that up for a boy who would probably leave at the end of summer and never look back?

But, oh God, I wanted to so badly.

I didn't realize how long I stood there staring until Everett glanced back at me, breaking my thoughts. Even from here, I could see the play of muscle across his chest, the definition in his arms and shoulders. It lit a fire inside me I desperately wanted to keep buried, but it was the ache in my heart that finally got my feet moving. I jumped into the Bronco and started it up, pulling away and back into town toward my sole remaining job.

I couldn't afford any entanglements right then, romantic or otherwise. But I couldn't help but wonder if I let this opportunity pass without grabbing hold whether I'd ever find anyone else I wanted as much as Everett.

chapter nine ❦

Lacey, do you know where Davy got that bump on his head?"

"Hmm?" I wasn't used to my little brother's teacher approaching me when I picked him up. Melinda Jones looked to be on the right side of forty, but I didn't know much more about the petite brunette, except that my brother adored her.

"Your brother came to class this morning with a bump on his forehead. I was wondering if you knew what caused it?"

Startled by her words, I shook my head. "I wasn't at home until after he went to bed last night. Did my mother say anything when she dropped him off today?"

The teacher looked troubled, which made me worried, but she nodded. "If you find anything out, please let me know."

Her cryptic statement stayed with me the whole way home. While I strapped him in his car seat, I examined Davy's head and in fact saw a small bump, barely visible against his pale skin, right above one eyebrow. "Baby, where'd you get that lump?"

"I hit my head playing."

The glum look in his eyes did nothing to assuage my worries.

I remembered the bruises I'd seen on his inner arm, and uneasiness plagued me all the way home.

My mother got home around five, and I couldn't even wait until she got all the way through the door. "Mom, where did Davy get that bruise above his eye?"

She blinked owlishly at me and then shrugged. "Must have happened at the school," she said, moving toward the fridge.

I shook my head. "Ms. Jones said it was there when he got to class today."

"What are you saying, Lacey?"

My mother had her back to me, but I could see the tension in her shoulders. "I'm not saying anything, Mama," I said, tensing for a fight. She'd just gotten off work at the post office; it was usually only when she was drunk that she got easily riled. "I just thought you should know what Davy's teacher said." Truthfully, I was hoping she had an answer to the unspoken worries in my heart.

She closed the fridge door and stared at the handle for a long moment. "You don't think," she started, and then paused. "You don't think your grandma is . . . ?"

I swallowed, trying not to let the idea overwhelm me. "That she's abusing Davy? I don't know."

My mother flinched at my statement, then slowly turned around. "She took him to school this morning. I don't remember seeing anything when we had breakfast." Then she shook her head. "No, my mother would never . . ."

"She does it to me." The statement was out of my lips, years of frustration coming to the fore. "Ever since we moved here, she's been nothing but cruel to me."

"Well, you're different. She actually liked Ben, but your daddy was, well . . ."

Her tone and words made my heart clench, and I tried to shake off my own pain. "Did she ever hit you as a child?"

I could see the answer in her eyes but also saw the stubbornness there. "Lacey May, you let me take care of this," she said firmly. "If someone's hurting my baby, I'll find out."

Her words, the strength there I hadn't heard in years, relieved me to my core. No matter what I thought of my grandmother, I didn't want to accuse her of abusing my baby brother. While it hurt that my mother would stand up for Davy and not me, at least she was going to do something.

"Yes, Mama," I said, relieved.

The tension in the room lessened, and we shared a small smile. "How about some dinner?" she asked.

"Sure." I swallowed as she turned away again, pulling items out of the fridge and pantry. It was nice having my mother back, even if only for the evening. I tried to put the marks on Davy out of my mind as we spent an evening together, free of my grandmother and almost back to the way we were before my life went to hell.

"Well, I say go ahead and fuck the boy."

I winced at the older lady's words, watching as the last customer I'd helped paused at the door, as if debating whether to stay and listen to this tidbit. I bit my lip as the woman glanced sideways briefly before finally deciding to leave. "It's not that easy," I tried again, wondering what on earth had made me say anything to my coworkers.

"Sure it is." Connie's gravelly voice held a note of certainty. "What's wrong with sex?"

I wanted to bang my head against the countertop. How was I supposed to make an oversexed older woman understand that I wanted to change?

"Sounds like you're doing fine," a small voice piped up from behind me. Elise set the bread down on the counter and started loading the long, thin sandwich loaves into the warmer. She tugged at the dark hair around her face and gave me a shy smile. "I think it's romantic."

I turned to Connie. "See?" I indicated the younger girl with both hands, some of my exasperation leaking away. "Thank you."

"Well, bless her heart but little Miss Prissy-Pants here probably isn't one to give relationship advice." Connie elbowed the smaller girl in the ribs. "No offense, sweetheart, but taking romantic advice from a virgin is pretty one-sided."

"That's beside the point," I said, and then sighed. "Maybe I should give up on men altogether."

Connie chuckled. "Where be the fun in that?"

Telling my coworkers about my dilemma probably wasn't my smartest move, but it felt nice to get it off my chest. At least, I'd thought so for about two seconds after opening my big mouth. I'd either been lulled into a false sense of security or was so desperate I hadn't really considered who was listening.

The sandwich shop had helped me some after being fired from the supermarket. It had been a little awkward coming in the next day and realizing my coworkers had heard about the confrontation and wanted all the juicy details. That I might not want to talk about it wasn't even a consideration; the small-town rumor mill had to be fueled or it turned on you. I'd had enough problems lately to risk that.

They'd thankfully upped my hours a bit but the additional hours didn't really equal what I'd lost with the other job. Add that to the fact I was now paying for gas for the Bronco, where before I'd been riding my bike for free, and I was leaking far too much money. Thing was, I liked the job; it wasn't much, but I enjoyed helping folks, and my coworkers were cool. I knew it wouldn't ever go anywhere, but it was so nice to not have to think about things too hard for the moment.

I wanted to say more, but behind me the bells on the door jangled, signaling another customer. Thankful to drop the conversation, I turned around. "What can I get . . ." I stopped as I recognized the newcomer, an uncertain smile tilting my lips. "Hey."

Clare seemed nervous, biting her lip and giving me a small wave. "Hey."

An awkward silence ensued. She obviously came for something, and realizing it might not have been to see me, I dropped back into my role. "What can I get for you?"

"Can we talk?"

The request startled me. I glanced back at Connie and Elise, and the older lady shrugged. "I think we can handle the hordes," she said in a dry voice.

"Thanks." Taking off the thin plastic gloves, I followed Clare outside. It felt strange to see her here. I'd barely gotten to know her, but thought we'd hit it off fairly well. "How'd you find out where I worked?" I said as we exited the doors.

"One of the baggers said she'd seen you in here once, I figured I'd check if you were still here."

"So, are you on your lunch break? Have I missed anything since I got fired?" My guess was that my exit was still the main source of gossip; it'd been less than a week since I was fired.

A short laugh burst from Clare. "I wouldn't know, actually. Right after you left, I quit, too."

I blinked. "Seriously?"

The redhead nodded. "Mrs. Holloway didn't seem to care, but Rob tried to get me to stay. He seemed pretty disturbed to learn you'd been let go so abruptly; I think if he'd known what was happening, he would have stood up for you."

"Yeah, well," I murmured, not really knowing what to say. "It was going to happen eventually."

"It sucked how it went down," Clare said fervently. "It was just wrong how you were railroaded like that. I told Rob that if a store manager would do that to one employee, how long before it would be me? I couldn't stay knowing the ax could fall for no apparent reason. Most of the other checkers felt the same way, but they need their jobs too much to speak out." She snorted. "Wish you'd cussed her out—heck, I wish I'd done it, too."

Her rant left me speechless. I'd assumed that people would have taken the juicy bit of gossip I'd offered on a silver platter and run with it. "I'm okay, I guess," I said after a stunned moment. "I had the sandwich shop, although I'll need more hours to make up the difference."

"Actually, that's the reason I'm here. I was wondering if you still needed another job."

That got my attention. No wonder she wanted to talk to me outside the shop. "Where at?"

"You know that country club on the north side of town? A member I go to church with recommended me, and I managed to snag a job as a hostess. Well, the same day we both quit, I go into work and several of the girls have already heard about it. The other coworkers were curious, and wanted to know what exactly happened."

I stifled a groan, wondering how far my dubious infamy had spread, as Clare continued. "Turns out, Mrs. Holloway isn't as popular as she thinks. Most people think she's a hag, which she is, but they're too polite to say it to her face, the cowards. So you've already got that in your favor, although I may have embellished your story a teensy bit."

"Embellished?" Apparently Clare liked to tell a story. I glanced inside to see Connie and Elise still watching us. "I'm on the clock right now," I hedged, hoping the hint would speed up Clare's tale.

"Oh, sorry! Anyway, I put in a good word to my boss and he wants you to come and interview!"

My eyebrows shot up. "Seriously?"

"Well, Norma-May's having her baby, and she used to wait tables for the bigger parties. It's one of those jobs everyone wants because the tips can double your nightly income, so when I asked about it I was surprised they gave it to me. I mean, I've only been there for a little while, I would have thought they'd pick somebody from this area over me . . ."

I groaned. "Clare."

"Anyway, there's a hostess job open. They're pretty keen

on filling it quick, so the sooner you put an application in the better."

I was speechless for a moment, unsure whether this was a lucky break or another setup for disappointment. Clare seemed to think my silence meant I was saying no because she added, "Please think about it? I know we didn't get to hang out that much but I feel really bad about getting you fired."

"I don't know, how soon can I interview?"

"What time are you done today?"

chapter ten ✤

Two hours later I was in Clare's car, wondering what I was getting myself into.

We drove through the gates of the club, passing several Mercedes and Cadillacs by the valet stand, and picked out at least two high-end Italian sport cars in the parking lot. I smoothed down my clothing as Clare pulled us around the back toward what I assumed was the employee parking lot. She parked and got out quickly, but I took an extra moment to look at myself in the mirror. *What was I doing?*

"You look fine," Clare assured me, opening my door and all but pulling me out of the car. "We're about the same size, although," she amended, her gaze dipping lower, "you may be a bit bustier than me."

When Clare had shown up at the shop the second time, just as I was getting off, she'd thrust a bag into my arms and pushed me into the backseat to change. That was probably for the best since all I'd had at the time were jeans and an old T-shirt. She'd given me a blouse and skirt, along with a pair of wedge heels that were a size too large but still mostly fit. They were spring colors, bright yellows and oranges, and definitely not from any discount stores. But even with the clothes

I still felt like an impostor, trailer trash among the social elite, and I worried I'd be called out.

Trying to tamp down my nervousness, I followed Clare through the wide entrance and into a series of offices. There was a bustle of folks filling the hallway and spilling outside, all dressed in matching formal wear. "They're getting ready for a wedding, it's all hands on deck right now," Clare explained as we pushed against the tide. "The main office isn't far."

The crush died down suddenly as we moved into the workout area, then past that toward the tennis courts. Ladies in small white skirts and racquets passed by, barely giving us a glance. For some reason not being noticed made me feel better. I preferred anonymity and wondered what they'd think if I'd shown up in cutoff jeans and a pair of flip-flops. *Doubt I'd blend in quite as much like that.*

I knew we'd passed into the main club when between one door and the next the furnishings suddenly got much richer. It was subtle things like the marbled floors, expensive wood paneling on the walls, and glass cases with pieces of art. The high ceilings had large chandeliers, and crystal fixtures lined the walls. The whole aesthetic managed to proclaim class without being too over the top, but it still made me nervous. *I don't belong here.*

"Earlier, I texted Drew—I mean Mr. Ford—that we'd be coming. He interviewed me in here last time. Hang on, I'll be right back."

Some of my anxiety returned as Clare disappeared around the corner. I picked through the business magazines on the coffee table by the couches and admired some of the artwork in the cases. Minutes passed, and I grew more apprehensive, wondering where Clare had gone. I poked my head around the corner where she'd disappeared, but it was just another hallway like the other we'd come through.

Not wanting to get lost, I explored my current surroundings a bit more. There was a second smaller waiting area through one archway, this one with refreshments next to a baby grand piano. I sipped on water while I ran my fingers over the lacquered wood, and then sat down on the bench. Lifting the cover as quietly as possible, I ran my fingers lightly over the keys. This definitely wasn't the place to run the instrument through its chords, but I let my fingers move across the keys in a familiar pattern, not pressing but remembering the sound from memory.

"Do you play?"

Startled, I accidentally pressed one key too hard, then covered my mouth in horror as the note reverberated loudly off the walls. I stood quickly to face the speaker, who was watching me with some interest. "I'm sorry, I didn't mean to do that."

The stranger didn't seem much older than me, maybe in his mid to late twenties, and unlike most of the people in the area he didn't have much of a Southern accent. He was tall and blond with a shrewd gaze, but despite having startled me, his even tone and answer made me relax. "You seemed to know what you were doing," he said, shaking his head at my apology. One eyebrow quirked. "I doubt the piano or our guests were disturbed by so light a touch."

"It's been a few years since I practiced," I replied, shrugging and looking back at the piano. "It's a beautiful instrument, though. I learned on a Steinway like this."

"So you *do* play. I thought as much." He held out his hand. "My name is Andrew Ford, pleased to meet you."

"Oh!" I reached out to take his hand. "I'm Lacey St. James. Clare said I should see you about a job?" As a matter of fact, where was Clare? I looked around but couldn't find her.

Andrew seemed to read my mind. "We're a bit short staffed tonight, and I sent Clare to check in with her supervisor. We've a wedding this afternoon and three people have already called in sick." He narrowed his shrewd gaze on me. "Your timing couldn't have been better."

I tried not to let my giddiness at his words show. A job in a location like this had to pay better than the little sandwich shop. "That wasn't my intention, Mr. Ford."

He winced a bit at the *Mister*. "You can call me Andrew for the moment since we're only talking. My father is Mr. Ford, not me." He indicated the piano with a jerk of his head. "Why don't you play something for me?"

I wasn't sure what to say. My jaw worked for a moment, then I sat back down in the chair and stared at the keys. "It's been a while since I played," I repeated in a shaky voice, suddenly nervous again as Andrew came around to the side of the piano. "What do you want to hear?"

"Surprise me."

Being given the choice of music, of course, made my mind go completely blank. To give myself time to think, I ran my fingers up the keys, playing an octave, then back down again to middle C. The dulcet sounds of the baby grand rang off the wood walls and I could tell immediately this piano was concert quality, far better than anything I'd played before.

Not wanting to make a complete fool of myself, I started off with Beethoven's *Für Elise*, one of the first classical songs I'd ever learned. My fingers danced across the keys, muscle memory still good even after years of neglect. The effort was flawless, and I was impressed despite myself.

"Not bad," Andrew said during a slower section. "How about something more lively?"

Without missing a beat, I segued right into Mozart's *Turkish Rondo*. As the decidedly upbeat tones reverberated through the small room, a smile tugged at my lips. I'd forgotten how much I enjoyed this, how much I loved the feel of the keys beneath my fingers. I made a few errors this time as my hands, which had been dormant so long, warmed up to the memory of the music I'd once cherished. But the sound of the music, *my* music, echoing around me was beyond compare.

"What about any modern tunes?"

A second later I heard Andrew chuckle as Katy Perry's "I Kissed a Girl" spilled from my fingers. I bit my lip, trying to hide my smile, and then segued into Lady Gaga's "Poker Face." Both songs were ones I'd taught myself as no sheet music had been available at the time, but they had been my favorite songs around the time I'd quit lessons.

When I glanced up at Andrew, he gave me a bemused smile. "Impressive. What's the toughest song you know?"

I ended the song I was playing and paused in thought, then as clapping sounded around me I realized with a jolt that we'd attracted an audience. The ladies I'd seen earlier by the tennis courts were watching me, as well as an older couple who were dressed as fancy as anyone I'd ever seen. I froze and gave Andrew an unsure look.

"Too late now," he said, reading my expression "They're already here, might as well continue the show."

This certainly wasn't the first time I'd played for an audience, but it had been a while. I suddenly remembered what I'd considered my toughest challenge on the piano. "It's been a while since I played this," I said, giving Andrew a rueful smile. "Don't say I didn't warn you if I botch it royally."

"Somehow, I doubt that'll happen."

Wishing I had his confidence in my rusty abilities, I waggled my fingers theatrically, then launched into Liszt's *Hungarian Rhapsody No. 2*. It was the last song I'd learned before my father—*stepfather*—had died. I expected to feel some pain for that reason since it brought back memories of him, but all I felt was the music spilling from my fingertips. The song wasn't easy, and I skipped most of the prelude and dove right into the hard parts.

Immediately I realized I'd forgotten more than I thought. Still, I managed to cobble it together enough so that few would realize it wasn't the original music. I made quite a few errors this time but the smile never left my face. With an overly dramatic flourish at the end, I received a round of applause from the people around the piano.

"I haven't heard that since Bugs Bunny played it on the silver screen," the older woman said, giving me a wink before wandering off with her husband. I bit my lip, trying to curb my enthusiasm and school my expression into something more stoic, but it proved too difficult.

The rest of the guests filtered away and Andrew looked

ready to say something else when an older gentleman stepped up to the piano. Andrew straightened when he saw the man, but he was ignored. The gray-haired man stopped beside the bench and peered down at me. "Are you auditioning for the piano position?"

"Um . . ." I look at Andrew, not sure what to say. *Piano position?*

"She is," Andrew answered for me.

The older gentleman nodded, keeping his gaze on me. Uncomfortable with his stare, I looked away. "Next time, use one of the side rooms so as not to disturb the guests. But you're hired." He looked at Andrew. "The Bozeman-Gautier wedding is behind schedule, make sure everything comes together in time."

"Yes, sir."

The whole exchange was just *odd*. I watched the older man disappear around the corner again. "If you don't mind my asking," I said as politely as I could, "who was that?"

"My father." Andrew didn't look all that impressed by the fact. "He owns the club and leads the board that runs it. If he says you're hired, then you're in."

"I didn't know I was trying out," I murmured, trying not to let my pleasure show. "He must have really liked my playing."

"Don't take it as a compliment, it probably wasn't your playing that got you the job."

The flat way he said it ruined my mood completely. I dropped my arms from the keys and looked away, but not before I saw Andrew's surprised look as he realized what he'd said. "I didn't mean . . . Shit. We had some drama with the girl before and . . . You're very talented, more so than the person you're replacing."

An awkward silence ensued, and then he pushed some paperwork at me. "If you're interested, fill these out and drop them off by tomorrow. My number is on the top, call me and we can set up a time for a tour."

I took the application paperwork and slid silently off the bench. I'd barely gone a step when Andrew's voice called out to me. "You really are good."

I paused to look back at him. He scratched his neck, looking suitably abashed, but continued. "I didn't think this little town would have anyone as good as you."

"I'm not from around here," I said, before turning away. His comment still stung, although something told me it wasn't personal, just leftover baggage from the previous piano player. He seemed nice enough, however, and I knew I couldn't turn down the job. I hadn't even realized how much I wanted something like this until it was offered, and now I could barely contain my excitement.

Andrew went back into the country club, and I walked toward the entrance, still looking for Clare. I pulled my phone out of my purse to check for texts and then pulled up my chat log with Everett. I was halfway through a text telling him about the job offer, when I stopped and stared at the words. It hadn't occurred to me until that point how dependent I'd grown on him. That feeling unnerved me, underscoring my uncertainty on what exactly our relationship was. Was he just a friend or something more?

Clare chose that moment to come racing around the corner, and I closed the clamshell phone, erasing the text. She was practically bouncing as she drew near, and spontaneously threw her arms around me. "Omigod, was that *you* playing the piano? That was so awesome!"

I smiled a bit at her enthusiasm. "Looks like I won't be working with you and the waitstaff."

"I guess! They told me when I went in that they'd already hired two other people this morning, so you wouldn't have gotten that job anyway."

"Oh." I'd gotten lucky then, really lucky. Talk about a change of pace.

"But cheer up! Your job is way better, plus I think you get paid more. The last girl bragged about that part all the time."

"Thank you." That didn't seem like nearly enough words to express my gratitude. "Thank you *so* much."

She just grinned at me. "What are friends for?"

"Are you working tonight?"

Clare nodded. "But I have enough time to take you back to your truck."

"What time do you get done?"

"About nine or so, why?"

"How much do you like live bands?"

chapter eleven

McHenry's was a relatively new bar in Oyster Cove, but very different from most of its ilk.

For one, McHenry's was on the north end of town, out toward some of the ritzier suburbs, not far from the country club. This seemed to give it permission to sell its drinks for double the price of other area bars, and what should have run it out of business made it the star attraction for area night-life. The place was always packed on weekends, and this evening was no different, with the college kids looking to party.

"I've never actually been here," Clare shouted into my ear as we squeezed through to the bar along one cinderblock wall. "I've heard it's one of the better bars in the area, though."

"The best in Harrison County," I shouted back, snagging a seat as one good old boy stepped away from the bar. "It'll be fun!"

I wished I felt as enthusiastic as I sounded, but to tell the truth I was nervous. Recognizing anybody in the sea of faces was difficult; there were people I very much didn't want to run into tonight. I couldn't see any of the construction boys, either, and tried to forget my anxiety by checking out Clare. "You look cute."

Clare was wearing probably one of the more conservative outfits in the club; her shirt was buttoned up to her neck and the breezy skirt sat just above her knees, but it still looked good. "Thanks, I don't go out much." She didn't seem uncomfortable, however, staring with wide eyes around the packed bar.

"Wait until the band starts, it can get wild." I'd seen Twisted Melody play before and they were decent, but I had no idea how well Cole would lead them. The band hadn't even started setting up on stage, but it was early yet. The DJ's song selection was pretty good, however, and I nudged Clare with my shoulder. "Come on, show me your moves."

She laughed nervously. "I'm a terrible dancer."

"Hey, you gotta learn somehow." Grabbing her free hand, I pulled her through the crowd toward an empty spot between dancers. When I hit the wooden dance floor, I realized suddenly just how much I missed this. There was a freedom in that place, lost in the crush of bodies around you. The music beat through me and I felt, if I closed my eyes, I could just dance my cares away.

For the moment, however, I pushed back the feelings, and twirled a laughing Clare in a circle. "Show me how you can't dance."

I found out quickly that she wasn't lying about her dancing skills. Clare moved like a wooden doll, but by the time she hit the bottom of the first bottle she'd begun to loosen up. The DJ played decent dance music, catering to the younger crowd instead of the older rock other bars played, so we stayed on the floor through several songs.

As she loosened up, so did I, allowing myself to feel the

music and move my body to the beats. My eyes were closed as I rolled my body to the sounds, but when I felt someone move up on me from behind, it pulled me out of the moment. Opening my eyes, I turned to see a younger man in a ball cap staring down my shirt. He reached forward to pull me close but Clare grabbed my hand, pulling me away.

"She's mine," Clare said, and I laughed at the boy's wide eyes as Clare crushed me to her body. He looked like he'd died and gone to heaven so I gave him a little show, gyrating my backside against Clare's pelvis. She took it in great humor, giving me a smack on the ass that had us both giggling.

When I glanced at the stage and saw the band setting up, I knew Cole had to be nearby and, hopefully, Everett. The club was more crowded now and, even in heels, I couldn't see above the sea of faces. I turned to Clare and said, "Come on, let's get you a drink."

Clare cheered, obviously already feeling the effects of the alcohol, and followed me off the floor. "This is fun," she shouted as we made our way through the crowd. "I've never gone out like this before."

"Seriously?" Clare was about my age, but it occurred to me that I didn't know much about her. For all I knew, she'd been raised in a convent. Grinning, I handed her my water bottle. "Here, drink this first." As she took a swig, I managed to catch the eye of the bartender. "Two tequila shots."

"Are you serious?" Clare stared at the amber liquid with wide eyes for several seconds before gingerly picking up the glass and lime slice.

"All right, let me show you how it's done first. Just remember: lick, salt, lick, drink, bite."

She stared at me with wide eyes. "You lost me."

Grinning, I grabbed the small saltshaker beside the drinks. I licked the back of my hand, sprinkled salt on the wet patch, licked it again, and then shot back the liquor. It burned going down, and I quickly bit into the lime slice. "Okay, your turn."

Clare looked apprehensive as she took the saltshaker from me, but it didn't take much encouraging before she started. When it came to the alcohol, she fumbled with the lime, coughing hard before finally getting it into her mouth. "That was terrible," she rasped, and I just grinned.

"I'll admit, it takes some getting used to." Maybe I should have ordered a better tasting brand of tequila, but I laughed when she held up two fingers to the bartender. "I'm the designated driver tonight so you can do these two. C'mon, you've got this."

Clare had downed the second shot, her face a mixture of pain and distaste, when someone bumped hard into my shoulder. I wobbled on my heels, stepping away from the other person, only to feel something cold run down my side. Stunned, I spun around just as Ashley poured the last of her drink on me, and then gave me a smug smile.

"Oops."

I gaped at her, completely at a loss on what to say. The wet material stuck to my skin, and I peeled the shirt off my belly.

Ashley gave me a toothy grin, waggled her fingers, and blended in with the crowd. Beside me, Clare gasped, "That bitch!"

"What happened?" Everett's voice cut through the noise as he materialized beside us.

"Nothing." I looked around to see people whispering and laughing. What fun I'd been having moments before evaporated. "I need to find some napkins," I mumbled, wanting only to disappear.

"Let me help."

I shook my head at Clare's offer and made a beeline for the bathroom. The liquid was cold against my skin, and I could already tell it was going to be sticky when it dried. Fortunately, my green top didn't show much of the stain, and I hoped the evening would be salvageable.

Everett was outside the door when I exited, still dabbing at the wet mark. "Is that the same girl from the night we met?" he asked as I leaned against the wall.

I nodded, not in the mood to talk. It felt like every eye in the room was on me and I just wanted to run. I turned to Everett, intent on making my excuses and leaving, and instead *stared*. The deep blue shirt he wore was fitted to his torso, dark jeans slung low on his narrow hips. The memory of the body I'd seen beneath that shirt proved the perfect distraction, the words I'd intended to say flying from my mind.

Two girls exited from the bathroom beside us, heads close together to be heard in the loud din. One of them with long dark hair and too much eye makeup looked Everett up and down then paused for a moment, trying to capture his attention. Her friend's eyes grew wide as they both stared, whispering excitedly.

Step off, bitches, he's mine.

The possessive thought startled me. Everett didn't even seem to notice the girls, who were alternately staring at him and frowning at me. I could see them psyching themselves up for an introduction and had the sudden urge to kick some ass.

Oh boy.

"I need to take a walk." Not bothering to see if he heard me, I pushed my way through the crowd toward the front door. Behind me I could hear the DJ's music die down as the band got ready to start their first number. I was only interested in getting out of that claustrophobic environment and shoved my way through the newcomers and out the entrance.

The night sky was cloudy and the humidity had increased, but I didn't care. Storms were common this time of the year but it hadn't yet grown windy so I wasn't too worried. I walked around the front of the building and leaned against the wall, glad for the alone time. Footsteps crunched behind me, and Everett leaned up against the wall next to me. "I thought you were going to walk," he said, flashing me a lopsided grin.

"Oh, a funny guy." I was antsy, but his presence helped calm me a bit. My shirt was plastered to my skin and I gave it a few good shakes trying to dry it out. "That was embarrassing."

"I don't know, I've always been a fan of wet T-shirt contests."

His comment surprised a laugh out of me. "Down, boy."

He leaned over and nudged me with his shoulder. "So, is this what you do for fun around here?"

"It's not normally this dramatic," I said, then smacked my forehead. "Oh yes it is. That's the South for you, gossip and drama."

That came out more bitter than I meant, and I let out a shaky breath. Leaning my head back, I stared up at the sky. The nearby grove of pine trees was outlined in the sky above, the moon's rays trying to penetrate the cloud layer. "Lately, the drama seems to always happen to me," I said after a moment. "I'm like a magnet for this kind of thing."

"What's that over there?"

I looked over to see him pointing toward the nearby trees. Following his finger I couldn't see anything moving. Just as I was getting ready to ask what he saw, a spark of light flickered then died, followed close behind by another. Understanding dawned. "They're fireflies."

He was squinting into the darkness, mouth slightly ajar, and looked cute enough to eat. I grinned widely, amused by his response. I had a similar reaction the first time I ever saw the insects; it was fun to watch someone else's first glimpse. "Want to see them up close?"

Not waiting for an answer, I grabbed his hand and pulled him toward the tiny lights. The bar butted up against a large pine grove not taken over by housing developments, and in no time we were tramping over needles and a few pinecones. The insects weren't normally easy to catch, but the cooler air had them lethargic enough for me to trap one against a tree.

"Here," I said, extending my cupped hands to Everett. "They don't bite, promise."

His hands slid over mine, and the heat from his palms was like an electric shock. My body stiffened and I bit my lip in the darkness, not wanting him to let go. But I gently pried my hands apart and deposited the small bug into his hands, watching it blink dimly between his fingers.

"It's smaller than I thought," Everett said, voice low as if worried he'd scare the bug. He brought his hands up to eye level, opening them slowly to see inside. The lightning bug stayed on his hand, calmly soaking up the warmth of his skin, before taking flight once more. It hovered around his head for a moment, flashing several times, before disappearing in the brush.

"Neat, aren't they?" I said as he stared after it. "They were one of the cooler things I found when I first moved here. I remember my mom gave me a Mason jar and told me I could . . ."

I trailed off as Everett loomed above me suddenly. Swallowing, I backed up against a tree as his hands spanned the thick trunk above me. Dipping his head low, he brushed his cheek against mine. "You're definitely one of the cooler things around here to me."

Words were impossible; even swallowing took all my remaining brain cells. He wasn't touching me, but his proximity was doing funny things to my body. My nipples ached, and a burning started low in my gut. I licked my suddenly dry lips and looked up at him through my lashes, at the full lips only inches from my face. My hands itched to touch his torso, to see if his body was as hard as I'd seen on the construction site.

"You smell good," he murmured, brushing his nose along the side of my head. I sucked in a breath as he moved to the other side, taking a deep breath. "What perfume are you wearing?"

As a matter of fact, I wasn't wearing any, which made his question even sexier. I clenched my hands, then, unable to stop myself, I reached out and laid them on either side of his torso. He clenched beneath my palms, all muscle and silk, as I traced the dips and curves with my fingertips.

He let out a ragged breath, and then nipped the top of my ear, playing with the skin between his teeth. It was my turn to gasp, my hand tightening against his belly. I curled my fingers in that silky shirt, desperate to pull him close and feel his body against mine. A small moan escaped me as he ran his teeth down my ear, flicking slightly at the skin with a hot tongue.

Headlights flashed from the parking lot, briefly illuminating our location before switching off. The light distracted me, enough to realize that we were essentially out in the open, even in the darkness. I crumpled the shirt in my fists, my numb brain trying to figure out what I was supposed to do, and then reluctantly pressed him back. Disappointment coursed through me as he moved away, and I took a deep breath. "This isn't the sexiest place to make out, you know."

"I don't know, I think having you back against a tree would be pretty fucking hot."

Whatever vocabulary I still had flew from my mind at the images that statement produced. I cleared my throat, but getting my mind on track was difficult. "There are ticks around here," I said, and then winced. *Way to be sexy, Lacey.*

He lifted me against him suddenly, and I squealed in surprise as he spun us around until he was the one leaning his back against the pine tree. I grabbed his arms for support, and he grinned down at me in the low light. "Is that better?"

I was straddling one of his legs, my breasts plastered against his hard belly. His biceps strained beneath my hands, and I let out a shaky breath. "Not really," I replied, my voice a bit higher than normal. "Now they'll just get on you."

He paused a beat, then laughed. "You sure are good at pillow talk."

I swatted him on the arm and he released me. "If I was doing pillow talk, you'd know it," I teased, then sucked in a breath as his head whipped around to look at me.

"You going to back up that statement?"

My body responded to the challenge, but I tried to back away. "I need to get inside," I said, pointing with both hands toward the club. There was something I was supposed to be doing . . . oh yeah. "I'm Clare's designated driver tonight, I need to make sure she's all right."

I was pretty sure the other girl could take care of herself, but I was grasping at straws. My reason was pretty flimsy as excuses go, but I clung to it like a lifeboat. Everett grinned down at me and nodded, then swept his arms to the side. "Ladies first."

The line into the club had grown since we'd stepped outside, but the bouncer at the door nodded us in. The lights had grown darker and the band was in full swing. As we got inside, I stopped and stared. "Is that Cole?"

"Yup."

If I hadn't known I was in some backwoods bar in Mississippi, I might have thought I was at an actual rock concert. Twisted Melody wasn't playing like a bar band tonight; the crowd at their feet was yelling and screaming as if this was a venue. They were right in the middle of the new Fall Out Boy song, and judging from the cheering you'd think they were the real deal. "He's pretty good." *There's an understatement.*

"He'll be happy to know you think so. Now let's find your friend."

Finding Clare in the dark bar was trying to find a needle in a haystack. I didn't see any redheads in the crowd, and I was starting to get nervous. It was silly; she was a grown girl, she could take care of herself. But I kept remembering her saying she'd never gone out like this before, and I felt protective of the girl who'd given up her job for me.

"Excuse me," I called, sidling up to the bar. The dark-haired bartender came over to me quick enough. "Have you seen the girl I was with earlier?"

"Yeah, she was with some dude in a cowboy hat. Looked pretty sloshed already, too."

I blinked. "She was drunk?" We'd only been outside a few minutes and, even if she couldn't hold her liquor, the shots shouldn't have put her low this fast.

"He bought her another drink, then they danced for a second." He hitched a shoulder. "I think she was getting sick so he helped her out."

Coldness flooded through my body. "Which way did they go?"

The bartender pointed with his head toward the front entrance and I didn't waste a minute. I didn't care if I was rude as I pushed people aside, making a path for myself where none existed. The second I was back outside I moved straight for the well-lit parking lot, trying to identify anyone that might be carrying a semiconscious redhead.

"What's wrong?" Everett asked, catching up to me.

"We need to find Clare *now*." Panic in my heart, I ran through the parking lot, almost twisting my ankle in the gravel.

Pulling off my heels, I started looking all around, ignoring the bite of the small stones into the soles of my feet.

Everett was going down a second aisle, keeping parallel with me. While I appreciated his help, all I could think about was getting to Clare as quickly as possible. Why hadn't I thought to ask the bartender how long it had been since he last saw her? Everett and I had been out less than twenty minutes, surely they couldn't have left that quick.

I was peering inside cars and trucks, trying to search as many as quickly as I could, and wasn't watching my path. Suddenly a sharp pain shot up my leg and I almost fell. I cried out, leaning against a jacked-up truck, and almost instantly Everett was beside me. "You all right?"

Lifting my bare foot, I saw dark blood against the pale skin. It hurt like hell and I hissed in pain when Everett probed it. "No, I'll be fine, I just . . ."

Out of the corner of my eye I saw another older four-door dually truck pull out, the headlights not even on yet. Through the window I barely identified that the silhouette driving had a cowboy hat, and someone slumped over in the passenger seat. Pushing off Everett and the truck, I stumbled past and out into the open, right in front of the truck.

There was a squeal of tires and the crunch of gravel, and the truck stopped in time to barely nudge me. I stood there, leaning against the hood in agony. The driver's-side door opened and a blond boy stepped out. "What the fuck!"

Staggering sideways, I limped to the passenger side and pulled open the door to find nobody there. Slamming it shut, I pulled open the rear door, then clambered into the backseat. "Clare, can you hear me? Wake up, sweetie."

"What the hell are you doing, bitch?"

Hands tugged at my hips, trying to pull me out of the car, then they slid off as something skidded across the gravel. I glanced back to see Everett standing between me and the pissed-off truck driver, who was on his ass several feet away. I couldn't see his face, but from the squared set of his shoulders, Everett looked ready for a fight.

"Stay down there until she's done."

Trusting him to deal with the cowboy, I shook Clare again. "Come on, girl, wake up."

When I tapped her cheeks, Clare snorted awake, blinking up at me. "Hey," she said, a sleepy smile crossing her face. Then almost immediately she grimaced. "I don't feel so good."

"C'mon, man, I was just taking her home."

The cowboy's words hit just the right button as rage consumed me. Momentarily abandoning my groggy friend, I backed out of the truck just as the cowboy climbed back to his feet. "What did you give her?"

"I didn't give her anyth—"

I launched myself into him, grabbing at his shirt and pushing him backward. "Don't you *fucking* mess with me, *what did you give her?*"

"You're crazy, bitch!" He pushed me away, knocking me sideways onto my bad foot. The pain made my legs buckle and down I went, right next to his booted feet. I saw one move backward as if he was going to kick me, then Everett slammed him to the ground. The sound of gravel and fists flying came from around the vehicle. For a moment I wasn't sure who to help, Clare or Everett, but when I heard my friend moan from inside the truck I chose to help her.

I half-helped, half-dragged the groggy Clare out of the backseat and onto her feet. My heel was fine to put weight on but kept digging into the soft gravel. Once we rounded the vehicle, Everett stood up quickly, staying between us and the cowboy. "Get in your truck," he said, pointing at the vehicle, "and leave."

"You're in a world of hurt, asshole." The man glared at Everett, wiping blood from his chin as he stumbled to the driver's side. "My buddies are gonna fuck your ass up good."

I wanted to launch myself at him and rip that cocky smirk off his face, but settled for hobbling over and grinding his hat into the gravel. He cursed but didn't come after it, jumping into the still-running truck and gunning the gas. Gravel flew up under the tires, pinging nearby cars and pelting us as he sped out of the parking lot, fishtailing out the narrow exit. I made a mental note of the license plate, searing the letters into my brain.

Clare squinted after the truck. "Why was I in there?" she mumbled in confusion, leaning heavily onto me.

I looked at Everett. "I need to take her home."

"We can take my car, you can't drive with that foot."

Dammit, he was right. Even wiggling my toes hurt like crazy.

The small car had just enough room for me to stay in the back with Clare. I was afraid she was going to throw up on my feet a couple times but mostly she seemed content to touch everything. "Your hair is so soft," she said, her head rolling on my lap.

"Where does she live?" Everett asked from the front seat.

It took us four tries to get an address out of the groggy

Clare, but eventually we pulled into a multistory complex. They were actually fairly upscale condos with a great view of the gulf. Everett carried her up the stairs and I followed, fishing around in her purse for the keys.

"Lay her on the couch." I turned on some lights to the kitchen, poking through the refrigerator. Pulling out two bottled waters, I grabbed a nearby dishrag and sat down beside an agitated Clare's head.

She grabbed my thigh. "I don't feel good."

"I know, honey." To Everett I said softly, "Can you find a small trash can or bucket?"

"Any idea what he gave her?" he asked, handing me a small bathroom garbage can a moment later.

"My guess is either E or a roofie. She seems more tired than wired so I'm guessing the second." I looked up at Everett, the corners of my mouth turning down. "I can't leave her alone like this."

"I know, I wouldn't ask you to anyway." He sat down on the wood coffee table as I wiped Clare's forehead with the wet rag, then pointed at my sore foot. "Here, let me see that."

I'd been putting this off, afraid what we'd find. Biting my lip, I lifted my injured foot onto his knee, wincing as he probed the tender skin. "There wasn't much bleeding, which is good," he said, "but I need to clean it out."

Ten minutes later, after rummaging around Clare's bathroom for some first-aid items, he packed some gauze around the cut and started bandaging my foot. "So, did you know that cowboy?"

I eyed him suspiciously. "Why?"

"You seemed really pissed at him."

I blew out a breath, tamping down the old anger. "No, I didn't know him, but . . . Well, I had a friend in high school who was roofied and raped. It ruined her life."

He looked up at me, hands stilling around my foot. "What happened to her?"

I just shrugged my shoulders, not wanting to get into it. He continued wrapping my foot, then put one of those little clips to keep it tight. "Promise me you'll go see a doctor if it gets red and infected."

For some reason, his protective command made me smile. "All right, I promise."

"You want me to stay?"

To be honest, I did. Clare was still playing with my hair, but her eyes were nearly closed and she was mumbling soft, incoherent phrases. "Do you work tomorrow?" I asked him, and then sighed when he nodded. "This isn't my house, and I don't know what Clare would want."

He nodded, lips twisting in obvious regret. "I'll go then."

"I got another job," I blurted out as he stood, not ready for him to leave. "Over at the country club. I get to play piano for the rich people."

A smile spread across his face. "That's fantastic, you must be over the moon."

I nodded, biting my lip. "I don't know if you can come see me play, though, I think it's a private club."

"Trent's family are members, maybe we'll stop by one day to see you."

"I'd like that."

He rounded the couch toward the door, then paused and leaned down to kiss the top of my head. His lips lingered for several beats, and I closed my eyes, savoring the moment. "You take the GED on Monday, right?" When I nodded, the corners of his mouth turned up. "One last practice session tomorrow night?"

I smiled back. "Definitely."

chapter twelve ❧

I knew she meant well, but Clare's apologies for her "behavior" at the club were getting annoying.

She'd awoken the next morning completely confused, not remembering anything of the previous night. When she asked me what happened, I made a judgment call and told her she'd had too much to drink and that Everett and I had brought her home early. I left out any mention of the cowboy or my fears that she'd been drugged, but Clare still took the news hard, thinking she'd ruined our night.

Everett had managed to get our cars from the bar to Clare's condo, so we weren't stranded. I said my good-byes to Clare and climbed into the Bronco, heading home. On the seat beside me was the paperwork Andrew had given me the day before to fill out, and I glanced at it repeatedly as I drove toward home. At the last minute, I turned into a shopping center a block from the trailer park.

"Can I borrow a pen?" I asked the girl at the counter as I paid for my ice cream. *Breakfast of champions.* Thankfully right beneath an air-conditioning vent, there was a seat open in the corner for me to fill out the papers.

I pulled out my phone and, after a moment's hesitation wondering if this was the right way to do it, I texted the number Andrew gave me.

< This is Lacey St. James, where did you want me to turn in the application again? >

Halfway through filling out the paperwork, my phone buzzed atop the table.

< I'm available in half an hour. Meet me out front of the clubhouse, I'll give your name to the men at the gate. >

I chewed the inside of my lip.

< Just FYI, I drive a 73 Ford Bronco. >

The next text was quick in coming.

< Sexy. Have valet park it next to my dad's Lamborghini, that should piss him off. >

The reply made me laugh out loud.

< You're going to get me fired before I'm technically hired. >

< I won't, trust me. >

I had no idea what to wear, except that I doubted the short

skirt I still wore from the previous night would be welcomed in a classy institution. Fortunately, I had a pair of jeans in the backseat, which at least covered more skin.

The guards at the gate didn't seem to believe I was being allowed inside, insisting on seeing my ID to compare to their list. When that checked out, they called into the clubhouse, presumably to speak to Andrew himself. The situation amused me, which was probably the whole point. Why be in charge if you can't have a little fun sometimes?

Once I got past the gate, the valet out front of the clubhouse seemed confused by my message. "Mr. Ford wouldn't say that." The young valet seemed nervous when I relayed Andrew's suggestion. He looked dubiously at my pride and joy, as if not sure where on the grounds he could hide the truck.

"I did actually say that." The blond man strode through the doors, towering over the smaller valet. His voice was good humored when he ruffled the younger man's hair. "Jasper, you need to live a little. I'd pay good money to see my dad's reaction."

"Respectfully, sir, it would be me your dad would fire if he caught it out there."

Andrew sighed. "You're probably right." He beckoned to me as I grabbed the paperwork from the passenger seat and handed the valet my keys. "Come to my office, we can discuss pay and do the paperwork, then I can take you on a tour of the property."

We walked through the doors and took an immediate left down a long hallway. Two glass doors later, Andrew held open an office door and led me toward a large desk. The window overlooked the outdoor pool one floor down. Palms and tropical plants lined the edges, and I could see several people lounging on the white chairs. Only one man was actually in the water, doing laps down the length of the pool. "Looks peaceful," I said, indicating the view.

"That's the way we engineered it. Looks can be deceiving, however, but image seems to be all that counts."

I wasn't sure what to say to that, and even Andrew seemed perplexed by his outburst. He shook his head slightly then indicated a chair. "Why don't you have a seat?"

He took the papers out of my hand as I sat down across from him. It felt weird to see someone so young in charge of such a place. I would have expected someone much older. Andrew was tall with wide shoulders, and in the polo shirt and khaki pants he could easily have been mistaken for someone older from behind. Maybe it was his air of self-assurance that belied his age, as if he was used to the weight of responsibility.

"Once upon a time we had a full-time piano position, but times changed and budgets grew tighter. The older folk still expect it, however, so we usually keep someone around. Our last player commuted from up near Biloxi every day, and she had some issues with tardiness, so I was hoping for a local."

"Do I actually have the job?"

Andrew smiled to put me at ease. "You do, we just need to iron out pay and benefits."

Benefits? I'd never had a job with any kind of benefits. This was my first music job, too, so I had no idea what to ask for pay-wise.

"We dealt with the last player like a contractor, paying the mileage to and from her house. Since you're a local girl we'll probably forgo that and just raise your pay a bit."

"Sounds great to me," I said enthusiastically, and then winced. "Sorry, I'm just a little excited."

He grinned, then handed me a folder. "You seem to have a good repertoire of songs already but here's some sheet music of our most requested songs. Do you have someplace where you can practice?"

I thought about the untuned piano in Everett's guesthouse and shook my head sadly. "No worries," Andrew said smoothly, "we can find you something to use. Maybe one of the churches could give you a room, or you could use one of the smaller pianos in the back. You don't seem to live that far away from here, so maybe that would be easier."

I froze when he mentioned my address. I hadn't wanted to put down my grandmother's mailing address as I didn't want to be judged, but it was all I had. From his expression, however, Andrew either didn't know or didn't care where I lived. "I'd love to practice here."

"That's settled then. Now, let me give you a tour of the facility."

True to his word, Andrew showed me around the main clubhouse. He even took me on a short trip along the golf course in one of the carts. If I hadn't long since given up on the myth of the Southern gentleman, I'd think Andrew was the real deal. He was charming, handsome, and, from the looks of things, rich.

He'd make a great catch, but he didn't seem interested in me and for that I was grateful.

Back at the clubhouse, Andrew said, "Membership isn't necessary to use the golf courses, but it is required to use the other—"

He cut off abruptly when a girl came shooting out around

a corner, slamming into him. Andrew caught her, holding her steady so she didn't fall to the floor. She gave a cry of dismay, however, as the contents in her arms spilled all over the ground at our feet. Golf balls rolled down the hallway, bouncing off the walls and out the door toward the course.

"Oh no, I am so sorry . . ."

"Clare?"

My friend turned wide eyes up to me, blinking owlishly. Beside me, I heard a deep chuckle, and then Andrew knelt to the ground. "It was my fault, Miss Bishop," he said, picking up the wire containers strewn about the floor. "Let me help you clean this up."

Andrew was staring at the ground so he didn't see the flush that suffused Clare's face. She shared a horrified look with me, and then mouthed the words *Oh my God* before dropping to her knees. "I'm such a klutz," she moaned, scooping up the golf balls.

"Here, let me help," I said, kicking over some of the ones that had rolled farther away. It gave me a chance to be helpful, and watch what was happening. Andrew's eyes never left the mortified Clare as she darted around the narrow corridor. Clare pointedly avoided looking at her boss, keeping herself busy while continuing to apologize.

There was something in the air I couldn't identify that linked the two, but it made me smile. I made a mental note to ask Clare what she thought of our boss the next time we were alone.

Andrew watched Clare disappear around the corner, and then seemed surprised to see me. "Would you like to see more of the grounds?"

I shook my head. "Thank you for the tour, but I need to meet somebody tonight."

"Let me walk you to the front then."

Nobody said anything as the valet drove my truck to the ticket counter, but the boy behind the wheel was smiling as he slid out. I didn't blame him, the truck made me feel that way as well. There were aspects to my new life that I'd wholeheartedly embraced, and jacked-up trucks were one. The old Bronco wasn't much to look at in some circles, but she could spin the tires on a dirt road and never failed to make me smile.

Everett had already sent me a text asking when and where we wanted to meet.

< I need to head home and get my books first. >

I pulled into my mother's parking spot, figuring I would be only a minute. The study aids were in a backpack on my bed, ready to go, and I was excited. The test was the next morning, and I could only cross my fingers that everything worked out. I'd barely gotten to the top of the steps, however, when the front door exploded open.

"You little *bitch.*"

Hands shoved at me and, caught off guard, I staggered backward against the low railing. My grandmother's enraged face filled my vision as she pushed me again, this time sideways. I gave a shocked cry as my foot came down on empty air. I barely managed not to fall down the stairs by slinging my arms out sideways and grabbing the rails, but still landed on my backside. Above me, my grandmother stood at the entryway.

"You fucking . . . I *knew* you couldn't be trusted!"

My heart racing, I scrambled backward on the gravel as she came down the steps. "Grandma . . ." I said reflexively, forgetting to call her by her first name like I usually did.

"Don't you ever call me that again. You're no blood of mine!"

Her words made my chest squeeze, my breaths going wheezy. I barely managed to get back onto my feet when she charged again, hands outstretched to grab me. It was fight or run, and I chose the latter, zipping around the Bronco to keep space between us. Her inexplicable rage both baffled and frightened me. I couldn't understand what was going on, except that my grandmother looked mad enough to kill me.

I'd seen her angry before, but never like this.

"You eat my food, sleep in my bed, and yet you . . . you . . ."

"And yet I what?" I rounded the truck again as she came after me anew. At any other time I might have found our merry-go-round amusing, but I felt as if I was fleeing for my life and didn't understand why. My grandmother had never hidden her distaste for me, but I was blood. I was family.

"I should have never let you through my door." Unable to catch me, Diana beat her fists on my truck. "You'll pay for what you done to your baby brother."

"What I . . ." My voice trailed off in confusion, then anger surged through me as I realized what she was saying. "Don't you dare pin that on me," I roared, pointing my finger at her. "You're the monster who did that, not me!"

She came around the corner again, face red with rage, just as another car pulled into the gravel beside us. I turned to see my mother staring at us wide-eyed, her face ashen. My little brother sat in the backseat, straining to see what was going on. Then I had to move again as my grandmother reached for me, her long fingernails grazing my arm.

"Mom," I called as she quickly exited the car, "you need to go. Get Davy out of here."

To my horror, she ignored me, unbuckling my brother from his car seat and pulling him up into her arms. There was a haunted expression on her gaunt face I'd never seen before as she ignored me, hustling toward the trailer.

"Mom! What are you doing?" We'd figure out something. My income could get us a new place, one where my brother was safe.

"Gretchen, get him inside while I deal with this piece of trash."

The words were like a dagger to the heart, but it was my mother's silent compliance that twisted the wound and made it gush. "Mama," I said softly, all of my disbelief and incredulity in that one word.

She paused for the briefest of seconds, not looking at me. "I can't," she whispered finally, and before I could even understand what she was denying, she hurried up the stairs and disappeared inside.

A rushing started in my ears as my throat closed even more, blocking off any air. Hands snatched at my arm, and I was tossed sideways, tumbling to the ground. All I wanted to do was curl up into a ball and cry, but the baseball bat I saw in my grandmother's hands goaded me into action. She swung at me, cursing, and I dodged in time to see it dent the rear quarter panel of my truck.

"If I ever see you go near that boy," she screamed as I scrambled to my feet again, "I will kill you. *Do you hear me?*"

She was readying for another swing just as I got to the truck door. I gave it an extra nudge with my foot, ramming it into her and sending her stumbling back. Pulling myself inside, I shut the door and started the car just as that metal bat connected with my driver's-side window. The glass shattered, spraying me with tiny shards.

I dropped the clutch, flooring it as the truck pulled backward out of the drive. My grandmother spun around, pulled by the momentum of the vehicle, but staggered after me anyway. I hit the brakes in time to miss a neighbor's fence, and then gravel flew as I drove off as quickly as I could. My lungs wouldn't allow me breaths but I didn't care—I had to get out of there.

Small moans came from deep inside me, punctuating every wheezing breath. I got as far as the main drag through town before darkness on the periphery of my vision made me pull off to the side. It felt like someone had put a clamp on my lungs. I couldn't get enough air inside, and the sobs that desperately needed escape were choking me.

Staggering out of the truck, I bent over at the hips, trying to steady my breathing. I'd had asthma attacks before but this was the worst one I could remember. It didn't help that I was crying, huge hiccupping sobs that did nothing to help the attack. Forcing myself to blank out everything else, I focused on getting my breathing under control. In, out. In and out.

Breathe in.

Breathe out.

The constriction around my throat lessened enough that I was no longer ready to pass out, but I knew I shouldn't be driving. I'd also managed to cut my legs by accidently rubbing tiny bits of glass into the skin. While I couldn't feel it, the blood was a red smear against my thigh. My injured foot was also throbbing, the pain intensifying as my adrenaline wore off.

Why, Mama?

All that was accomplished right then by thinking about what had happened was that my breathing grew more labored. So I emptied my mind and focused only on taking breaths. Shallow ones at first because that's all my labored lungs would take, then eventually deeper.

I pulled my cell phone out of my pocket and dialed Everett's number. To my surprise, I got a computerized voice saying my call could not be completed as dialed. Baffled, I hung up and tried again, with the same result. A desperate hiccup escaped me as I tried calling for a third time, then flipped the clamshell closed when I heard the same tones. Frustrated and in desperate need of help, I did exactly what I swore never to do.

I keyed in Macon's number and pressed Send.

A big part of me prayed that he wouldn't pick up, that it would go to voice mail and I wouldn't have to speak with him. Unfortunately, Macon picked up on the second ring. "Hello?"

My jaw worked but I couldn't get any words out. The logical side of my brain was screaming at me to end the call, but I couldn't get my body to do it. My heart was broken, continuing to shatter into smaller and smaller pieces, and I couldn't bear it. Macon had been the one I'd always called before, and no matter the situation he'd been there for me. Even if I regretted it later, even if I knew he might ask me to do things I couldn't stomach, I knew that I could count on him to be there.

"Hello? Who is this?"

The words wouldn't come. I squeezed my eyes shut, willing him to hang up the phone, but he continued to ask. His voice grew more belligerent the longer I stayed silent. Finally, he said, "Look if this is some kind of joke . . ."

A sob I'd been trying to hold inside escaped me, and Macon cut himself off mid-sentence. "Lacey?"

The belligerence was gone, replaced by a cajoling voice I knew only too well. The familiarity and dread it produced made my skin prickle, but I couldn't bear to hang up. Not now that my world was falling apart.

"Lacey, baby, is that you? Do you need my help?"

My phone beeped in my ear, and I pulled it away to see an unfamiliar local number listed on the tiny screen. I hadn't given out my new number to many people, so it had to either be work or someone I knew. Staring at the numbers made me realize what a mistake I'd made. If I was trying to start a new life for myself, why was I calling a remnant of the old one?

"Look, Lacey, if this is you, then I don't have all day. Where are you?"

Macon's voice was getting irritated again, and that finally propelled me into action. *What was I thinking?* Remaining silent, I ended that call and switched to the unknown number. "Hello?"

"Oh good, I was afraid you wouldn't pick up an unknown number."

I almost melted to the floor when I heard Everett's cheerful voice. "I tried calling you," I started, but my voice hitched at the end. God, I hadn't realized how much I needed to hear his voice.

"Lacey, you all right? What happened?"

"I was kicked out of my grandmother's house." There was so much more than that—my suspicions about my brother, my mother's betrayal, the fact that Macon now knew my number—but I couldn't say any more.

"Where are you?"

Some small part of my brain was amazed I'd give some-one I'd only known a short while that information while not Macon, but I shoved that aside and gave him my location. "Stay there, I'll be there in five minutes."

The phone immediately went dead, but his words managed to give me one last push into resuming my normal breathing. I made my breaths slow and long, the constriction gradually easing from around my lungs, until I saw that ratty little hatchback pull up beside me.

"You okay?"

I nodded. "I had an asthma attack." It was my second in almost as many weeks. Maybe it was time to get a refill on my old asthma inhaler medication.

"Come on, I'll drive."

It wasn't my normal habit to follow orders, but I got into his passenger seat meekly and put on my seat belt. The ride was quiet, as though Everett knew I needed space to think. I wouldn't have been able to talk about it right then anyway, and I appreciated the silence. Even thinking about it made me want to start crying, and I knew if I started, I wouldn't stop.

There were several cars parked out front of the mansion, as if for a party. Everett bypassed them all, heading around back toward the multistory guesthouse. He shut off the car and got out first, moving quickly around the front to open my door. The gesture was gallant, which a part of me appreciated, but all I could do was exit the vehicle silently.

He unlocked the doors to the guesthouse and let me inside, turning on lights as he came in behind me. I saw immediately that someone had cleaned up the place; the sheets were off the furniture, and there wasn't any dust to be found. "How did you know I was coming?" I asked, my attempt at humor falling flat.

"If I'd known you would be staying, I might have done more."

"Staying?"

Not answering me, Everett moved on ahead of me toward the stairs. "Come on, let me show you the upstairs."

There were three levels, each with numerous bedrooms like a hotel. It reminded me of servants' quarters, although it didn't look like it'd been used in years. The décor in the upper levels, while simple, was dated; some of the curtains and bedspreads looked threadbare, as if they'd been sitting for many years. They were, however, dust-free, as if an army of maids had gone through and cleaned it all out.

"The refrigerator downstairs has nothing but beer in it right now. We can move some food over from the house or you can come there in the mornings to eat."

"Everett, really, you don't need to . . ."

He shook his head. "There's something else I'd like to show you."

I followed him downstairs again. He stopped by the

piano. A small smile tipped one corner of his mouth. "Try it again."

The keys were clean, the dust gone from the shiny black surface of the cover. I gave him a look, then lowered myself onto the bench, brushing my fingers along the keys before pressing down a three-chord note. Gone was the discordant harmony from before; the sounds that emanated from the strings were crisp and clear. "You had it tuned," I said, a small smile forming on my lips.

"I told you I wanted to hear you play."

I looked up to see those blue eyes staring down at me. A lock of dark hair fell across his forehead, but Everett didn't seem to mind. He leaned a hip against the side of the piano, cocking his head to the side. Swallowing, I turned my attention back to the keys, performing a quick scale. The notes rang perfect through the room. "What do you want to hear?"

"Surprise me."

The request made me pause. I had a number of songs in my repertoire, most of which I hadn't played in years. One simple song, however—among the first I'd learned—rose to the surface, and I began the refrain for Andrew Lloyd Webber's "Memory." The notes echoed through the room as my fingers danced across the keys. I knew this one, it was one I had often used for practice, and hearing the somber tones took me back to simpler times.

"That's from *Cats*, right?"

I nodded and continued playing the melancholy notes. The tension I'd been carrying finally eased, the soft familiarity of the song washing it away. When I came to the end of the song it was like saying good-bye to an old friend. "Did you ever get to see a Broadway play?" I asked, closing the cover of the piano.

Everett shook his head. "My parents went to several, but it wasn't really my thing."

"What did you like to do?"

"Lacrosse, rowing, debate. Don't laugh, but I was even in the chess club for my freshman year."

"You weren't in band, then?"

He shook his head. "I just like hearing you play."

His confession made my heart do little flip-flops. We stared at one another for a long moment before I looked back at the keys. "I should probably be going."

"You're welcome to stay here. We've got more than enough room for you."

The thought of imposing made me shake my head. "What would the owners say having some unknown girl move into their guesthouse?"

"You have too much pride. Learn to take some help when it's offered."

"Everett . . ."

"Do you have any other options?"

His blunt question stopped me in my tracks. Truth be told, I didn't. The only other thing I could do was sleep in my car, or see if my uncle Jake would take me. He was my grandmother's friend, however, which meant he would probably let her know my location. Right then, I needed to stay as far from that as I could.

"It would only be for a short while, until you get back on your feet. I doubt they'd mind all that much as long as you didn't overstay your welcome."

I looked around the downstairs area again. The furniture, despite being older, was definitely richer than anything I'd ever lived with. Even the piano, while not as fine as the one in the country club, was better than most I'd played. I felt like an intruder inside a place like this, but Everett was right. I had no other options.

"Fine, but only temporarily," I said finally. "I'll sleep on the couch just to make sure I don't get comfortable."

"Suit yourself."

"Are you having a party? I saw a lot of cars out front."

"Trent invited all the guys from work over to watch a game. The family here has a huge TV. There's pizza and beer, if you're interested." The thought of greasy pizza made my stomach twist, and I shook my head. "Well, do you want to do that one last round of studying?" he asked as I stood and moved across the room to sit on one of the couches.

"I can't. Not tonight."

"But tomorrow is . . ."

"I know, but I . . . can't." I leaned my head back against the couch, staring at the ceiling. "My books are all still at the trailer and I just . . ."

"I get it," he said gently. "What I don't understand is why your family is being so hateful."

I shrugged. "It's always been like this. My mother withstands our life now by drinking, but I . . ." *I don't want to be like her.* It killed me to see my mother like this, compared to the woman who'd actually raised me. "My grandmother Diana just doesn't approve of me."

He nodded, and then looked at me thoughtfully. "There's more, isn't there?"

My face felt pinched as I nodded. "You know what I told you before," I said, my voice thick, "about my real dad being a not-so-nice guy? Well, he was killed just before I was born." I took an uneven breath. "My grandmother shot him."

He went still at my words. Some inner part of me started screaming, *Why are you telling him this?* Because I needed to see if he'd run. I needed him to see how messed up I was, just to see what he'd do. I also knew that if he disappeared from my life, it would break something inside of me, steal that last ounce of hope I held on to. But I had to know, before my heart got any more involved.

"What happened?"

I swallowed at his words. "My mom tried to leave him and headed over to my grandmother's house. He followed and came after her with a knife. My grandmother had an old twelve-gauge shotgun and got him when he broke into the house."

"And your mom?"

"As soon as I was born, she packed everything into her car and drove across the country, looking for a fresh start. Then she met my stepdad, and the rest is history."

Silence greeted my words, and I shut my eyes tight. I couldn't look at him, too scared of what I might see in his eyes.

"So your grandmother blames you for his mistakes."

Bingo. It was the first time I'd ever told anyone else that story, and somehow saying it aloud made it worse. Tears welled up again and I angrily dashed at them with the back of my hand. The couch dipped as Everett sat down beside me. "Is there anything I can do to help?" he asked softly, reaching up a hand to cup the side of my head.

I didn't look at him, but the contact made me want to weep more. Scooting sideways a bit, I laid on the couch and rested my head on his thick thigh. There was a moment of silence, and then his hand began stroking my hair. Closing my eyes, I shut out everything in my mind and focused only on his hand stroking my hair and the rumble of the fan above our heads.

chapter thirteen ❧

I don't think I can do this."

"Sure you can. You'll be incredible."

I wished I had even a tiny amount of his confidence. A sandwich-board sign was on the curb with GED in big letters and an arrow pointing toward a nearby building. The test was being held at the local middle school, and I could already see several people going inside the assigned building. "Maybe I should postpone this for a little bit."

"You're not going to postpone anything." Everett got out of his tiny hatchback and circled around to my side, opening my door. "I know this isn't the best timing," he said, "but we've been practicing for this for weeks. You'll be just fine."

His sincerity was touching, but I wasn't so sure about it myself. When I still wouldn't move to get out of his car, Everett sighed and squatted down on his heels. "You'll be fine," he repeated softly, and I finally turned my head to look at him. He had that lopsided smile on his face that made my heart beat faster, and he reached out and took my hand. "All you have to do is pass, and I know you can do better than that."

Watching as more people filed inside, I swallowed and

then unfastened my seat belt. The morning skies were overcast and the wind was blowing, bringing an unseasonal chill to the summer air. The weather perfectly matched my mood, but I followed Everett inside quietly, looking around. Most of the people there were older than me, although a couple of kids still obviously in high school dotted the area, accompanied by their parents.

I signed in and sat down, playing nervously with my thumb. Everett sat quietly beside me, not saying anything but lending support. I leaned into his shoulder, grateful he was there. If it had been me by myself, there was a very good chance I would have left the test for another day. I wouldn't admit it, but I appreciated his tenacity in getting me here this morning.

"If I can have your attention, everyone." The larger woman who had been helping with sign-in was speaking. "We're ready to administer the test. If those of you taking it would please follow me."

"Showtime," Everett murmured, and I took a deep breath before standing up. Everett's hand stayed in mine briefly as I stepped away, alone. I looked back to him as he gave a small wave and then followed the crowd into the testing area.

"I totally failed it."

"You don't know that."

"Sure I do, because that's how my luck has been lately. It would be a miracle if I passed it."

I wasn't sure why I was going out tonight of all nights, but here I was in the Bronco all dressed up, with Clare sitting beside me. The overcast skies from earlier had turned into a full-blown storm. Trees whipped above me in the wind as I parked outside Calamity Jane, rain pelting down on the truck and falling through the open space next to me. It'd be a while before I could replace the window my grandmother had shattered with her bat.

The parking lot was almost empty compared to normal, but a little rain wasn't going to deter most folks on a game night. It was still early, so more people would come as the night went on.

Despite the fact Everett had driven me to the testing area that morning, I hadn't actually seen him for most of the day. He'd run errands, so I decided to get in some piano practice and almost lost track of time. My fingertips were tender, no longer used to the hard keys like before, but the feeling was glorious.

I could remember a time when I'd disliked the mandatory practice times, but it had been difficult to stop myself tonight. The stress I'd been carrying from the test melted away within five minutes of playing some Beethoven. Visiting the various songs I'd learned to play in happier times was no longer a chore, but a delight. Even learning the new material that Andrew had given me was fun, and I hoped that feeling wouldn't go away anytime soon.

"Look," Clare said as we slid out of the truck, "try to stay positive. If you passed, yay, crack open the champagne bottle, etc. If not, you do it again. Simple as that."

"You sound like Everett," I said, scanning the parking lot, but the only familiar vehicle I saw was the band's van. We hurried inside, eager to get out of the rain. Despite what appeared to be an emptier parking lot, the interior of the smaller bar was packed. As Clare headed for the restroom, I noticed that the band was already set up in the back corner but prerecorded music blared from speakers set up along the walls. The room was divided into three different areas: the bar and tables, the dance floor, and what was the main attraction for the coastal club.

I'd never ridden the mechanical bull, but the feature was one of the highlights of the club. Right now people were gathered around cheering for the lone cowboy who was hanging on for dear life to the shuddering contraption. Laughter and good-natured jeers spilled from the area as he was ejected from the bucking device, but his replacement was ready to take her place. Whereas the cowboy had been violently jerked around right from the get-go, the lady was moving much slower with smaller lurches. Her breasts bounced underneath the white tank top, much to the amusement and cheers of the men around her.

The whole display made me roll my eyes.

Across the room, I saw Trent seated next to two of his coworkers, but I didn't see Everett. I wasn't ready to go over there just yet since I didn't know them all that well, so I hit the bar.

Cherise sidled up to my position and lifted her brow. "Got your ID on you, babe?"

The few times I'd seen her before, she'd never asked me for proof of my age. I was surprised enough to almost give her my real driver's license . . . almost. My heart beat a little faster as she scrutinized the fake card. "You know this doesn't even look like you," she said, smirking as she gave it back to me. "But I don't want to be shut down on my first night so I'm checking anyone who comes up to the bar. Might want to spread that around."

I grabbed my beer and leaned sideways against the bar

as Cherise moved to another person. The whole thing about getting a beer was more habit for me than any need to drink. Earlier after the GED test I'd been tempted to drown my sorrows, but I was serious about turning over a new leaf. Alcohol turned me into somebody I didn't like, let me do things I regretted when I was sober. Still, it would be weird for me to be in a bar without a beer in my hand.

Clare pulled up next to me at the bar, and I grinned over at her. "Glad you could make it."

She returned my smile. "I figured I'd give having fun another shot after the mess last time."

I held up a finger. "I swear if you apologize one more time, I'll boot you back out that door."

Her smile widened. "Fine, my lips are sealed." Clare looked around the bar. "So, where's your new guy? I've been dying to meet him."

"Oh, I can definitely introduce you." I peered around her at the entrance, trying to see if my other invitee for the night had arrived. "As soon as I find him, that is."

"Has he come to see you play at the club?"

"I haven't had my first official day just yet." I bumped her with my shoulder. "Have I thanked you lately for helping me out with that?"

"Not today, but I'm willing to listen again if you'd like."

I laughed, and then took a sip of my beer to hide my expression as I looked past her. Clare caught my gaze and turned around. Her eyes widened in surprise. "Hi."

Andrew gave her a small wave. "Hi."

I took pity on him immediately, although I kept my mouth shut. He looked like he'd just stepped out of the country club, with his slacks and polo shirt. All that was missing was a sweater tied around his neck to complete the image. He looked totally out of place in the bar, but when Clare smiled up at him, I saw him visibly relax. "Would you like a drink?" he asked, offering his arm.

Clare hesitated only for a second before winding her arm through his. "Sure." She slanted a look at me, and her eyes narrowed at my wink. "We're going to talk later," she murmured before being pulled farther down the bar.

That went pretty well. Clare and Andrew looked good together, and I wanted to see them both happy. I'd seen how he'd watched her at the club, and my hunch appeared to have been correct. They stayed where they were chatting once they got their drinks, and I crossed my fingers that my first attempt at matchmaking wouldn't be a colossal failure.

"Mm, you smell nice."

"I smell like a wet dog, got caught in the rain too long." I bit my lip to keep from smiling, and then gave Everett as prim a look as I could manage. "You're late."

He leaned onto the bar beside me, almost touching, and gave me a secret smile. Butterflies danced around in my belly, and I tried to cover my reaction by motioning toward his friends. "Want to join everyone else?"

"Maybe I'd rather keep the pretty girl to myself."

I made the mistake of looking up at him and was struck by the piercing glow of his eyes. Everett wasn't doing anything inappropriate, wasn't staring down my shirt or leering at me, but something about his gaze made my skin break out in goose bumps. Against my better judgment, I took a quick swig of my beer, trying to calm my racing heart.

He's just a boy, I tried to tell myself, but as he leaned closer toward me I felt my heart rate speed up more.

"I couldn't get you off my mind today," he murmured, his voice somehow still audible over the sounds of the bar. I could feel his breath on my ear, the sweet scent of his cologne filling my nose. "You have a bewitching way of making me want you always around me."

My gaze fell to his chest, unable to maintain eye contact with him. The hot promise I saw there made my knees weak, and this was too public a place for me to . . . what? Kiss him again? Jump his bones? Because that's exactly what I wanted to do.

I'm not that girl anymore, I thought, but the repeated vow was growing feeble, even in my mind. Staying firm in my resolve to steer clear of men, however, grew more difficult the longer I was with him. Would it be so bad if I let my guard down just once, and maybe allowed myself to have some fun?

Do you really want to risk it?

"Let's go see what Trent and the guys are up to." Grabbing my beer off the counter, I took a step toward the far table, only to have Everett's arm suddenly blocking my way.

"Lacey, look at me."

I didn't want to, but it was as though my body wasn't under my control. Everett was studying me, head cocked to the side. When I looked away, he reached over and gently took my chin in his fingers, turning my head until we were eye-to-eye. "I won't go any faster than you want," he murmured, leaning in close to make sure he was heard. "But I'm going to tell you the truth as I see it." He stroked one cheek with his thumb. "You are by far the most beautiful girl in this entire room."

My legs went weak at his words and I struggled to keep my composure. Off to one side, I thought I saw Ashley's face in the growing crowd, but I couldn't be sure. Sweeping aside my worry, I held out my hand. "So," I asked, taking his hand, "do you New Yorkers know how to dance?"

Not waiting for his answer, I pulled him out toward the dance floor. The music beat through me as I rolled my body, letting the rhythm pick me up. Hands crept around my hips, holding but not directing me as I danced. I let go of all my worries, allowing the music to take me.

The hands on my hips moved up, sliding along my sides and back down over my hips. Smiling a little, I rolled my body back, until I brushed against his wide chest. Closing my eyes and blocking out my surroundings, I danced for him and was rewarded as his fingers dug into my skin. One hand snaked around to my belly, pulling me back against him so we were together. I gave a small gasp as we began moving together, and I snaked one arm up and back to circle his neck.

"God, you're sexy."

The words set off a series of sensations inside me, making me bolder. I felt almost drunk, high on life, and I turned around so I could see his face. Perhaps that was a mistake; his eyes glittered in the low light, promising all sorts of sensual delights, and his reaction to me only made me bolder. Molding my body to his, we danced.

"Not bad, New York." It was easy to forget my crappy

life on the dance floor like this, where there was nothing but the music and bodies moving in sync. I don't know how many songs we danced to before I finally became totally conscious of how close his lips were to mine. He was staring down at me, the sleepy look in his eyes making me aware of the hardness I felt poking me in my belly. I swallowed as we both stopped dancing and he gathered me close.

"You dance well yourself," he murmured, and I knew he was going to kiss me.

"Why don't we get something to drink?"

My blurted words surprised him, but he let me go as I stepped back. His hand didn't leave mine, however, and emotions warred inside me as I pulled him off the dance floor. *What the hell, Lacey? This isn't some random guy you picked up, this is* Everett.

I tried to keep my regret from showing as I pulled us toward the table with all his buddies. Plastering on a smile, I waved silently as the construction crew made us room around their tables.

"Saw you two out there," Trent said, laughing as I blushed. "Didn't think a girl who moved like that could blush."

Everett gave him a hard jab to the ribs, enough that Trent winced. "Okay," the blond boy said after a minute, "let's pretend that was the beer talking."

"How many have you had?"

Trent grinned. "Enough to lose my brain-to-mouth filter."

"Haven't seen you around lately with those treats," Vance said, giving me a good-natured grin. "It's only getting hotter and hotter outside, so wouldn't mind if you showed up at work again sometime."

"Well, I'm up." Cole stood up from his chair, eyes on the stage. "Try not to get into any fights without me."

"Can't promise you that," Trent called after him. He winked at me. "That's half the fun of these places."

Beer bottles already lined the tables, and I added mine to the throng. "How long have y'all been here?" I asked, surveying the damage.

"An hour or so." Trent grinned as my eyes widened. "What? We were thirsty."

Snorting, I leaned back in my chair and surveyed the bar. Everett's arm snaked around my shoulders, and I hid a smile at the move. The smile, however, disappeared as I saw Ashley staring at me from several tables away. She gave me a nasty smile and I looked away, a sour pit forming in my belly.

"Trent here's gotten himself off the day-to-day grind," Everett said, pointing with his beer toward his friend.

"Yeah, Dad thinks I should learn some of the office stuff. Get ready to take over the business when he leaves for vacation."

"How long is he going to be gone?" I asked, trying to put Ashley's presence in the bar out of my mind.

"Winter's a tough time for construction, so my dad is letting me have the reins while he heads west to winter in Arizona."

"You're not going back to college with Everett?"

Trent and Everett shared a look. "I'm, uh, not going back

to college after summer. Mom's not happy, but Dad thinks it's a good idea and so do I."

Everett's fingers made lazy circles on my shoulder, and I leaned my head back against his arm. Tilting my head sideways, I frowned as I saw Ashley talking to Daniel, the youngest of Everett's coworkers. When she pulled out a cell phone to show him something, a sick churning started in my gut. "I'm going to get another beer."

Everett turned toward me as I stood up. "Is everything all right?"

I tried to speak, but couldn't figure out what to say. My eyes turned back to Ashley and Daniel, and Everett followed my gaze. Whatever he was watching on the girl's phone had him riveted, and I suddenly needed to get out of there.

"Listen, if it's about your friend . . ."

"She's not my friend." I stood up quickly, then realized every pair of eyes around the table was on me. I flushed. "I just need some air, I'll be back."

"Lacey . . ."

Ignoring Everett, I scooted my chair back to leave. Everett stood to follow me, and then suddenly Daniel was there between us, shoving the phone under Everett's nose.

"Dude, you gotta see this." His voice was slurred, the result of too many beers for someone not used to alcohol, but his words were still understandable. "Your girlfriend's got a video online."

The bar was loud: people talked and music blared, the cacophony making it difficult to hear much if you weren't close to someone. Yet I could hear the tiny groans from that cell phone, the familiar jeers and sounds from the video as if I were watching it myself. Horror engulfed me, rooting me to the spot, as Everett stopped, his eyes on the small screen.

No, please don't watch that. It was the moment I'd been dreading, and there was nowhere for me to hide. Everett's eyes flickered from the screen to me, and I wanted to run, to get out of there and away from my shame. But before I could take a single step, I watched as Everett twisted, his fist coming up to make contact with Daniel's face.

The phone flew from the Daniel's fingers, bouncing off a table and onto the floor. Nobody was watching its trajectory, however, too focused on the fight. Daniel dropped like a stone but Everett followed him, raining blows. I covered my mouth in horror as the table full of boys leaped to their feet, shouting and throwing themselves on Everett. His arm was pumping up and down, his elbow visible in rhythmic bobs above the table. Hands grabbed at him but nothing slowed down his pummeling. Only when Vance stepped in and wrapped his arms around Everett's torso, lifting him high into the air, did I see what was happening.

Everett's face was contorted in rage, and as I watched he snapped back and his elbow connected with Vance's face. The black man lost his grip as Everett threw himself back on the prone Daniel. There was shouting around me, and I stumbled back as two bouncers in black shirts waded through the circle of people.

God. I covered my mouth, horrified, and backed away. Everett was pulled to his feet, one arm held behind his back by the big bouncer. He had a gash along one eyebrow, but the anger fled his face as his eyes captured mine. The inexplicable pain I saw there made my heart hurt.

I suddenly wanted to cry. *This is all because of me.* The boys were trying to reason with the bouncers but were ignored, as Everett was held immobile. Not sparing a glance for Daniel, still on the floor, I turned and raced toward the front door, unable to take the cloying bar anymore.

chapter fourteen · 🥀

Outside, the rain came down in buckets, but I didn't care. My boots sloshed through the puddles in the gravel as I ran away from the bar toward the ocean. Calamity Jane was only a block off the water across the highway, and in this storm there was nobody on the road. By the time I'd reached the water's edge, I was soaked and breathing hard. The normally placid waters of the Gulf were choppy, waves crashing against the sandy beaches. The area was illuminated by the nearby pier, but I wanted only to be left alone.

Every painful memory came roaring back, blindsiding me with their intensity. I felt dirty all over again, as if everything had happened yesterday. Waking up alone in a strange bed, sore in places that scared me; my thin dress sticking to my body, pasted there by unknown fluids. I had no idea where I was, no memory of the previous night, but I'd known I needed to get out of there.

"Lacey, wait."

The memories continued to play through my head like a bad movie. Walking home along two miles of country roads, without shoes or underwear because I'd lost both somehow during the night. Being thankful that neither my grandmother nor mother was back from church when I arrived home. Stuffing that tiny party dress in the bottom of the garbage can, then bathing in scalding water for two hours, trying to scrape off the memory of the slime on my skin. Hoping that I could somehow forget the whole night ever happened, even when I couldn't remember a single thing.

Then going to school Monday morning and learning that events I didn't remember in the slightest had been recorded and broadcast to everyone in my school. I was instantly labeled a slut and a pariah, shunned by the girls and relentlessly pursued by the boys.

"Lacey!"

Somebody grabbed my arm, and I reacted instinctively, attacking the person who held me. Some sane part of my mind told me I knew this person, but another more broken part only wanted to lash out, to hurt the ones who'd done this to me. Lost in my memories, I blinked as I fell back onto wet sand, the real world crashing around me once more.

Lightning flared over the water and I saw Everett standing above me, as soaked as I was by the storm. The blood from his eyebrow was a dark line running down the side of his face. I couldn't see his expression but realized from the way he held himself back that it was him I'd mindlessly attacked. Remorse and mortification set in and I scrambled to my feet, looking around. The rain had plastered my hair to my head and I had to look an absolute mess, but I couldn't find it in me to care.

"Are you all right?"

I started to nod my head, and then shook it instead. "No, not really." My voice was a croak, barely audible over the storm.

"Let me take you home."

There were no questions about the video, no remarks on my reaction. He didn't seem at all curious about why I ran away and, somehow, that made me want to explain it all the more. But what could I say? *"I'm sorry you had to see that? I thought with you I could start over?"* There wouldn't be any do-overs, though, would there?

"Come on, let's get somewhere inside and we can talk."

I didn't want to talk about it, though, not really. Lightning flashed again, illuminating the dark waters of the Gulf. Oddly enough, I couldn't take my eyes away. I'd never been on the beach in a storm before. The normally placid waters were roiling, waves crashing against the shore and reminding me of the Oregon beaches.

"Lacey . . ."

"I want to go for a swim." The urge to see if the ocean was as strong as it looked was overwhelmingly powerful. Maybe it could sweep away my pain, end this wretched existence I called my life. I hadn't taken more than a step, however, when Everett's hand grabbed on to my arm.

"What are you doing?"

Everett's grip was like steel, but his voice washed over me like the tide. I was so tired of fighting everything: my grandmother, my reputation, that video. My eyes blinked slowly as I stared at the waves. They were beautiful, illuminated by the lightning, and suddenly I wanted to see if they were as cold as the waters of my childhood. I tried to pull my arm out of Everett's grip but he held firm. "Let go."

"No."

Anger bubbled up from deep inside, and I shot him a look. "Everett, let me go."

"To do what? Go drown yourself in the waters out there?"

No. Yes. I didn't know what I wanted to do, except to wade into the turbulent ocean. It was just a little swim. I tried again to pull myself free, harder this time, but his grip was like iron. Not thinking about anything except escape, I lashed out quickly with my fist, twisting in his grip. The move must have surprised him because he relaxed his grip briefly, enough for me to slip free, then I was racing toward the water.

The wet sand offered me the perfect grip for running, but I'd only just reached the high tide point when something slammed into me from behind. We fell to the ground, Everett's arms pulling me sideways and up so that his body absorbed the blow.

"What the *hell* are you doing?"

"I don't want to do this anymore, let me *go.*"

"Do what anymore?"

"Live my life here, in this hellhole."

"So what are you going to do?" Everett rolled me over, pinning me to the sand. "Swim away in the middle of a storm? Are you trying to kill yourself?"

"*I don't know!*" I wanted to fight something, to rail against the world, but Everett held me still against the ground. Unable to move, unable to fight, the despair burst forward from a dark part of my soul. "I can't take this anymore," I sobbed. "If dying is the only way out . . ."

"Don't say that, don't you *ever* say that."

The intensity in his voice startled me out of my misery. Everett shook me, his grip like iron. "I can't let you go, Lacey," he said, releasing one of my arms so he could stroke my face. The skies illuminated his face again, and the desperation I saw there mirrored my own. "You can't do that, or I'll follow you."

Water dripped from his face onto mine, but the despair I read across his features told me they might as well have been tears. When I didn't struggle, he let my hands go, framing my face with his hands. "You can't leave me," he murmured, and the anguish I saw in his eyes broke my heart. "Don't go, please . . ."

His face hovered above me, his lips only inches from mine. Around us the storm raged, but for right now there was only the two of us. It took barely a tilt of my head, the smallest of movements, for me to brush my lips across his. I tasted salt mingled with the rain, and wondered if they were his tears or mine. Then Everett's lips parted, deepening the kiss, and my brain lost focus on everything but his taste.

There was desperation in his kiss, a hunger that answered a similar need inside me. I twined my arms around his neck, pulling him close, sighing into his mouth. Every situation weighing on my mind fled at his touch, and I sighed into his mouth as he gathered me up.

"Don't leave me," he pleaded against my mouth, his lips trailing down my neck. I sighed, enjoying the feel of his body on top of mine as he slowly chased away the lingering darkness in my mind. His touch was like a balm, distracting me from the pain until it was only a memory, not a monster ready to swallow me whole.

This close, even in the darkness, I could see the beautiful lines of his face. His hair hung down from his head, the shaggy locks limp and dripping from the rain. The bedraggled look somehow struck me as amusing, and I gave him a small smile. "You look cold."

"So do you."

I touched his cheek, running my fingers along his face before leaning up and giving him another feather-soft kiss. "Can you take me home?"

Everett's eyes searched mine, and then I saw the edges of his eyes crinkle slightly as he smiled. "I'll drive you."

He helped me to my feet, but wouldn't let go of my hand. I don't know if he was afraid I'd take off running toward the water or just wanted to hold my hand, but I didn't protest. The crash of the waves lessened as we crossed back toward Calamity Jane hand in hand.

Everett led me over to his car, but as he opened my door I saw Trent walk over from under the awning. He took in our bedraggled faces and soaked clothes, then gave a lopsided grin. "Glad you found her."

I looked away from Trent, just wanting to hide in the car, but paused as the blond boy called my name. "I remember you from school now. It was shitty what happened to you back then, and I'm not going to let it happen again now."

Flushing with shame, I ducked quickly inside the car door. Outside, I heard Everett say his good-byes, and then he got inside the car and drove out of the parking lot. "We'll get your truck tomorrow, I promise."

The mansion was only a few miles away, and we spent most of the drive in silence. I snuck peeks at Everett, who kept his eyes focused on the rainy road ahead. He pulled up behind the house and came around to open my door, but when I started toward the guesthouse he grabbed my hand.

"Come on, we have some towels upstairs."

I followed him inside the back entrance, acutely aware of his hand in mine. The lights inside were all off, although the exterior around the compound was kept lit. I followed him blindly as we weaved around furniture, my heart fluttering as we went up the stairs.

Everett rummaged through a hall cabinet and then threw a large towel over my shoulders. "Here, use this to dry off real quick."

I drew it around me, not realizing just how cold I really was until I had the terry cloth over me. Everett must have noticed because he began rubbing my shoulders. "We should probably get you out of your clothes."

I knew the moment he realized exactly what he said because his hands stopped trying to dry me off and he cleared his throat. His uncertainty made me smile, but I kept quiet, not wanting to ruin the moment with a joke. "I can get you some clean clothes from the guesthouse while you take a shower."

"They're all in my truck," I said, shaking my head.

"Well, maybe we can borrow from the people who live here. There's a girl's room just down the hall, her clothes will fit you."

"You've gone through the drawers?" I quipped, and flushed at the shrewd look he gave me.

"Never know when I might want to suddenly become a cross-dresser."

The deadpan statement made me laugh, and I clapped my

hand over my mouth. In the low light, Everett grinned and handed me another towel. "Take a shower and get the sand off you, I'll have clothes for you when you get done."

For a guest bathroom, it was pretty darned big. There was a white metal tub to one side that looked deep enough to sleep in, but the shower was insane: four jets, two on each side, as well as one traditional showerhead.

"Yeah," I murmured to myself, wadding the now-sandy towel onto the floor near the tub, "I gotta try this."

I wasn't sure how long I stayed in that bathroom, but I couldn't remember the last time I had this much fun. The shower itself had numerous settings as well as a waterproof keypad that let you play music, but I wasn't in the mood for songs. I took my time, not leaving the shower until the water was lukewarm even on the highest heat settings. The new towel Everett had given me was big enough to wrap around me twice and nearly came to my knees, so I wasn't afraid to open the door and step outside.

The lights in the hall and interior were still off, but I blinked as I saw a row of small candles on the floor. A smile tilted my lips as I followed the tiny votives, padding quietly over the wood floors in bare feet. The hallway was long, curving around a corner to the left before opening up into a large bedroom. My jaw dropped as I stared around the room, lit only by the glow of what seemed like a million candles.

"I thought you'd never get done in there."

Arms wrapped themselves over my shoulders as Everett moved in behind me, laying his chin on one shoulder. "It's the master bedroom," he murmured in my ear, sending chills up my body. "You can stay here for the night."

"But . . ." I was speechless, looking around the room. Setting this up must have taken him forever, as well as lighting this many candles. "You did this for me?" I whispered.

He nuzzled my neck, lips laying a soft kiss just behind my ear, and my breath hitched in my throat. "I thought you deserved something nice after the day you've had."

I turned in his arms and stared up into his eyes. Everett had a small smile on his face and, despite the opportunity to look down my towel, kept his eyes fixed on mine. He stroked my cheek with one hand. "Everyone deserves some happy memory, something they can . . ."

My kiss silenced him. I looped my arms around his neck as his grip tightened across my back, pressing me against his body. His clothing was dry, meaning he'd changed, but the thin pajama pants did little to hide the telltale bulge. *So he's not as unaffected as I thought.* As an experiment, I pressed my hips forward, rubbing his chest with mine, and heard his breath hitch.

"Why did you really do this?" I whispered, staring up into his eyes.

His throat worked, hands tightening against my back. "Because every girl should get a proper first time."

I knew exactly what he was saying, and drew in a shaky breath. "I've had mine," I murmured, but before I could get lost in the darkness he shook his head.

"No, you didn't." Everett lifted up my chin until I was forced to look at his face. "Yours was stolen from you. What happened was cruel and unforgivable, and you deserve better."

"And you think you can give me one better?"

"I'd like to try, more than anything in the world."

His offer made me want to cry. A loud, cynical part of my soul cried out, *He's a boy. He doesn't care about you. He just wants sex.* But the candles, the truth I saw in his eyes, told me there was so much more. Torn, I laid my hand on his chest, feeling his heart beat beneath my palms. I wanted him so bad it hurt, and yet . . . "I don't want to be that girl anymore."

He took my hand and kissed the palm. "Then start over. Be whoever you want to be. Lacey, if you say no, then I'll walk away and still be your friend tomorrow." He stroked my cheek again. "But please say yes."

I stared up into his eyes, then with a shaky hand I pulled out the little knot to the towel wrapped around me. The terry cloth stayed in place, held there by our pressing bodies. "Help me with this?" I whispered, my body tightening with longing as his eyes sharpened.

Everett skimmed his hands up my sides, lifting my arms and raising them above my head. I held them there as he carefully unwrapped the large towel from around me, shivering from far more than the cold. I swallowed as the towel, no longer held in place, slipped from my body.

"You're so beautiful."

Drawing in a trembling breath, I lowered my arms around his neck. His fingers slid down my back, following my backbone before fanning out over my hips. Then, with barely any noticeable effort, he grabbed my backside and picked me up. Yelping in surprise, I wrapped my legs around his waist, then stared down wide-eyed into his smiling face.

"I gotcha," he said, winking, and then one hand went behind my head, pulling me down into a kiss. I sighed, parting my lips to accept the flicks of his tongue as he walked us across the room to the bed. He laid me slowly back onto the large mattress and carefully crawled over on top of me, straddling my body. I clung to him, even when he let me go, but Everett didn't seem to mind. My hands went down across his chest, then started tugging at his shirt. "Take this off."

He quickly complied, pulling it over his head. Biting my lip, I ran my hands along the bare torso I'd been dying to touch for so long. His touch mirrored mine, and I arched my back as his palms brushed across my aching nipples. He flicked them with his thumbs and I groaned.

"You're so sexy," he breathed above me. His hands moved across my skin, and I arched my back more to give him better access. He dipped his head and I gasped as his mouth closed over one nipple. A needy groan exploded out of me as Everett dragged his teeth over one breast, then across to the other.

His hands moved around to span my belly, sliding down across my hips. He grasped my thighs and spread my legs, and I closed my eyes, trying to block out the sexiness of his gaze locked on mine.

It was his turn to groan as he bent down again, his lips meeting mine, his kisses growing suddenly fierce. I met him, lips and tongues clashing as he jerked his hips forward, pressing against my aching sex and making me gasp. Small needy sounds came from my mouth as I tried to push down his pants, desperate for more.

"I have something else in mind."

His kisses trailed down my neck and down my belly, and I jerked as I felt lips press over me. A cry tore from my lips as his tongue flicked out, brushing over the hard bud of my clit. I grabbed at the sheets above me, hanging on for dear life as his mouth worked magic, drawing guttural cries from my throat. By the time he lifted his head, I was a quivering mess, my body already worn out by pleasure.

Everett stalked up my body, trailing kisses along my torso as I sank my hands into his hair. "I want to be inside you so bad," he murmured against my skin, lips moving along my jaw. "I want to feel you around me, make you cry my name as you come."

I grabbed his head, pulling his lips to mine, as he maneuvered himself over me. He didn't move any closer, however, even when I wrapped my legs around his waist silently urging him on. When he did lower himself over me finally, he still didn't go inside, instead sliding his hard shaft through my wet folds. I dug my nails into his back, urging him on with my cries, but his will was like iron.

His grip tightened on me and I thought for sure this was it. I was ready to take him, desperate to feel him inside me, but I wasn't prepared when he rolled us sideways, reversing our positions. I blinked down at him in the candlelight, and Everett just grinned. "Your turn."

It never occurred to me until that minute, but I'd never had sex on top of a boy like this. There was a certain vulnerability to the position, but power as well, I realized, as I sat on his hips, feeling him hard against my backside. I ran my hands across his torso, testing out the field, and heard his small groan when I raked my fingernails lightly across his muscles. A slow smile spread across my face as I leaned forward, sliding my backside up and down his shaft.

His fingers dug into my hips. "Tease," he gasped, and I laughed.

No matter the position, there were things my body desperately needed. Teasing wasn't enough, and as I lifted my hips and settled him at my opening, I saw his lips part. When I pressed down, letting him fill me, his chest stuttered. "God," he moaned as I reached the base, then lifted myself again. His hands ran up my torso as I began riding him, slow at first but with longer strokes in and out as I found our rhythm.

The memory of us dancing earlier at the club flashed across my mind, and as the DJ's music filled my head I rolled my hips. Everett's hands tightened around my knees, his head arching backward, so I did it again. "Fuck, you feel good," he groaned and I licked my lips, twisting my hips and squeezing around him until he moaned.

I leaned forward and gasped as the position rubbed him against something inside my body. He must have liked it, too, because he surged up inside me, and I cried out.

The world tilted, and suddenly I was back down on the mattress with Everett looming above me. There was no mercy in his face as he stared down at me, only hard need. He surged inside me, stabbing deep, and I cried out in pleasure. His need matched my own, and I scrabbled at his back, tilting my hips up to meet his thrusts. Guttural cries were pulled from his throat as his teeth grazed my shoulder, and I hooked my ankles behind his back.

My orgasm rose quickly in the face of his intensity, and I gave a startled cry as it broke over me. Everett lifted his head and our eyes met. I cried out again as he thrust hard inside me, the move sending waves upon waves through my body.

He gave a hoarse shout, and then his body shuddered above mine.

I closed my eyes, trying to catch my breath. Everett, spent as well, lowered himself over me, pressing me into the mattress with his weight. I wrapped my arms around him and we stayed like that for a minute, just catching our collective breath.

"So," I murmured when I could breathe right again, "you up for another go?"

Not even bothering to raise his head and look at me, Everett held up one index finger. "Give me a minute to answer that."

I smiled and gathered him close. Tiny tremors still shook my body occasionally but I was loath to give this up just yet. My fingers drew tiny circles on his back, moving up and down his spine, until he finally stirred. Pulling himself out of me, he wrapped his arms around my body and pulled me sideways until we were spooning. He nuzzled my hair and kissed my ear. "That was nice."

"*Nice?*" Twisting in his arms, I turned to see him grinning at me. "Just nice, huh?"

"Really nice? Incredibly nice? What about holy-cow-I'd-do-it-again-if-I-weren't-so-spent nice?" He pulled me closer so that my breasts pressed against his chest. "Would *incredible* be a better word?"

"You're getting warmer." I pushed his dark locks back from his face, enjoying the silky feel of his hair through my fingers. "Are you this charming with all the girls you meet?"

He shook his head. "Just the ones I like."

"How often does that happen?"

The edges of his smile tipped downward and something dark flickered in his eyes. Then just as quickly, it was gone. "Not too often, actually."

Realizing I'd struck a nerve, I flicked his ear as a distraction. "So you're saying I should feel lucky?" I said in a prim voice, and was rewarded by another smile. "Because, for all I know, that was just a one-time experience."

The fingers doing slow circles over my hip bone stilled. "One-time?"

"You know, the kind that can't happen again." I made a show of looking at my nails as Everett sputtered. "Maybe you only have it in you to do this once tonight, and that would be okay, many men . . ."

Everett growled, and suddenly I was on my back again. He stared smugly down at me. "Challenge accepted," he murmured, lowering his lips back to mine.

"What's the best thing about New York City?"

"Why do you want to hear about New York so much?"

"Because it isn't here." I propped my chin on my hands on his chest, staring up at his face. "How long have you lived there?"

"Mostly I just went to a boarding school there. My family lived elsewhere, only coming to see me for the holidays."

I frowned. "That sounds like a really cold childhood."

Everett shrugged. "It was all I knew at the time. Eventually, my parents began spending the summer in the state as well, preferring the company I guess. I was in the city more often than at home."

"So what's a city-boy like you doing in someplace like Oyster Cove?"

"Well, I went to college with Trent and then followed him here when I needed to get away from family." He poked the tip of my nose with a finger. "Question is, why are you still here?"

I let my head fall against his belly, muffling my answer. He lifted my head, raising his eyebrows, and I sighed. "There was always one more reason to stay, one last piece of the puzzle to figure out before I could go."

Everett gave me a droll look. "So you always made excuses," he translated.

"Precisely." I laid my cheek against Everett's chest. "Whether it was my brother's day-care bill, or my truck was out of commission, there was always something holding me back. Usually it came down to money, and how much I lacked whenever things got really bad."

"Where would you go?"

I hitched one shoulder. "Somewhere I could play the piano. Some place nobody knows anything about me."

"What about your family in Oregon?"

"Why do you always ask about them?"

The question came out more confrontational than I'd intended, but Everett answered anyway. "One of the biggest influences in my life was a man completely unrelated to me. My parents haven't played a big part of my life. This man would come regularly to see me in New York, send me cards and gifts for my birthday and holidays. Anytime things got bad, he would be the first person to show up to help."

I digested that for a moment, laying my head against his

chest again. "I may need to contact them soon anyway," I murmured, feeling reluctant to even say the words. "I think my baby brother's being abused."

Everett was silent for a long moment. "Is that why you got kicked out?"

I nodded my head, misery rising up. "My grandmother accused me of doing it, and my mom didn't bother to defend me."

"Which do you think is doing it, your mom or your grandmother?"

I shook my head. "I don't know, and that's the worst part of all. Whatever I do, I need to do it soon for my brother's sake." I laid my cheek on his chest, tightening my arms around his chest. "Do you have any siblings?"

"None."

"Did you ever wish you did?"

Everett shook his head. "Would you move back to Oregon if you could patch things up with your family?"

The change in subject wasn't subtle, but I let it slide. "It's a lot more expensive to live there than here . . ."

"All I hear are more excuses."

I stuck my tongue out at him. "New York sounds good, too," I quipped, and Everett stilled. It was too late to take back my words, and I felt like kicking myself. "Bet that sounded crazy-stalkerish," I said glumly, expecting he wanted to run.

"No, it's just . . . surprising."

"Why?"

He didn't answer immediately, which only made me feel worse. Now was too early in, well, whatever we had for me to get possessive. The thought of him leaving again at the end of summer made my heart hurt, however. Embarrassed by my revelation, I tried to roll away only to have Everett's arm snag me back against him. "Did I say you could leave?"

The imperious question made me throw him a frown, which quickly became a laugh as he made a face at me. "Oh yeah, so sexy," I said, giggling as he rolled over atop me.

"I'll show you sexy," he growled, pressing me onto the mattress and taking my lips with his. I answered his need with my own, wrapping my arms around his neck and tilting my body up to accept him.

We stayed like this all night, waking one another up as the hunger dictated. Once I woke him with my mouth and rode him to completion. Another time, I awoke to find us spooned together with him already inside me. Every time was magical, and with each successive coupling we slept more and more soundly until finally it was light outside.

When I awoke the final time, the bed beside me was empty. Light streamed in through the nearby windows and I pulled the sheets up to my neck. Candles dotted the walls, burned or blown out by now. I was alone in the large room, and I wasn't sure how I felt about that.

My whole plan for a new life had been to stay away from boys and focus on *me* for once. I'd been doing well until I'd let Everett in as my tutor. Now I was back to square one, naked and alone in a strange bed at a boy's house. How was this any different from before, the life I'd been desperate to leave?

I stretched, reveling in the delicious soreness. *Because it's Everett's bed.*

As desperate as I was for a new life, there was nothing

about the previous night I could regret. I rolled my head sideways, smiling at the candles on the small stand beside the bed. They had burned down overnight, but just seeing them reminded me of the romance.

I'd never met anyone like Everett. The myth of the Southern gentlemen, as least in my experience, was a lie. Everett may not have been Southern, but he'd never been anything but the perfect gentleman, almost too good to be true. I'd been burned so many times that I'd almost given up on men.

Apparently, there were still a few good ones scattered here and there. Somehow, one had managed to land here in Oyster Cove.

I looked around the room, and to my surprise I spotted a small pile of clothes at the foot of the bed. A torn-off sheet of paper laid atop them, saying simply, "For you." I had no idea whose clothes they were but they did appear to be roughly the right size. I cleaned up quickly in the bathroom before stepping outside into the hallway.

The house really was like something straight out of the *Gone with the Wind* set, at least until you noticed the big flatscreen TV above the fireplace. The furniture looked period as well, although whether they were indeed antiques or modern replicas I hadn't the eye to tell.

For some reason, the bodies of boys draped over the dainty antebellum chairs amused me. All of Everett's coworkers from the bar were here, although I hadn't heard them arrive at the house last night. I tiptoed downstairs, trying to make as little noise as possible, but I needn't have bothered. Loud snoring came from the far area as Vance somehow managed to sleep sideways in an armchair half his size. The couch held

Trent, who, as I watched, snorted in his sleep, sounding for all the world like a pig.

"You up for breakfast?"

Everett's whispered voice came from an opening at the far end of the room as he peeked inside. I carefully avoided furniture and passed-out boys, moving into the massive country kitchen with high ceilings and thick tile.

"You work today?"

I nodded. "Later this afternoon."

"Too bad." Everett snatched me close, and I pursed my lips to keep from laughing too loudly. "Because I have plans for you . . ."

Giggling came from inside the other room, definitely not from any of the boys laid out on the furniture. Frowning, I leaned back, peeking into the other room just in time to see two skinny girls, a blonde and a brunette, escape out the front door. Cole was coming down the stairs, a big grin on his face. "Being in a band is *awesome*," he announced loudly, jolting several nearby awake. Trent groaned, grabbing his head in obvious pain.

I rolled my eyes and leaned into Everett. "Looks like we have a few more people to cook for this morning."

He laid a quick kiss to my lips. "I'd love the help."

chapter fifteen ❧

I stared at my reflection in the bathroom mirror, trying not to freak out.

The box of hair dye, now empty, that had been sitting in my truck for what felt like forever teetered on the edge of the sink. The model's hair a gorgeous chestnut, so unlike the new reality of my existence. I'd bleached my hair for years, even before I'd moved to Mississippi, and had grown used to the lighter color on my head. Despite following the instructions on the box to the letter, I now had hair that was several shades darker than the model's, the fried locks having soaked up the dye like a sponge. I was left with almost-black hair atop my head and down around my shoulders. Some of it would wash out, that much I knew from experience, but that didn't stop my mini freak-out.

Just seeing my reflection made me want to hyperventilate. The dark mane plastered to my head like a hoodie looked *wrong*. I'd wanted a change, something different to symbolize the life I was leaving behind, but nothing anywhere near this drastic.

Even after two showers, the color didn't appear to be fading at all. It clung to my face, making my skin seem practically translucent in comparison. The effect was startling, but if I wasn't being critical, it wasn't totally horrible.

Well, look on the bright side, I thought. *At least my eyebrows don't seem so dark anymore.*

Seriously, small comfort.

I'd decided to do the dye job spontaneously, opening the box and mixing the contents before I'd given myself time to think it through. Now I had little time to get ready for my first official day at my new job. I'd been practicing daily over at the club, but today was to be my first real gig playing before an audience. While I'd grown up doing recitals for my lessons, this felt much more real and daunting.

Having hair that made me look like a Goth chick didn't help the anxiety.

It had been three days since I'd run out of the club, and it surprised me how quickly life had fallen into a rhythm. I was no longer staying in the guesthouse out back, although I used the piano there to practice on a regular basis. More often than not, the living room served as a crash pad for much of the crew, but they seemed to accept me as another roommate. There were no jokes about my presence, for which I was grateful, but I tried to be useful.

That was a job in and of itself, cleaning up after a house full of guys, but it had been so long since I'd been this happy in a home. I'd wanted to celebrate the change, so while the dye job was spontaneous, the sentiment wasn't. It was going to take some serious time to get used to the "new" me, however.

Drying my hair quickly and relaxing somewhat as it lightened ever so slightly, I gathered up my things and opened the bathroom door to see Everett standing outside. I froze, staring at him in shock, as he blinked at me. "I thought you were at work," I blurted out.

"What happened to your hair?"

All my anxieties rose to the forefront, and with a pained cry I slammed the door in his face. Immediately, he began knocking. "I didn't mean it like that."

"What are you even doing here?" I asked through the door. "I thought you were working today."

"Boss let us off early. C'mon, Lacey, let me in."

I chewed my lip for a long moment, and then unlocked the door for Everett. It took him a moment to open it and peek around the frame. "Safe to come in?"

A reluctant smile tugged at my lips as I pulled nervously at my clothing. I thought I was alone in the house so had on only a shirt and pair of panties. I saw the moment he noticed, but to his credit he kept his gaze on my face. "Now," he said, shutting the door behind him, "let me take a look at the new you."

Pressing my lips together tightly, I ran my hand through my hair, then did a little pirouette. He wasn't looking at my hair when I faced him again, and raised his eyes guiltily. The tiny grin on my face widened, and I took a step forward. "Do you like it?" I asked, running my finger along the center of his chest.

His throat worked as his eyes darkened. He reached up and ran the dark strands through his fingers, and I leaned my head into his hand. Everett skimmed his knuckles down my shoulder, my hair gliding through his fingertips. This close, I could smell the sweat and dust on him, but instead of turning

me off it just made me want to lean closer. Beneath all that
was a scent I associated only with him, one that made me want
more.

"I like it," he murmured, bending his head down beside
mine. I thought he was going to kiss my neck, but he only nuzzled my hair. "I like it a lot." His hands moved around behind
me as he pressed forward, curling around the globes of my ass
and squeezing. "I like everything about you, no matter the
color."

I wound my arms around his neck, and tilted my head to
meet his lips. His kiss was hungry, needy, and the same desire
rose quickly inside me. Everett was unlike anyone else I'd
dated. Sex with him didn't make me feel degraded or like I
was being used; instead, it was *awesome*. If it weren't for his
job, I doubted we'd leave the bedroom. As it was, I took every
minute with him I could get.

He growled against my mouth, then hooked his thumbs
under my panties and pulled them down. I trailed my lips
down his neck, removing one arm from around his neck and
massaging the heel of my hand down his crotch. His sharp
intake of breath made my pulse speed up, my own breathing
coming faster. He was hard as a rock, and I didn't protest
when he lifted me up and set me atop the granite counter. I
pulled at his shirt, suddenly desperate to touch him; he must
have felt the same because his hands went to my sides beneath my thin top. Arching against him, I pulled him close to
me, desperate to feel his hard body against mine.

I was already wet by the time I felt the blunt tip of his cock
probing at my folds. I opened myself wider, and gasped as
he surged inside me. His hands grasped my bottom, fingers

digging into the soft flesh, while I clung to his shoulders. My cries bounced around the large bathroom, echoed by Everett's hard panting.

"Lacey," he murmured, the strained word music to my ears. I laid kisses over his face as he pounded inside me, raking my nails along his torso and down around his taut backside. Everything about him turned me on, and I could feel my climax rushing to the surface. I leaned my head back against the mirror and Everett took full advantage, reaching down my top and pulling out one breast. His tongue teased my nipple, and just like that I was sent over the edge. With a loud cry I came, my body trembling from the release.

"My turn," he said in a low voice. He picked me up, keeping my legs wrapped around him, and stalked out of the bathroom and onto the bed, pulling off first my shirt, then my bra. There was no finesse in his desire, only raw need as he bore me back, and I reveled in being so desired. His teeth scraped over my breast as he wrapped my legs around his ribs and pushed inside me again. I braced against the headboard to keep from being pounded backward from his thrusts. I could still feel the pleasure of my orgasm coursing through me, and his rough strokes only emphasized the sensations. Soft cries poured from my lips, echoed by Everett's rough grunts.

"Oh God, I'm . . ." His teeth dug into my shoulder almost painfully, and with a hard groan he came. I put my arms around his shoulders, reveling in the way his body bucked against mine. Nuzzling the side of his neck, I ran my fingers through his soft hair. Work in the hot Southern sun had put some natural highlights in his hair, but it was still about as dark as mine now. "So I take it you like my hair?" I murmured as he laid atop me.

"I like *you*," he said, laying a kiss on my temple. "But yes, your hair is nice, too."

"Just nice?" I raised my eyebrows. "All that just for *nice?*"

"Do I need to prove again how much I like it?" he growled, pinning my hands to the pillow beside my head.

I giggled, sliding my knee along his side. "You sure you're up for more?" I teased, then my humor faded at the intense look he gave me.

"There's more than one way to prove how sexy I find you." It was his turn to grin wickedly as his lips trailed down my breastbone and over my belly. I was already trembling as he set my legs over his shoulders, then he parted the folds and dipped his head down.

I was almost late for work, but I couldn't keep the smile off my face.

The playlist was the same songs I'd been practicing, but I was still nervous when I first walked out to the piano.

Growing up, I'd had my fair share of recitals where I'd played for large audiences, but I knew within five minutes that this was different. Whereas with a recital the player was the center of attention, here I faded into the background. Very few people looked my way; I'd get the occasional glance as people walked in through the door, but for the most part I was left to my own devices.

That suited me just fine.

The piano was a good one, and my fingers danced across

the keys. Muscle memory only took me so far, so I was glad I'd been practicing as much as I could the last several days. The club itself wasn't nearly as formal as I'd imagined, although I did see some older patrons come in like they'd stepped off the TV set of *Dynasty*. For the most part, people were in shorts and looked casual, which made sense with the heat spell. I wasn't sure what I'd been expecting, but it was a surprisingly pleasant atmosphere.

I wore a simple black dress I'd picked up for relatively cheap, a belt, and some heels. It wasn't my job to stand out but to blend in, and I did that well. It allowed me the chance to watch people as my fingers flew over the keys, and a few I recognized. The gentleman with the loud belly laugh near the window played Santa Claus during the holidays, and the older couple in the corner had watched my impromptu piano audition.

"Why don't you take a short break?"

I finished the song and looked up to see Drew next to the piano. "That would be nice," I said, smiling and standing. "Where's the break room?"

"Go ahead and get a drink at the bar, it's pretty quiet right now. I've had a couple people ask about you already, wondering if you're available for hire at other functions. Would you mind if I passed along your phone number to them, or would you rather they asked in person?"

I tried not to let my excitement show, but it was hard. "Go ahead and give them my number," I said, and Drew matched my smile.

"You're definitely a better player than our last girl, and

people have noticed. Now go take your break, these folks can take some canned music for a little while."

I headed over to the bar and sat down next to a girl about my age. She was dressed as fashionably as anyone I'd seen in my little town. A large Louis Vuitton purse sat at her feet, and she had on a tweed jacket that looked too warm for the summer heat. She was skinny with dark hair that only accentuated her pale skin, and reminded me of the mean girls I'd gone to school with. When she looked over at me, however, I saw only curiosity on her face.

"You're the piano player?" At my nod, she tipped her head toward my instrument. "You play really well."

"Thanks," I said, smiling. Her mouth curved up in what could only be called a Mona Lisa smile, difficult to read. I wasn't getting any cruel condescension from her, just a polished diffidence that was designed to keep people away. She was talking to me, however, and it would have been rude not to respond.

"How long have you been playing?"

"Since I was a kid. I had a long break there for a while, life got kind of rough."

Her lips twisted ruefully. "It does that a lot, doesn't it?"

I hadn't meant to make her sad, and struggled to repair the damage. "Do you play music?"

She shook her head. "I never really had the knack for tunes."

"So what do you like to do?"

"Travel . . . and shop."

She seemed embarrassed by her admission, as if not knowing an actual skill was something to be ashamed about.

"Well, if it's any consolation," I said, indicating her clothes, "you're really good at the shopping part." Her clothing was the epitome of style, not the casual elegance I saw with the locals. It made the girl stand apart, although something told me that wasn't deliberate on her part.

"It's what I wanted to go to school for," she said, tugging on the jacket around her shoulders. "I always loved fashion and design; I thought it would be incredible to do it myself."

I frowned. " 'Wanted'? Why the past tense?"

Her mouth opened and closed, and she looked at me curiously. Finally, she held out her hand. "I'm Skye."

"Lacey," I said, shaking her hand, then waved my finger around. "Are you from around here?"

"Mostly just visiting."

"You like it?"

She seemed at a loss for words, as if not quite sure what to say to my question. Finally, Skye smiled, a real one this time. "It's nice. Very different from what I'm used to, though."

I nodded emphatically, returning her smile. "I moved here from Oregon a few years ago. Believe me, it was a tough change."

Her smile widened as if she'd found a kindred spirit. "Where are you living now?"

"I'm here in Oyster Cove, although I recently moved out of my grandmother's home." That was certainly one way of putting it. "Do you know the Plymouth plantation house down near the water?"

"I do, as a matter of fact."

"Well, a friend is letting me stay there until I can get back on my feet again. I guess it had been vacant for a while." I held back the information as to who and why, not wanting to get Everett into trouble.

Skye's smile froze, and she looked down at her drink. "Oh, so someone is living there again?" When I nodded, she gave a faint sigh. "It's a really beautiful house."

"Yeah, I envy whoever got to live there. Can't imagine why they'd leave it empty for so long."

The bartender handed me my drink but I stayed in my seat, curious about the girl. I got the feeling she was holding something back, but I didn't know her well enough to press for details. Despite the country club setting, something about the girl was different from the people surrounding us. She was sitting alone at the bar, a fish out of water, and that was a feeling to which I could relate. "How long are you going to be in town?"

"I don't know." Skye shrugged, swirling her drink. "Maybe I'll see you around?"

I nodded. The practiced hardness I'd seen on her face before was gone, replaced by a melancholy I was afraid I'd somehow caused. I bit my lip, wanting to continue our conversation, but realized I needed to get back to work. "I'll be here," I said, offering my hand, which she shook. Skye's grip was soft, almost frail, and I lightened my own so as not to hurt her. Reluctantly, I stepped away from the bar and went back to my piano, picking up my set where I left off.

When I next looked back at the bar, Skye was already gone.

chapter sixteen ✦

Everett

"Y̶ou know, if you're really as into this girl as I think, you should tell her everything."

"Trent, man, give it a rest."

"Tell her the truth . . . worst-case scenario, she dumps your yuppie ass."

The very idea made Everett's chest squeeze, and he gave his best friend a dirty look. "Just pass me the wrench."

Trent handed him the tool and Everett stuck it down inside the hole, tightening the fastening. "There, that ought to do the trick."

"The old man would be proud."

Everett snorted. "Your old man would think I should have done that faster."

"Still, not bad for a city slicker."

Trent went to turn back on the water as Everett dusted himself off. He surveyed his handiwork with no small amount of pride. If he'd been with his parents, the small sprinkler repair would have been done by a plumber. There was no way Everett's father would have gotten himself dirty or done it himself.

But I did. That knowledge felt great.

"Don't get cocky," Trent called over his shoulder, as if reading Everett's thoughts.

Rolling his eyes, Everett stepped off the lawn, not keen to get wet when the water came back on. Before the fix, the sprinkler head had been a geyser. Hopefully the repair would work, or Everett would never hear the end of it from his friend.

He peeked around the side of the house to see if the familiar Ford was in the driveway but couldn't get a good look. Lacey was due home from work any minute, and Everett was nearly jumping out of his skin to hold the girl in his arms. It was like a burning in his gut, the raw *need* to touch her, to *taste* her, to feel her against his body. She was in his head, in his thoughts nearly every waking second. He couldn't get enough of her, and that both thrilled and terrified him.

Getting involved with a girl like her had never been in the plans. Technically, she wasn't quite local since she'd moved from Oregon, but it wouldn't have mattered anyway. Everett needed the girl, didn't feel right without her by his side. She plagued his thoughts day and night, and since he'd felt her beneath him, her needy nails on his back, and heard her soft moans, that was all he could think about.

There was a hiss from nearby, bringing him back to the present. It was the sheet of water hitting him square in the belly, however, that finally got his full attention. Cursing, Everett danced out of the crooked sprinkler's path, and then stared down at his drenched shirt and pants. From across the lawn, Trent howled with laughter, and Everett gave him the finger.

Fortunately, aiming the new sprinkler head in the right direction was easy enough, and five minutes later, Everett headed back up toward the house to change, Trent still chortling behind him. "Dude, you look like you pissed yourself."

"Fuck off," Everett said good-naturedly as they rounded the house. He stopped when he saw the large vehicle in the driveway. "When did Lacey get home?"

Trent jabbed Everett in the ribs with his elbow. "You should try focusing on the real world once in a while," he said, ignoring Everett's scowl. "She drove in when you were prancing around in the sprinklers."

The thought of seeing Lacey again quickened Everett's pace, but Trent held back. "I'm going to get lunch, you want anything?"

Everett nodded absently, heading for the house as Trent split off toward his car. Inside the house, he didn't see Lacey in the living room or kitchen, so he headed up the stairs, taking them two at a time. Just the thought of her made his dick strain against his jeans, his heart rate going into overdrive. The need to touch her was intense; he could almost feel her presence in the house, and it made him hornier than ever.

Lacey was standing in the center of the bedroom, wearing only a bra and panties. Her work clothes were lying on the floor, and Everett noticed the shorts and tank top on the bed. She turned when he came through the door and her eyes widened as he collided with her, sweeping her into a fierce kiss. He didn't stop until she was pressed against the wall, her body molding into his as if they were made for one another.

She gave a tiny sigh into his mouth, surrendering to the

kiss, and it only inflamed him more. His hands went to her ass, covered only by the thin cotton panties, and he lifted her off the floor. She squeaked, surprised, and wrapped her legs around his waist. His actions made her own movements grow bolder; she tugged at his shirt, helping him out of it, then running her nails along his shoulders and back. "I missed you," she murmured as Everett's head dipped to her neck, sucking at the delicate skin.

There was so much he wanted to say at that moment, emotions threatening to explode from him, but no words would come. He'd missed her and wanted her and needed her, and now, having her in his arms, pressed against his body, it still wasn't enough. He needed to possess her, to know that she was his. Tearing his hands from her body was one of the hardest things he'd ever done as he unhooked his jeans, letting them fall down to the floor.

Lacey's hands didn't stop their movements, running over his body like tiny coals setting him ablaze. He wasn't the only one affected by their coupling; her breath was coming in short pants, her hands growing needier, tugging at him for more. He laid his mouth on her throat again as he freed himself, then pushed her panties down. She helped him, dropping one leg to let him remove the offending cloth, but Everett couldn't wait. Winding his arm under her knee, he lifted her leg and spread her wide before surging inside.

Lacey gasped, and for a moment Everett stopped, worried he might have hurt her. The nails in his back, however, told him otherwise, and when she arched into him with a loud groan he drew back and pressed in again. Lacey's head went back against the wall, her lips parting slightly, as Everett pounded into her. "God, you feel so good," he murmured, his voice raspy as if he hadn't used it all day. She was like a warm silk glove around his cock, but it was more than that.

This was Lacey. Here was everything he wanted, and he took it.

He felt it when her body exploded, and smiled at her shocked cry. Everett enjoyed giving this girl pleasure. Her muscles trembled around him, only adding to his own sensations. He didn't stop, driving inside her willing body, not caring when her nails made tracks across his shoulders.

"Condom?"

It took a second for the whispered word to register for Everett, so caught up was he in the moment. Desperately, he looked around for a small foil packet within reach, but the closest was on the other side of the bed. He bit back a groan, trembling against her as he stopped his pace, then felt her small hand push against his shoulder. Disappointment tore through him but he released her legs, letting her slide to the floor as he stepped back.

Lacey's hair covered her face so he couldn't read her expression as she slid down the wall, then kept on going until she was on her knees before him. Everett stared down at her, stunned, as she winked up at him, and then took him inside her hot mouth.

"*Fuck!*" Everett braced his hands against the wall in front of him, his entire body shaking. If he thought it was incredible before, it didn't hold a candle to being inside her mouth. He closed his eyes and laid his head forward, one hand moving down to tangle in her silky hair. Her tongue skimmed along his length, flicking the tip of his cock before pulling him deep again. She wrung the orgasm from him, and he gave a hoarse cry as he came inside her mouth.

"Goddamn," he whispered, panting hard. Everett shuddered again as Lacey ran her fingernails up his calves and thighs, then he stepped back and helped her to her feet. "You are so fucking hot," he breathed, his brain unable to register anything else at the moment.

She gave him a smug smile, then kissed his cheek. "Welcome home."

He wanted to laugh at her words, but only managed a single breathy chuckle, still too wrung out. God, but she was so fucking fantastic. He'd tell her if he could string two words together, but that was proving impossible right then. All he could do was stare at her naked ass as she picked up her discarded underwear and bra.

Lacey peeked over her shoulder at him. "Can I get dressed now?" she asked, a saucy note in her voice.

Everett grinned, but before he could answer, somebody knocked on the door. "You guys decent?"

Everett laughed loudly at the question.

"Yeah, okay, stupid question," Trent said through the door. "We, uh, have a guest. You mind coming downstairs?"

He sounded worried, which in turn worried Everett. He let Lacey go, picking his pants up from the floor. "This isn't over," he murmured, kissing Lacey swiftly before she darted for the bathroom.

Trent was waiting a respectful distance away from the door, an anxious look on his face. "Dude, you need to get downstairs."

The utter seriousness on Trent's face melted away the last

of Everett's euphoria. He looked nervous, and Everett braced himself for bad news. "What's wrong?"

Trent opened his mouth to speak, only to be cut off as a woman's voice called from below, "Everett?"

Everything inside Everett stilled as he recognized the familiar voice. His hands curled into fists. "You *let* her in the house?"

"No way, man, she let herself inside."

Everett glanced back at the room he'd just exited, and then at Trent, who looked pained. Dread filled him as Everett moved down the hall and stared downstairs.

"Hello, Everett."

Anger bubbled up at even the simplest greeting. He barely remembered going down the stairs, so quick were his steps. "What the hell are you doing here?"

"I have as much right to be here as you."

Everett shook his head, unable to formulate words. Stalking to the entrance, he opened the door. "Get. Out."

Part of him was surprised when, after a short pause, the girl complied. "Everett, I just want to talk."

He slammed the door in her face.

"You knew she'd find you eventually." Trent stared back at him, a resigned expression on his face.

"It doesn't matter."

Trent didn't seem inclined to let the matter rest. "Dude, she's your—"

"*I don't care.*"

Trent looked down at Everett's clenched fists, and then sighed. "Fine, I'm shutting up."

"Everett?"

His eyes closed as he heard Lacey's voice behind him. "Is everything okay? Who was at the door?"

There was a brittle note to her words, and he wondered how much she'd seen, but when he turned all he saw was concern on her face. *Where to even start?* Everett could only stare as Lacey came down the stairs, stopping at the base. She looked between the two boys, and Everett saw her swallow. "What's going on?"

Everett's mouth worked soundlessly for a moment, then he blew out a breath. "There's probably some things I should tell you about me," he started.

"Who was she?" Lacey cut in, the darkening suspicion in her eyes breaking Everett's heart.

"*She* lives here, too, and doesn't like getting kicked out of her own house."

The annoyed voice made everyone whirl around. Skye stood near the back door, managing to look both elegant and pissed. "You forgot I still had a key," she said, waggling a keychain in her fingers.

"Skye?"

The other girl's eyes flickered to Lacey, and both girls stared at one another. Lacey looked between Skye and Everett as if trying to make sense of everything.

"This is your house?" Lacey asked.

"I said I've seen it many times," Skye said, not unkindly, "because it's our house." Then she cast a glance at Everett. "Are you going to tell her, or should I?"

Everett's chest squeezed as he saw comprehension dawn

on Lacey's face. "But you said . . . I thought you two were . . ." She trailed off, a confused look on her face as she looked at Trent, then back to Everett. "You lied to me?"

"Lacey . . ."

She stumbled back a step, her eyes not leaving Everett's face. Then she whirled around and stomped away toward the back door.

Everett ran his hands through his hair, breathing hard. *Fuck!*

"Everett, please . . ."

He whirled around on Skye, pointing a finger at her. "You, out of the house. I don't want to see you when I get back in."

Skye shrank back from Everett, and a pang went through his heart. Part of him wanted to cause her pain, to make them even, but her gaze only made him sadder. He glanced at Trent. "Make sure she gets out."

Abandoning Skye to his friend, Everett raced after Lacey, trying to figure out what to say that would fix everything.

chapter seventeen ❧

Stupid, stupid!

I ignored Everett's calls, heading outside and away from everyone else, not wanting them to see me cry. All I wanted to do was run, keep running, get away from anyone and everything that let me down. My life consisted of one major disappointment after another, and I was tired of it all.

He lied to me. Why do they always lie?

"Lacey!"

Everett's voice wasn't far behind me, and I just quickened my pace. "Leave me alone," I yelled, rounding the house and making a beeline for my truck. I saw Skye being escorted to her car by Trent but ignored them, my only goal being to get out of there as quickly as possible. I'd barely touched the door when Everett's fingers wrapped around my other wrist, stopping me.

It would have been so satisfying to turn around and slap him, but I stood stock-still, not moving a muscle. I heard his ragged breathing, but he stayed quiet, as if unsure what to say. My heart hammered, threatening to burst from my chest, and when his thumb stroked my wrist, my chest constricted painfully. "Let me go."

"Lacey, let me explain, please. . . ."

"No!" Wrenching my hand out of his grip, I whirled around. "I'm sick and tired of being lied to."

"I didn't lie to you, though!"

"You told me you were house-sitting," I spat. "You made me think you were here just for the summer, that you were visiting." The anger rose inside me like a sick bile, making me choke on my words. I pulled my truck door open, but Everett leaned against it, his face desperate.

"My parents had a house here," he said, "but this isn't where I grew up. Please, Lacey, just listen."

"I thought you cared about me, now I find out I never meant anything to you because you have a *wife*."

"A what? No no no, Lacey." He tried to cradle my face, but I shook his hands off, too filled with disgust. "Skye isn't my wife. She's my *sister*. The house belongs to our parents."

"Your sister?" That confession only made me angrier, and I stabbed him in the chest with one finger. "You told me you didn't have any siblings."

He raked a hand through his hair. "I don't have a relationship with her—none whatsoever. But yes, I do have a sister."

"Then why didn't you just say that? How am I supposed to know what's true and what's not?"

"I'm so sorry, Lacey."

Everett looked wrecked, apologetic lines etched deep into his face, but it wasn't enough for me. "Goddammit," I moaned, pushing past him onto the grass, "I'm sick to death of all the lies. You tell me you're from New York . . ."

"I am," he said, but I wouldn't even look at him. "I grew up there. It's practically all I know."

"I shouldn't be surprised you would disappoint me, too." I laughed, the sound high and wild. "Everyone I ever cared about or looked up to has done it, why not you? First my father, and then when the police . . ."

"Police?" Everett asked when I trailed off. "What happened?"

"Screw you." The old, familiar anger surged through me, and the urge to hit something was overwhelming. I wanted to curse him, drive him away, but mostly I just wanted to leave. "Let me go," I said, hating how my voice broke.

"If I let you go, you won't come back."

He was right about that. All I wanted to do at that moment was run away from the hell I was living in. Anywhere had to be better than here. I stayed motionless, staring at a patch of grass, as Everett moved in close. "Who else lied to you?" Everett murmured, tucking an errant bit of hair behind my ear. "Help me understand."

I leaned into his touch, hating myself for that weakness. "After that night, after the video of what happened to me circulated through my high school . . ." My breath shuddered in and out. "I went to the police and told them what I knew. That I'd been raped, and could prove it." I swallowed, still able to feel the horror of that moment now. "I was so stupid, so naïve. I was sure that, if I showed them the video, they would arrest the boys and stop all of the abuse toward me. I thought . . . I thought they could fix it, that they would make it all go away.

"Do you know what they said to me after I'd shown them the whole thing?" I felt my face crumple, and I fought against breaking down. "'You seemed to be enjoying yourself.'"

"Oh, Lacey."

"I-I thought if they saw it, they'd believe me." A hiccupped sob escaped me. "Someone recognized one of the boys as a son of a deputy in the building. One of the deputies knew my grandmother and called her, saying I was making false accusations at the police department . . ."

Everett wrapped his arms around me, holding me upright when I would have collapsed. I was trembling so hard that speaking was difficult, but I tried. I had to make him understand. "Meanwhile, they showed the v-video to several people and wouldn't give me my phone back, saying it was evidence . . ."

"God, Lacey, I'm so sorry."

"I knew I'd made a mistake, but it was too late. I didn't say anything more, but by the time my grandmother showed up, nobody believed me. She only made it worse, letting them all know who my father was, and what she'd done to him, as if that were proof somehow . . ."

Everett's arms tightened around me and I trailed off, trembling against him. He pressed me back against the Bronco's door but there was nothing sexual in his touch, only comfort. I squeezed my eyes shut and laid my forehead against his shoulder, unable to stop the tears from leaking out. I'd never told anyone my side of the story, although people knew the details. In their versions, however, I was the villain not the victim, the girl trying to ruin the lives of three fine boys.

"My parents weren't around most of my life."

Everett's words pulled me back to the present, but I didn't move, only stood there in his arms as he continued. "My sister and I were raised by nannies, then later in boarding schools.

Yes, this house belongs to my family; yes, I was born in Gulf-port. But my parents wanted more, they wanted New York, and by the time I was eight I barely had any memory of living full time in this place."

I wrapped my arms around him, clinging tightly like he was a lifeline as his voice droned on. "We came here every year, making it more like a vacation home than our family's legacy. I looked forward to those vacations because it meant I had my parents to myself. I played with Trent, got to know his father, but I never really belonged. What used to be some-thing that lasted all summer, though, gradually lessened to a month, then to a few weeks, then to maybe a week. Mean-while, we stayed in boarding schools during the year and rarely saw our own parents."

He took a deep breath before continuing. "My father was an investment banker who worked his way up to chief financial officer at a major firm. He's poised to take over now as CEO, taking over for some billionaire who wants out. My mother is a writer and motivational speaker who spends more time on the road than at home. They rarely called, wrote, or contacted us while we were in school, but made up for it with extravagant gifts. Looking back on it, I was miserable, but at the time I didn't see it that way."

"Why didn't you just tell me that?" I asked. "Would it have been so hard to tell me the truth?"

"Yes," Everett said quietly. "Because I don't want to be that person anymore. I wanted a fresh start. A chance to be a bet-ter man." He trailed off, and I looked up into his pinched face. He looked pained, as if remembering that part of his life hurt, something with which I could relate. My eyes met his,

and he stroked my face. "Being raised like that does something to you, makes you want to bring others down to your
own level of misery. I was a good son, did everything to make
my family proud. With others, though, I could be cruel. It
helped alleviate the boredom and made me feel better, at least
for a little while."

"So what changed you?"

A shadow came over Everett's face, and he swallowed hard.
"Getting away from all that," he mumbled, looking away. "I'd
done things, caused irreparable damage to lives . . ."

"Like what?"

His brow furrowed, creases I'd never seen before forming
around his eyes. "Please don't make me tell you that," he pleaded,
suddenly looking old, "not right now."

Something inside me rebelled, made me want to force him
to tell me. The raw anguish I saw in his eyes, however, stopped
me. I knew what it was like to hold in a secret that broke me,
but the fact that he wouldn't say anything scared me. "Would
it change how I feel about you?" I whispered.

The lines on his face deepened. "Maybe."

I swallowed and looked away. "But why did you lie to me?"
I asked, my voice ragged.

"Because I wanted you to see the real me, who I am now."
He stroked my cheek again, arms tightening around me. "My
family's wealthy—not just well off, but filthy rich. That might
not surprise you, but for years it defined who I was in the
world. I could have anything I wanted, and I took it all."

Some of my emotion abated, and I stared at him curiously.
"You're one of the most selfless people I know."

I watched the tension melt out of him at my words. "Thank you for saying that," he said, exhaling a shaky breath. "I wanted to change but didn't know how. The life surrounding me was stifling—I think you of all people can understand that—and next to impossible for me to leave. So, when the chance came, I chose a college as far away from my previous life as I could get and left it all behind, hoping for a clean slate."

"What did you find?"

The first signs of a smile tugged at one corner of his lips. "I found out I wasn't a big fish, even in a small pond. It was so weird, being a complete unknown; I was starting fresh like I'd wanted, and I took advantage of it. I also reconnected with old friends—Trent was going to the same college, and we clicked like we had as kids."

"I'm glad you got your happy ending," I murmured.

Everett must have heard the longing in my voice and stepped back. "I shouldn't have lied to you," he said softly, "and I can't apologize enough for that."

"Just promise me, no more lies, okay?" My voice wavered, but his relieved smile made my belly do flip-flops.

"Promise."

Skye had left sometime while Everett and I were arguing. I decided not to bring it up. It was on the tip of my tongue to ask what his deep, dark secret was, but I stopped myself in time. At that moment, it felt too good to be in his arms, and I selfishly wanted to keep that happy feeling.

I just hoped it wouldn't end up biting me in the ass.

* * *

The argument was still going through my mind the next day at work when Skye showed up at my piano. "I need your help."

I pursed my lips, not sure what to say. "I'm working right now."

"I know that and I'm sorry, but can we talk on your next break?"

A quick look at the clock told me I was due any time now, but I hesitated. "I don't know what happened between you and your brother," I murmured, "but it's not really my business."

"Please," Skye pleaded softly, and I glanced up at her. Her thin face was pale, even behind the makeup. She looked desperate, her blue eyes so very much like Everett's, and I felt myself relenting. "I just want to talk."

"Fine, give me five minutes," I said, and saw her shoulders sag with relief.

"Thank you. I'll meet you out in the lobby."

I'd expected her to say the bar, but she walked away before I could say anything. Intrigued despite myself, I finished my set and told the hostess I'd be taking my break, and then went out to find Skye. She wasn't in the main lobby, so I checked the side room with the couches and saw her seated at the far corner.

She stood when she saw me, and I noticed she looked a little wobbly on her heels. "Thank you for agreeing to speak with me," she said, her hands twisting around her small purse.

I waved a hand, uncomfortable by the formal way she spoke. "I don't know how I can help you, or even if I should."

"I'm dying."

The melodramatic statement got my attention, but I just folded my arms and waited for her to finish. She must have seen the disbelief in my eyes because she reached up and, with only a moment's hesitation, tugged at her hair. My mouth fell open in surprise as it slid sideways, revealing the pale skin crown atop her head. I stared, dumbfounded, too shocked to think of decorum. Whatever I'd been expecting, this wasn't it.

"The cancer's spread to my organs, and chemotherapy isn't reducing the spread fast enough." Skye twisted the wig in her hands, clearly uncomfortable with the nakedness. "There's a good chance I won't see next year, and I can't leave my relationship with Everett like it is now."

It took me a long moment to find my voice. "Does he know?"

"That I'm sick?" She shook her head. "He has no idea. And I don't want him to know, not yet anyway. That's not why I'm here. I came to make amends."

Shaken, I sat down on the arm of the couch beside me. "What happened between you two?"

She bit her lip and looked away. I didn't think she would answer me but finally she said, "What has he told you about us growing up?"

"That your parents were absent for most of your lives, and you two don't have a relationship."

A humorless smile tipped her mouth. "That's certainly a nice way to put it. We were like every bad stereotype you see in movies, the people who were cruel just because they could be. Maybe that's why . . ." She trailed off, indicating herself with the wave of a hand, then she sighed again. "There are some things money can't buy, and apparently health is one of them. Not that Mom and Dad aren't trying; they're paying and donating as much as they can to get me fixed. I should be thankful they've finally deigned to give me any attention at all."

She didn't sound thankful, and if what I'd heard about them was true, maybe they didn't deserve it. "They haven't told him?"

Skye shook her head. "My parents tend to forget they have kids at all until something goes wrong. I'm sure he hasn't spoken to them in ages. He disappeared right after the court ruling . . ."

"Court?" Everett had gone to court for something? How much did I not know about this boy?

Skye looked uncomfortable, but persisted. "Please, can you help me?"

I wavered, unsure what to do. My eyes flickered back to her bald head, and pity stirred in my heart. "What do you need me to do?" I said quietly as she readjusted her wig. I knew it helped give her the semblance of a normal life, but my heart ached for her.

"Just give me a chance to talk with him. You saw what he was like the other day—he won't speak to me. I just want to apologize, do what I can to repair things, let him know he's not the only one who's changed."

I considered her for a long moment before finally speaking. "Trent and the guys are organizing an end-of-summer party at the house." The words came reluctantly; I still wasn't sure if inviting her was a good idea. "It's happening this Sunday. Find me first, and I'll make sure he sees you."

"Oh, thank you."

I thought for sure she was going to break down into tears, or hug me, but she held her ground. The gratitude, however, emanated from her in waves.

"And please don't tell him I'm sick. I'll let him know, but I want to apologize first. I want his real forgiveness, not just his pity."

"I don't know what he'll do. Whatever happened between you, I don't think he's forgiven it."

"You've already been tremendously helpful. Thank you so much." This time she did hug me, an awkward affair as if she wasn't sure how a hug was done. I thought back to what both she and Everett had said, the cold and distant home life. Perhaps something as simple as a hug was foreign to her. I couldn't imagine having rich parents, or being stuck in boarding schools most of the year. My life up until my stepfather died had been good, and only recently could I look back on it without feeling pain.

"I, uh, should probably get back to work."

Skye stepped away as a couple walked past us. "I guess I'll see you on Sunday," she said, giving me a tiny smile, then walked away.

I blew out a breath and sat down on the couch, wondering what kind of mess I'd involved myself in. It felt as though I was always learning something new about Everett, but the story came in bits and pieces, incomplete. I knew there was more, something that for whatever reason they were keeping from me, and I wasn't even sure whether I wanted to know.

I stood up and moved back toward my piano as a large group moved toward the exit. I noticed a familiar face rounding the corner. Frozen for a moment, I recovered then hurried after the smaller woman. "Ms. Jones!"

My brother's teacher turned at the sound of her name, and my heart fell when I saw her expression tighten when she saw me. Melinda Jones had never been anything but nice to me, but from her pinched look of distaste, she could barely stand the sight of me. I knew immediately that my grandmother had likely spread even more lies about me. It was almost enough to make me turn around and walk away.

Almost.

"Ms. St. James. I had no idea that you worked here."

The apparent rest of that phrase, *Or I would never have come*, was left unsaid. Southern gentility prevented her from saying how she really felt, although it was written all over her face. I wiped my palms on my dress, suddenly nervous, and asked, "How is Davy doing?"

"He's well, no thanks to your treatment."

I flinched at her words, which confirmed my suspicions. "The last time we talked," I said, keeping my voice low, "you said there was something suspicious going on."

"Why are we having this conversation, Lacey?"

It was weird to see her closed-off face. Before, she'd always smile at me, her gentle but firm persona keeping the preschoolers in line. Having her disapproval aimed at me hurt, but I couldn't back down. "Because I haven't seen my little brother in almost a week," I said, "and I need to know he's okay."

The teacher's eyebrows lowered. "A week, you say?"

I nodded vigorously. "Not since my grandmother kicked me out of the house."

She looked away, emotions warring on her face. "Lacey," she said after a minute, "your little brother hasn't been in my class since Tuesday."

"What?"

"After I spoke with you, I talked to your grandmother as well. She promised to fix the situation—those were her exact words."

And she had. That was the same time I'd been thrown out.

"But on Tuesday, I noticed your brother was withdrawn and had fresh bruises on his arm. This time I brought it up with the supervisor, who called in your mom. She claimed it was your fault, but I haven't seen Davy since then. Technically, he's still enrolled, just not attending." She peered at me. "You really haven't seen him this week?"

Sitting back down on the couch there, I drew in a shaky breath. The idea of running out of work and tracking down my brother was tempting. As was evidenced by his teacher's reaction, however, everyone thought I was the abuser. What would I do when I had him then? Run to Mexico? Go into hiding? Every scenario I thought up was laughable, except one.

"I need to call someone," I said, wanting to cry from the dread in my heart.

Melinda's expression softened, and she laid a hand on my arm. "If you need me to help in any way, please don't hesitate to ask." She rummaged through her purse and handed me her card. "I'll do whatever I can to help your brother."

I nodded and walked away, looking for someplace private. Winding my way down the network of hallways, I finally found a small bench outside the main areas and sat down.

With shaking hands, I pulled my cell phone from my bag. The old numbers were still in my head from a childhood of talking on the phone with my grandparents. I pressed them into the keypad and lifted the phone to my ear, heart jerking crazily as it began to ring.

Someone answered on the third ring. "Hello?"

Aunt Jeanine. I almost said her name. I hadn't heard from any of my stepfather's family in years, and yet the instant I heard that voice I was taken back to when I was a child. Questions ran through my head: Where were my grandparents? Why hadn't they answered the phone?

"Hello? Is anyone there?"

I tried to speak, to say anything, but my throat closed up. Clutching the phone to my ear, I opened my mouth but nothing would come out. Emotion choked me, and I suddenly felt like crying. I needed help, but they were nearly a whole country away. Could they really do anything?

There came an exasperated grunt over the phone, then the click as she hung up.

Dammit! I punched in the numbers again quickly, but closed the clamshell before I could press Send. Doubt washed through me and I covered my eyes, trying to control my shaky breaths. It wasn't my asthma that threatened to choke me this time but my own fear and weakness. *What do I do?*

chapter eighteen

B oys are so predictable."

"Totally."

I picked up the big twenty-four case of beer and hefted it inside the shopping cart. "How much more of this are we supposed to get?" I asked.

Clare smirked. "According to their list, we'll need another cart."

"Typical." I stacked another case on top. "Enough for now. This should last them tonight at least. We'll get more the day of the party."

"You're not going to have any?"

I shook my head. "Not much into alcohol these days."

Clare nodded as we meandered through the beverage aisle at the supermarket. "What's next?"

"Chips, dip, and hot dogs. Not the most original menu."

"I'm sure by the third beer most won't even care." I glanced up at her. "Thanks for hanging out."

"Admit it, you just wanted me for my ID card."

"Well, I needed someone over twenty-one, but you were my first choice, honest." I looked over at my friend. "So, you're coming to the party this weekend, right? You never gave me a definite answer."

"I'm pretty sure I work that day, but I might be able to come later that afternoon."

"You'd better. I haven't seen you much around the club since you moved to catering."

We fell into an amicable silence as we headed back to the meat section. I eyed Clare for a moment and then asked the question that was first and foremost on my brain. "How are you and Andrew doing?"

A small smile played across her lips. "Good, I think. He's a nice guy. What about your boy?"

I shrugged. "We had our first big fight. Things are better since then, it's just . . ."

"Just what?"

"I worry about all the things I don't know about him, what happened before we met and such."

"What, do you think he's a serial killer or something?"

That imagery startled a laugh out of me. "I'm pretty sure it isn't that," I said, then bit my lip. "I hope."

"Well, it takes time to get to really know somebody. You can fall in love the minute you see a person, but that doesn't mean . . ." She trailed off, lost in thought. "Sometimes you just know that person is for you, that they fit. You love even the rough edges, mistakes and all, because you just know they're for you."

I stared at Clare curiously. "Are we talking about Andrew here?"

The question seemed to surprise her out of her daydream,

and she flushed. "He's a nice guy," she repeated, checking out
the items on the opposite aisle so I couldn't see her face.

"You just said that—"

"Well, look who decided to show her face in public."

I froze at the familiar female voice and turned to see two
of my exes standing behind me. Ashley was tucked up under
Macon's arm, her expression a mixture of triumph and scorn.
Macon, ever the golden boy, seemed perfectly content with
his situation, but his eyes still ran up and down my body. It
made me shiver, but I kept my reaction inside as I turned the
shopping cart away.

"What, you're not even going to say hello to your friends?"

The condescension in Macon's voice made me grit my
teeth, but I kept right on walking.

"Don't worry, baby," Ashley cooed, "she's just jealous."

I rolled my eyes. *Jealous? Seriously?*

"She can do way better for herself than either of you!"

Oh, Clare. I appreciated how my friend stood up for me
but would have rather avoided a confrontation "Come on,
they're not worth it," I murmured, and knew that Ashley
heard me by the sharp intake of breath.

"I was your friend, and you ditched me for some dick-
head," she hissed.

"You stole my card and used me as nothing more than a
chauffeur service, and you expect me to just take that?" I
couldn't hold myself back; the memories welled up and
brought the anger with them. "You were never my friend unless you needed something."

"Whatever," Ashley said, waving me off, and I had to fight

not to slap her silly. She wrapped her arms around Macon's waist and stared up at him dreamily. "She was never as good to you as I am," she said, turning his head so he looked at her and not me.

He didn't answer, just kissed her roughly, pinching her ass in full view of the public. I wrinkled my nose at their display and the amount of tongue they used, then nudged Clare, who looked ready to say something else. "Let's just go."

Macon broke off the kiss, his eyes swinging back to me. "Come on, baby, you know I'd take you back in a heartbeat," he said in that soft croon that had once made me melt. "Why don't you come back home?"

I gawked at him. Macon didn't seem to realize what he was saying in front of his new girlfriend, or otherwise he just didn't care one way or another. The hurt look Ashley gave him made me feel pity for the girl, right up until she turned to glare at me, as if his propositioning me was my fault. Disgust filled me at the entire display. What had I ever seen in either of them? "You two deserve each other," I muttered, walking away.

Ashley tugged on his arm. "Leave her alone, baby, let's go."

Macon ignored her pleas, following after us. "You're not still with that fucking city-boy, are you?" he said, all softness gone from his voice.

I bit my tongue against saying anything as Ashley tugged at his arm. "Macon . . ."

He rounded on her, shaking her off. "Don't fucking tell me what to do."

Ashley staggered sideways into a magazine rack, spilling several candy bars and tabloids to the floor. She looked

stunned by what happened, and I stepped between her and
Macon. "Hey, leave her alone!"

The commotion had attracted unwanted attention, but I
held my ground, glaring up at Macon. He'd noticed the additional stares from shoppers, and the charm slid over his
face like a mask. "She just slipped," he said reasonably, moving
around me to pull Ashley to him. "You've had a little too
much to drink, haven't you, baby?"

She seemed unsure, a bit confused, and my heart went out
to her. I remembered a few times when I'd "slipped" or "made
a scene" while out in public with Macon. His smile could
charm people into not believing their own eyes, that no, he
hadn't pushed her, she'd just tripped. It was never his fault;
he was the hero of those situations. You were the clumsy one,
the stupid one, he was just trying to make you a better person. From there, it was so easy to fall into the trap that a cuff
to the head, bruises on your arm, were for your own good.
Such bullshit.

The sudden knowledge that someone could twist power
like that made me sick.

"He pushed you, Ashley," I said, staring at her. "It's not the
first time, either, right? It only gets worse the longer you're
with him."

He turned Ashley's face to his, giving her an angelic smile
that had no business being on the face of such a devil. "I'd
never hurt you like that. It's all lies, baby."

He laid a soft kiss on her lips, and I knew I'd lost when she
clung to him. He hugged her close and gave me a triumphant
look that only made me sick to my belly. Turning away, I
pushed the cart quickly up a nearby aisle, wanting only to get

away. This time, they didn't follow, but the memory of them together stuck with me.

"God, what an asshole," Clare muttered beside me.

"Come on, let's take this home." Steering the cart back toward the front of the store, I made a beeline for the register. It shamed me to think I'd once been so stupid to put up with that, and I wanted to be away from them both as quickly as possible.

chapter nineteen 🌸

Everett

The party was in full swing, but Everett couldn't take his eyes off the dark-haired girl across the pool.

Lacey was wearing a bikini and lounging on a chair with her friend Clare. She laughed at something her friend said, leaning over to whisper something, then as if feeling his gaze she looked across the pool. Her smile widened and she raised her hand in a little wave, which he returned.

"What's got you so quiet today?" Trent asked. The blond boy was dripping wet but didn't care, plopping himself down beside his friend.

"Yeah, I'm just thinking about what's coming next when summer's over."

"Yeah," Trent echoed, then followed Everett's gaze. "Brother, if you were anyone other than my best friend, I'd be all over that."

Everett knew his friend was teasing, but that didn't stop a stab of jealousy from tearing through his heart. Trent must have seen it as well because he elbowed Everett hard in the ribs. "Seriously, what's up with you?"

Sighing, Everett tore his gaze from Lacey and stared up at

the sky. Words warred inside him as he tried to figure out what to say. "I'm just nervous."

"About what?"

Everett leaned his head sideways and gave Trent a droll look. Realization dawned on his friend's face. "Ah," was all he said, and they sat in silence for a moment.

"Have you ever been given something you don't deserve?"

The feeling behind the question was far more than he normally revealed, but the guilt was eating him alive. More than anyone else there, Trent knew Everett's story, knew what had happened in his past. If there was anyone he could go to for advice, it was Trent, but right now his normally talkative friend seemed unsure what to say. That only made Everett more uncertain. He cleared his throat. "They say we're punished by our sins, not for them. Maybe it would be better if . . ."

"Goddamn, you're being all emo and shit today. So my dad's thinking of asking you to stay on permanently."

Everett blinked at the sudden topic change. "Huh?"

"We talked about it yesterday and my dad thinks you need full-time work. He's serious about asking you to stay on after summer's done."

"I . . ." Everett didn't know what to say. "I didn't realize that was an option."

"Well, it's not glamorous work, but you've already got two years of a business degree under your belt. Might get you off the work sites quicker than most, and since he likes you, he figures he'd give you an option besides college." He shrugged. "He wants to help you out."

"My family hasn't lived here in a long time."

"Never doubt the good ol' boy system; it can span generations. They used to be good friends way back when, so now it might work out for you. No need to make any decision now, just throwing it out there."

It was as though a huge weight had been lifted from Everett's shoulders. Until that moment, he hadn't quite realized how desperately he wanted to stay in Oyster Cove. This summer, this free and unencumbered summer, was the first taste of true normalcy he'd had in what felt like forever, maybe for the first time ever. His life here, though—the happiness—was fragile, and easily broken. He felt at home here, like maybe he could start his life anew, but he wasn't sure he deserved any of it.

He didn't say anything to Trent, just drank his beer and watched Lacey. The small white bikini showed off her curves, but she was no more risqué than any of the other girls milling around the pool. Even though there were some pretty girls at the party, none of them captured his attention like Lacey. Her friend left and she lay back on the chair, enjoying the sunshine. A couple local boys walked past, craning their necks to admire the view, and Everett's fingertips dug into the concrete beneath him.

A hand cuffed him upside the head, enough to knock him off balance. "Snap out of it. You're young, you've got a kickass girlfriend, and summer's not over yet." Before Everett could answer, Trent plucked the bottle from his hands. "And I'm cutting you off before you get any more annoying," he added, guzzling the last of Everett's beer.

"Hey!"

Trent smirked, and then nudged Everett with his shoulder. "You gonna stay over here like a lovesick asshat, or go talk to the girl before she falls asleep?"

As he asked the question, Lacey stood up and made her way back toward the guesthouse. Everett rose as well. "See you in a bit," he said, snagging his friend's full beer and grinning at Trent's squawk. Lacey disappeared inside and Everett quickened his pace.

Most of the food and drink was just outside the main house beside the barbecue, but they'd left the guesthouse open to hold the extra food. Few people stood around it, most milling about the pool, and Everett moved in quietly, looking around for Lacey. Just as he'd expected, she was over in the small kitchen, pulling items out of the refrigerator. From behind, she looked positively delicious, and Everett felt his cock stir. He snuck up behind her, listening as she hummed the same tune that'd been blaring outside a moment ago, then put his hand on her waist and leaned down to kiss her neck. "Hey, beautiful."

If he'd been looking to surprise her, he obviously hadn't been sneaking well enough. Lacey turned in his arms, grinning up at him. "I was wondering when you'd deign to talk to me," she said, twining her arms around his neck.

He dipped his head for a kiss, running his hands over her backside and the thin material of her swimsuit. "You seemed to be having fun," he murmured against her lips.

Her smile widened. "Jealous?"

"Maybe." He pulled her against him, loving the feel of her silky skin beneath his fingertips. Glancing at the door, he pulled her sideways into a darker corner of the room, mindful of visitors. "Is it terrible if I want you all to myself?"

She gave a contented sigh. "Not at all," she whispered, lifting her lips to his, then stopped when there was a whisper of movement behind them. They both froze, then exchanged looks of surprise when they heard it again. Pulling apart slightly, Everett stepped sideways and peeked around the corner. "*Someone's in there,*" he mouthed to Lacey, who covered her mouth with one hand when there was another bump.

A glance at the dark-haired girl in his arms told Everett that they were thinking the same thing. Creeping sideways, Everett moved around to the closet beside them and wrapped his hand around the doorknob. He waited for another bump, and then jerked it wide open.

Clare gave a small shriek and pushed away from Andrew, in the process hitting her head against the wall. Lacey peeked around the door, and then smothered a laugh as her friend struggled to fix her clothing. "This isn't what you think," she said, then went red as she heard her own words.

"Fancy meeting you at a place like this," Lacey said drolly, grinning when Clare stuck out her tongue. Both of them had their clothes on so whatever they'd been planning hadn't gone too far. Andrew had the same placid expression on his face, but Everett recognized the possessive look the other man gave the blushing girl beside him. He stepped out of the way and let them exit, and heard another smothered giggle from Lacey behind him.

"Everett, this is Andrew, my boss." Lacey's smirk encompassed him as well, but her eyes positively danced when she looked at Clare. "He must be *really* nice."

"I'll see you outside," Clare said to Lacey with as much dignity as she could apparently muster, then walked away, pulling the taller boy behind her. Lacey bit her lip until they stepped outside, and then met Everett's eyes.

They burst out laughing.

"Oh my God, did you see her face?" She giggled uncontrollably.

"They should have been a little more quiet," Everett pointed out, enjoying the smile on Lacey's face and her uninhibited glee.

"Come on, that space is tiny. Anyone would be all elbows in a space like that, it'd be hard not to make noise."

Everett waggled his eyebrows. "Care to make a wager on that?"

The look she gave him sent Everett's pulse racing, but nothing like the small smile that curled her lips. Grabbing the band of his shorts, Lacey pulled him into the closet, and Everett made sure it closed securely behind him.

"You can wipe that silly grin off your face."

Lacey was leaning heavily against Everett, but looked up at him and grinned. "I totally won that wager."

"I suppose so if moaning loud enough to be heard through walls counts."

"But I still won."

She didn't seem embarrassed in the slightest, almost smug instead, which only made Everett's grin widen. He pulled her to the couch and let her sit on the arm, then leaned down and kissed her softly. Her lips were swollen from his kisses, and she looked thoroughly pleased with herself. A dark red spot stood out on her collarbone, Everett's handiwork. It awakened something fierce inside of him to see his mark on her, and he wanted to drag her back inside that closet for an encore performance.

Sighing, and obviously reluctant to leave, Lacey stood back up and went over to the far table. "I need to take this out and head inside to freshen up a bit. Could you check on the drinks?"

"Yes, ma'am!"

She gave him a droll look before sauntering outside. Everett watched her leave, eyes fixed on her swaying hips and backside, then, with a grin, followed her out.

The drinks were on the far side of the pool, right beside Cole and Vance. Cole was leaning up against the wall with a girl under each arm. He leaned his head down to whisper in one girl's ear and she giggled. The other girl, disliking being ignored, slid her hands along Cole's belly and a bit lower, teasing the edge of his already low-slung swim trunks. A smug smile slid across his face and he gave her a kiss, egging her on. "You came just in time," he said as Everett walked over. "The last of the ice just melted. Grab one now if you want it cold."

"Apparently I'm in charge of drinks."

"Then hop to it." Cole leaned forward. "You all done in the guesthouse?"

So much for privacy, Everett thought, shaking his head. "It's all yours, unless someone else is already inside."

"Best get a move on then, the ice is inside the house." Cole stood up straight, pushing the two girls ahead of him, who tittered but seemed as eager as he was.

Heading into the house, Everett made a beeline for the

kitchen. The large icebox below the refrigerator had two more bags of ice, which would hopefully last them through the afternoon. He pulled them out, dropping each a few times against the tile floor to break up the ice, then turned around and stopped in his tracks.

"Hi, Everett."

He stared at his sister, hands fisting around the plastic ice bag. "I said you weren't welcome here," he growled.

"I invited her."

Everett swung a stunned look over to Lacey, standing off to the side. She stepped toward him uncertainly. "I'd like for you to hear her out," she said haltingly, her eyes not leaving Everett's. "Please."

"You don't know what happened between us."

"No, I don't, and I've never asked. But Everett, I'm asking you to just hear her out. I don't know her at all, but I think she's being sincere."

"That's just it, you *don't* know her." If it had been anyone other than Lacey, he would have gone off about them meddling with his life. As it was, he was barely managing to restrain himself. Just looking at his sister brought up all the old anger, all the old fear. "She's a good manipulator," he ground out, not caring whether his sister heard. "Whatever she's told you is probably a lie."

To his consternation, Lacey shook her head. "I don't think this is a manipulation," she said, laying her hand on his arm. "Please, Everett, just talk to her."

It pissed him off more than anything that Lacey had been taken in by Skye, but those pleading eyes softened something inside his heart. He wanted to talk to his sister like he wanted a hole in the head, but . . . "I'll give her one minute," he muttered, "but nothing more. Then I want her gone." Lacey looked ready to argue, but he cut her off. "Please. There's a reason I cut her out of my life."

Lacey laid a hand on Everett's cheek, and he automatically leaned into her touch, needing the comfort. She reached up and kissed his stiff lips, and he saw the understanding in her eyes. "I'll be outside," she said, kissing his cheek before stepping away and disappearing outside, closing the door behind her.

Silence fell, neither of them wanting to speak first. Everett stared sideways out the window, emotions warring inside him. He needed her gone, away from their family's house as soon as possible. *The happiness, it never lasts, does it?* "Say what you need and leave, Skye," he gritted out.

"Everett, look at me."

"Just tell me what you want and—" he roared, but the words turned to ashes in his throat when he finally looked at her. At first, he couldn't quite comprehend the sight before him: the pale dome atop his sister's head, the dark hair dangling limply from her fingers. He blinked several times, unable to figure out her angle this time. "What the *fuck?*"

"I didn't want to tell you like this, but now I see that there's no other way." Even from their distance apart, he could see the way her jaw trembled as she said, "It's terminal."

"I don't believe you."

Even as the words came out of his mouth, Everett could tell they lacked any conviction, but Skye's eyes still widened. "You think I shaved my head and lost thirty pounds to lie to you?" she said in a breathy voice.

Uncertainty nagged at Everett, but he shook his head, not wanting to listen. "You were always skinny," he said, swallowing back his doubts. "And if you thought it would get you what you wanted, I wouldn't put it past you to—"

"I'm *dying*, Everett!" Skye's cry echoed around the large open space, off the wood and tile floors, and through Everett's head. "I've already been through four rounds of chemo, but it wasn't enough. I didn't go to the doctor when I started feeling sick, and it was already so advanced."

"If you're sick," Everett challenged, "why didn't anyone tell me? Why wouldn't Mom and Dad say anything?"

"Because I asked them not to say anything to you." She swallowed. "I couldn't bear your rejection at the same time as treatment, having you tell me you'll be happy I'm gone . . ."

A lump formed in Everett's throat as Skye broke down in tears, leaning against the large dining table. His head was a muddied mess of emotions, but when he looked at the frail girl in front of him, he couldn't feel anything but a deep sadness. Once upon a time, each of them had been the only family the other had. Time and bad decisions had warped them, and apparently Everett wasn't the only one trying to move past that.

"There's got to be more they can do," Everett said, and his heart squeezed at the stunned surprise in Skye's gaze. "Other treatments, anything."

"There are, but I may have put off going in for too long." She looked away, her knuckles going white where she held the table. "I thought I deserved to be miserable, to be sick, but I never imagined it would be this bad." She turned bright eyes up to look at Everett. "You're not the only one who suffered when Emily died."

The sound of her name made Everett tense. "She didn't die," he bit out, "she was killed, as surely as if someone had put a gun to her head." He drew in a shuddering breath, emotions draining away into some black hole. The emptiness was so much easier to cling to, allowing him the chance to breathe. "Emily Hunt's death was my fault, and I'll have to live with it the rest of my life."

"No . . ."

"Go home, Skye," he said, interrupting her. The truth was clear as day to Everett, as if someone had removed a veil from his mind. "Despite everything, I don't think I can ever hate you." He met her eyes, and for a moment all he could see was the bossy little girl who, when they were growing up, had followed him everywhere. "You're my sister, and you're dying. I wish there was a way to take this pain away, to go back to the way we were, but I can't."

She took a step toward him, but Everett held out a hand. He could feel himself shutting down emotionally; this was too much to take all at once. "Go home, and maybe . . ." He couldn't bring himself to say the words. "Just go."

Skye must have been expecting this because her expression didn't change, but Everett felt misery emanating off her. They stared at each other for a long moment, and then Skye sighed and looked away. "It took death for both of us to change." Skye's throat worked as she swallowed. "I wonder if that means anything."

Everett didn't know what to say to that, but right then the

door opened beside them, breaking the somber mood. Skye fumbled with her wig as Trent poked his head inside. "Hey, where's the ice?" He spied Skye almost immediately and cringed, then looked from her to Everett. "Everything all right?"

"Yeah," Everett said, his voice deep with emotion. Looking at Skye now, he saw how very frail she looked, as if wasting away. She'd always been skinny, but this was so much more, far beyond anything healthy. "Keep me updated this time," he said, unable to find it in himself to give more support than that. His chest felt empty, this latest news having squeezed out all remaining emotion.

Skye picked up her purse from the table and quietly moved to the front door. Before she could open the door, however, Lacey walked back inside, looking worriedly between the two siblings. "Everything okay?"

Skye nodded, giving the other girl a wan smile that didn't reach past her lips. "Thank you for your help," she said softly, then slipped past into the summer heat.

Lacey turned to Everett, but he looked away. The two bags of ice were still at his feet, water pooling across the tile floor. He picked them up and headed out the side door toward the pool, but Lacey moved in his way.

"Everett."

He stopped and laid a quick kiss on her cheek before continuing past her and outside. He needed a beer, and badly, but that wasn't the real problem. The conversation with Skye had stirred up old memories, brought back emotions and insecurities he'd been trying to overcome. Looking at Lacey, realizing just how good he had things right then . . . it didn't seem fair. He didn't deserve any of this, didn't deserve to be happy or free or alive. None of these things he could tell Lacey, the girl who hated lies, and was right in the center of one that would strike home.

There was no way she'd ever forgive him if she knew.

chapter twenty ❧

"Who's Emily Hunt?"

I'd hesitated in asking anything for as long as I could, but I needed answers. Trent had been sitting quietly next to Vance and Cole, nursing his beer and looking out over the crowd. At my question, however, he choked, coughing hard. "Where did you hear that name?" he wheezed, his eyes watering.

"Everett was having an argument with someone and the name came up." I didn't mention that I'd been listening near the door when I heard it. Not that I didn't respect Everett's privacy, but I wanted to make sure he made amends with his sister while he still had time. Otherwise, I knew he'd regret it for the rest of his life.

Trent's eyes traveled across the pool and I followed his gaze to see Everett sitting alone, a beer bottle dangling limply from his fingers. He was staring off into space, the same thing he'd been doing for the last half hour, as if deep in thought. I'd let him have his space, even as curiosity burned bright inside me. I understood his pain, at least in part, but I needed answers and Trent was the only one I figured knew him well enough.

"He, ah, hasn't told you about Emily?"

His response was worrisome, but I tried not to let it get to me. I shook my head and Trent fidgeted nervously, looking between Everett and me. "Come on," I pushed, more curious now because of his reluctance, "who is she? An old girlfriend?"

Trent ran his hand through his hair, looking back over at Everett. He seemed desperate to get the other boy's attention, but Everett was too lost in his own thoughts to notice. "I, uh, stay here for a second."

I blew out a breath, impatient, as Trent pushed off and headed around the pool. At almost the same time, Clare plopped down beside me. "Fun party," she said, looking over at me. "What's got you so serious suddenly?"

"Can I borrow your phone?"

She shrugged a shoulder and fished it out of her pocket, handing it to me. I kept an eye on both Trent and Everett as I opened up the Web browser and inserted the unknown girl's name. On a hunch, I added Everett's name and pressed Search just as Trent reached Everett's side.

I knew something was wrong when Everett's head snapped in my direction but I tried to ignore him as the results loaded. The very first article to come up stopped me in my tracks:

NEW YORK TEEN COMMITS SUICIDE
OVER CYBERBULLYING

Oh, my God.

"Lacey, you're white as a sheet. Is everything okay?"

I ignored Clare and scrolled through the rest of the articles, then clicked on one from CNN. Skimming the article, I backed up and clicked another, then another. My body trembled and I clutched the expensive phone too hard. I felt like I was ready to either explode or break down, but when Everett reached for me I swatted him away furiously.

"Lacey, please let me explain."

I tuned Everett out, poring over the next article. Naked pictures on the Internet; thrown out of her boarding school; finally committing suicide to escape the pain and unwanted notoriety; her former boyfriend, Everett Ward, being investigated for releasing the pictures; classmates reporting that Ward circulated the photos around school. The image of a young girl with dark hair and trendy glasses, smiling into the camera. I zoomed in on that happy picture, and then turned the phone on a stricken Everett. "Who is she?"

Everett flinched at the picture, pain cutting creases at the corners of his eyes, and it was as though my heart had been ripped out of my chest. An aching black hole remained, sucking away all my emotions, leaving me an empty shell. I turned dull eyes on Everett. "Who is she?" I repeated in a dead voice.

"Lacey . . ."

"WHO IS SHE?"

My shout brought all eyes on me and Everett, but I didn't care anymore. Everett wasn't looking at anyone else, either. His eyes begged me for something, but he still wouldn't answer my question. Rage filled me and I thrust the phone in his face, almost hitting his nose. "Did your pictures kill this girl?"

He recoiled at my words, falling back onto a nearby chair. I was relentless, however, following after him. "Did they?"

The anguish and guilt on his face confirmed my worst fears, but his one whispered word fell like a hammer. "Yes."

"Oh God," I mumbled, feeling everything crumble away inside. I staggered to my feet and pushed my way out, not caring as my bare feet hit the gravel area beside the house. Small rocks bit painfully into my feet but I barely noticed, wanting nothing more than to get away from it all.

A hand closed around my arm and I lashed out, my fist cracking hard on Everett's jawline. "Don't you fucking touch me," I screeched, pulling free and racing toward the front door. There were a few people milling about inside, but I didn't care. I was after one thing only, snatching up my purse and storming back outside.

"I swear, it's not what you think."

His words were like salt in an open wound. I had so many words to say but nothing would come out except sobs, so I kept my mouth shut and ran toward my truck. Everett followed after me, begging me to listen, but I covered my ears, blocking him out. Each breath I took hurt and I wondered if I was having an asthma attack. My heart was breaking into little pieces, shattering more with each step, and I wasn't sure how I'd survive it.

"God, Lacey, don't go. Don't leave like this, please."

"What was I to you? Redemption? A summertime amusement?" The words poured out of me, unable to be restrained any longer. "Did you think that 'saving' me would somehow fix what you did to Emily?"

He fisted his hands in his hair. "It's not like that," he said, his eyes wild. "I love you!"

I laughed in his face, startling him. There was a tinge of

hysteria to the sound, and I forced myself to stop. "That's all this was, wasn't it? Some desperate attempt to redeem yourself? And I was perfect, wasn't I? Another girl damaged by the same damned thing."

"Lacey, listen to me! I didn't even know what happened to you until I was already in love with you." Everett grabbed my shoulders, pushing me back against my truck. "I did everything I could to fix what I did to Emily, but I couldn't take any of it back. I even tried to plead guilty in the lawsuit, but my family wouldn't let . . ."

"Lawsuit?" I struggled in his grip, but he held me fast.

"Please, Lacey, don't . . ."

I kneed him right in the balls, putting every ounce of power I had into the leg lift. His whole body tensed and a small sound escaped his lips as he tried to contain the pain, to no avail.

"You don't deserve any forgiveness," I spat, pushing him sideways onto the ground. Seeing him in pain like this should have given me some comfort, but it just fed the aching disappointment burning inside me. "Have your lawyers get you out of that," I snapped, yanking open the Bronco's door and climbing inside. Fishing the keys out of my purse, I jammed them into the ignition and twisted hard, and the old Ford engine roared to life. Not caring whether I ran over Everett, I stuck the truck into reverse and veered sideways, past the line of cars in the driveway and over the immaculate landscape. The tall truck bounced over the curbs, across the small road parallel to the water, then onto the highway.

A smaller car, moving at speed, veered away as I tore onto the two-lane road, but I just swerved around it. I knew I was driving recklessly but couldn't bring myself to care. My truck rattled and shook at the excess speeds as I flew past the other cars, weaving in and out of traffic. Tears blurred my vision, making it all the more dangerous, but my foot was like a lead weight on that pedal. All I could think about was escaping, leaving the hellhole of a coastal town in my rearview forever.

My brain could do nothing but scream, too overwhelmed by emotion to think rationally. Clarity was impossible, except to realize I had no clarity and that me being behind the wheel was a bad idea right then. Plus, when I finally looked at my gas gauge, I was dangerously close to empty. I finally slowed down to a reasonable speed and then pulled off at the nearest gas station. There weren't many cars in the small station so finding a pump was easy. I turned off the truck and just sat there, the silence almost too much. Leaning forward, I laid my forehead against the steering wheel and finally let the tears fall.

God help me, I wanted to go back. Even knowing what he'd done, ruining a girl's life like that, I still wanted to turn around and run back into Everett's arms. My shoulders shook and I covered my mouth to keep the loud sobs from escaping. I was in public—anyone could see me—but it was too late for me to stop now.

He's just like Macon, doesn't care about anyone or anything other than himself.

Except that wasn't true and I knew it. That only made it harder for me, trying to wrap my mind around the Everett I knew and the boy whose actions had silenced another girl forever. He'd admitted to doing these things, to driving a girl to suicide, and even though I sensed his desperation to atone was genuine, I couldn't forgive him. And yet, I still needed him so very badly, wanted him to hold me and tell me it was going to be all right, and that knowledge tore me apart.

"Hey, sugar, you're not looking so hot."

The familiar voice startled me, and I looked out my window to see Cherise peering up at me. The bartender cocked her head to the side as I furiously dashed at my tears, and then motioned for me to get out. I paused for a moment, then slowly opened my door and slid to the ground. My cheeks were wet and I brushed them with the back of my hand.

Arms unexpectedly folded around me. "You look like you need a hug."

I stood frozen for a moment, not sure what to do, but when she started stroking my head a flood of emotions broke loose. My father had done the same thing with me growing up, and the memories and my current situation hit me hard. I clung to the other woman, hiccupping my sobs, feeling out of place doing this at the gas station but unable to help myself.

"Aw, sweetie, I'm so sorry."

"You already know what happened?" Somehow, that wouldn't have surprised me, but Cherise shook her head.

"Not a clue, but it doesn't matter. You can tell me or don't, I've no use for gossip."

I shook my head. "I'm leaving this town. I can't go on like this."

"Like what?"

"With everyone judging me over a mistake I don't even re-member, thinking I'm nothing but trailer trash."

"Darlin', you do know I've lived in trailers, too, right?"

I winced at her words, feeling my cheeks heat up with embarrassment. "I didn't mean . . ."

"I know that, I'm just saying where you live doesn't make you who you are." Her mouth twisted down as she surveyed me. "Boy, somebody's worked you over good, haven't they?"

A fresh round of tears welled up. "I just need to get out of here."

"I can understand that. But where will you go?"

"Anywhere has to be better than this."

"That may be, baby, but do you know how much money you have? Do you have clothes, any toiletries you might need?" When I couldn't answer her, she sighed. "You might not believe it, but I've been in your shoes. Looking back, I wish I'd had someone reach out and give me a little help."

"You don't need to help me . . ."

"Of course I don't, but I'd like to do what I can. Question is, would you accept it?"

I gave a wet sniffle and looked up at her. "What are you offering?"

"You want out of whatever it is you're in right now. Well, maybe you're not much for trailers, but I've got somewhere you can stay for free as long as you'd like. It would give you someplace to sleep, a chance to get ready for leaving, and enough time to quit your job proper."

My denial stuck in my throat as the sense to her plan started trickling past the desperate parts of my brain. I was ready to leave this instant, but that didn't mean that was the best option. Helplessness shot through me as I suddenly thought of Davy. If nothing else, I needed to make sure my brother was out of harm's way before leaving Oyster Cove forever. I still didn't know how to help him, but I couldn't leave him behind.

"Come on and fill up on gas while you think about it."

I complied, and by the time my tank was full again I'd made my decision. "Just for tonight," I said, and Cherise nodded, looking serious.

"Stay as long as you need to, but just remember to say good-bye to me whenever you do head out."

I followed her Chevy north away from the water, not quite sure what I was getting into. She turned off the main roads, eventually ending up on a small dirt road that led out toward the middle of nowhere. The homes around us were all rural, but everyone we saw waved as we went past.

Cherise's house, when we finally arrived, was set back in a long driveway and nearly invisible from the road. I had no idea how far her land extended but the surrounding trees hid the neighbors' homes. I parked next to her truck, getting out and following after her.

"I've got two options for you: you can have the couch in the house, or the entire single-wide trailer I've got out back. I can promise that both are free of bugs and have electricity, plumbing, and air-conditioning. Let me show you the trailer first."

Having lived in a mobile home park with my family for a few years, I'd learned how to spot a nice trailer. The one Cherise showed me was obviously old, but the interior was well maintained. "I had this brought out here for my mother to live with me," she said as I looked around the living room. "She decided to go back to her previous situation, so this is mostly empty. There're sheets and towels in the hall closet. Refrigerator doesn't have much in the way of food, but I think there's some instant grits and oatmeal in the pantry. Microwave works, and you're free to use whatever you need. What do you think?"

I looked around the small trailer, laid out much like my grandmother's but different in so many ways. My grandmother had never been much for decorations; her walls were empty of everything except the cheap laminate siding. This place by contrast had something on every wall and open table surface. It was cluttered but homey in a way I hadn't seen in so long, the kind of place that one walked into and immediately felt comfortable.

A slow, reluctant smile spread over my face. "I like it."

"Good, because I was afraid you'd want to see the inside the house. Believe me, the bed here is more comfortable than that ratty couch I have."

"It'll just be for tonight," I said, feeling as though I was imposing, but Cherise waved away my protests.

"Baby, stay as long as you need. I could rent you the place for cheap, too, if you're interested."

I stared at her, stunned by the offer. "I . . . How much?" I stammered, looking around the place again.

"We'd figure something out, I'm sure. But don't worry about that right now. It looks like you've done enough worrying for one day, honey. Now, make yourself at home. I've got some chili cooking; you're welcome to a bowl or two."

"Thank you." The words didn't seem like enough. "Thank you so much."

Cherise grinned. "No worries, girl. Like I said, I just wish somebody'd done the same for me."

When she left, I took a seat on the couch, leaning over

until I was laying my head on the arm. Light still streamed through the threadbare curtains, giving the trailer a faint glow. The furniture was outdated and mismatched, probably all thrift-store finds. Unlike my grandmother's trailer, this one had an abundance of, well, *everything*, but looked comfortable and lived-in. It was a better home than anything I'd been in for a while, although nowhere near as grand as Everett's family home.

Everett.

I swallowed the sudden lump in my throat as his anguished face flashed through my mind. I replayed our conversation in my head, trying desperately to find something redeemable in the exchange. He hadn't tried to defend himself, hadn't denied any of it, and I'd seen the defeat in his eyes almost from the beginning. It killed me how much I wanted to forgive him, but I couldn't. I just . . . couldn't.

Dragging myself through the trailer on unsteady legs, I moved to the bedroom and climbed into the bed. Pulling the covers over my head, I pressed my face into the pillows and cried and cried.

chapter twenty-one

S issy!"

I had been looking at gardening tools, but my head snapped around at the familiar child's voice. Abandoning my cart, I looked wildly around. "Davy?"

A small body rushed around the corner of potted plants and then slammed into me full speed. "I knew it was you!"

Oh my God. It felt so good to hold my little brother. Tears pricked my eyes as I knelt down and wrapped him in my arms.

"Mama said you had to go," he babbled, still hugging me tight, "and Granny is mad at you. I'm not supposed to ask where you went, why not?"

I pressed my lips together and just hugged him tight. I would have sworn he'd grown since I'd last seen him; his arms and legs certainly looked longer. I'd been watching him grow up his whole life, taking care of him myself for much of it, and that I missed anything at all made my heart hurt. "Where's Mama, Davy?"

"She's working. I'm here with Gramma."

I scanned the aisles, looking for my grandmother, but she

was nowhere in sight. "You shouldn't have run off from her," I said, smoothing back the hair from his face.

His face fell. "But I wanted to see you."

Pulling him into a hug, I tried to think about what to do. My grandmother was here, so whatever I did would still make the entire situation my fault. "Baby, you can't just . . ." I cut off, running my finger over his brow. There was a red bruise there, and as I pushed him away I noticed a purple mark on his neck. "What happened?" I said sharply. "Did someone hit you?"

Almost immediately, he shut down. "Nothing," he mumbled, looking down at the floor.

I bit my lip. "Honey, if someone's hurting you, you need to tell me."

He grew suddenly shy, twisting around uncertainly. "Gramma said . . ."

"Davy!"

The screeching cry echoed from somewhere inside the store. I recognized the voice immediately, and instinctively pulled my brother into my arms, rising to my feet. He laid his head on my shoulder, arms wrapping around my neck. A second after the shout, my grandmother rounded the corner, followed by a security guard, and zeroed in on me and my brother. Even from this distance, I saw the anger on her face as she recognized me, and she ran down the aisle. "Davy!"

I took a step back, but there was nowhere for me to go. I turned wide eyes to a nearby clerk who was watching us curiously, and then my grandmother was there, trying to pull my brother from my arms. "Give him to me."

"Sissy, no!"

His cry made me hold harder, and I twisted him away from my grandmother. "Let go of him," I cried, lashing out with my arm and pushing my grandmother a few steps back.

"I want to stay with you," Davy said in my ear, loud enough for everyone to hear. "Please, Sissy."

The older woman's face twisted in anger and she marched toward us, hands outstretched. "Why you little . . ."

"What's going on here?"

The security guard following my grandmother had finally caught up, and he stared at both of us in equal turn. My grandmother stopped her charge but leveled a finger in my direction. "She's trying to kidnap my grandson!"

"No, I'm not!" I stared at her, openmouthed in shock, and then turned to the security guard. "I'm his sister, he followed me over here."

Diana threw herself at me, only to be blocked by the guard. "Give him to me," she hissed.

I just hugged him close, too shocked to move, as the guard looked back at me. "Is she his legal guardian?" he asked, pointing toward my grandmother.

I had no answer to that. Right then, my grandmother darted forward and snagged Davy's arm, ripping him from my grasp. "You little shit," she snarled, setting him on his feet. I thought she was talking about me until her hand cracked across Davy's cheek. I lunged forward, intent only on ripping her face off, but was stopped by the security guard.

"I'm afraid I have to ask you both to leave now," the

security guard said, and even though his eyes looked troubled he didn't seem willing to step in.

"Come on," my grandmother said, dragging Davy away, her long nails digging into the tender skin of my brother's arm.

"Sissy," he called, eyes wide with fear and confusion, and I let out a sobbing breath. The guard remained in my way, as if knowing I'd try to go after him, but I was helplessly rooted to the spot. Davy kept calling after me even after he'd disappeared around the corner leading to the parking lot, but I heard his pleas in my mind long after his voice was gone. All I wanted to do was curl up and cry. I hated feeling this powerless; there was nothing I could do to save my brother.

"Ma'am?"

I looked up to see the security guard watching me. He pulled a card out of his pocket. "This is my contact information. If you need anything to help that boy, I'll do all I can."

"And my name's Alfie," the thin clerk behind the register said. "Alfie Ray. I saw it all and think you should have decked that old lady."

The imagery made a corner of my mouth tip up briefly, but it felt wrong to find any humor in the situation. I took the card and thanked both men, then hurried out toward my truck. A few others had seen the debacle, and I felt their eyes as I walked outside. I didn't care at all what they said, however; I'd done absolutely nothing to be ashamed of, and none of them had offered to help.

I pulled myself up into the Bronco and just sat there, staring out over the other cars. There was no sign of my grandmother and baby brother, but I wasn't expecting to see them anyway. I wanted to beat on something, preferably my grandmother, but that would be useless. I had no real way of helping my brother, especially since my mother seemed to have convinced so many people that I was the one abusing my little brother. There was nothing I could do.

Unless . . .

Pulling out my phone, I quickly keyed in the Oregon phone number I still remembered, but it took me a long moment before I pressed the Send key. It only rang twice before someone answered. "Hello? Who's this?"

The almost belligerent tone of voice stopped me in my tracks. I couldn't breathe, but I also couldn't hang up. Stuck at an impasse, I struggled to get the words out, even just a greeting. Unfortunately, the person at the other end didn't seem to have any trouble with her words.

"I know this number, you called here before. Are you going to hang up again like last time? If you ever had any decency, why can't you come out of hiding and fucking talk to us face-to-face?"

My aunt's familiar voice was darker than I'd ever heard before. All the air whooshed out of my lungs as if I'd been kicked in the chest, but she wasn't finished. "You stole everything we had left of my brother, and I will *not* let you ruin our lives again."

My jaw trembled as despair threatened to overwhelm me. "A-Aunt Jeanine?"

The tirade stopped instantly, and there was a stunned pause on the phone. "Who is this?"

Some of the belligerence was gone from her voice, but I couldn't stop shaking. "L-L-Lacey," I stammered, wanting only to curl up into a ball and cry.

"Lacey? Oh shit, honey, I thought you were your mother!"

The trembling through my body wouldn't stop, and a tear spilled over one cheek. "Can I please talk . . ." *To Grandma Jean?* I couldn't even finish the simple sentence, too overwhelmed by pain. It would be so easy to hang up, try to forget the words that made my heart ache, but I couldn't. My brother needed them, and that thought was the only thing that kept me on the line.

"God, Lacey, I'm so sorry, I . . ."

There was a shuffle on the phone and the murmur of voices as I struggled to pull myself together. Her apology soothed something deep inside me, but I was still a ball of nerves. Thankfully, nobody was around to see me. I was a hair away from becoming a total wreck, and I wouldn't be able to be coherent with strangers.

"Lacey? Oh honey, is that really you?"

I really did almost lose it then. Clutching the phone hard, I gulped back my tears. "Hi, Grandma."

"Oh my God, it *is* you." More muffled voices, then my grandmother's tinny voice away from the phone: *"You can apologize in a minute.* Oh . . . Oh, honey!"

I could tell from her voice she was just as overwhelmed as I was. She sounded more frail than I remembered, but I knew that voice well. I could almost see the big smile lighting her wrinkled face, and a tiny flame of hope lit in my heart. "Hi, Grandma," I managed, and the happy laugh I heard across the phone made me bite my lip.

"Oh baby, how are you? How is everything? We've missed you so much."

"Really, we have," my aunt's voice came over the line. "Ignore what I said before, I was just angry, and *so* not at you. Your cousins are going to be over the moon when they hear from you!"

My face crumpled, happiness bringing out a fresh set of tears. I covered my mouth, unable to speak for a moment. "I'm good," I said finally, biting my lip to keep it from trembling. "How about you?"

"I'm still alive and kicking, but tell me about you. Oh baby, it's so good to finally hear from you!"

I started crying again, this time out of regret over my own stupidity. For nearly five years, I'd listened to my grandmother telling me over and over that I was unwanted. She had planted the idea in my head that my Oregon family wanted nothing to do with me, that I wasn't really their family because I wasn't blood. Never mind that I'd known them from the time I was two, that I didn't remember a life without them. She drilled it into me that my stepdad was my only connection to them, and with him gone, I was nothing to them.

In that moment, I hated my grandmother Diana with every fiber of my being.

My grandma Jean babbled in my ear, but I barely understood the words, just took pleasure in hearing her familiar, beloved voice. Apparently my aunt and cousins were all there and wanted to talk to me, too, but I had to get out what I needed.

"Grandma, I think I need your help with Davy."

She listened intently as I haltingly told her what I'd discovered, my fears and uncertainties. It felt wonderful to have someone else to confide in, and while this was the most mature conversation I'd had with my grandma Jean, she didn't treat me like a child. The fact that she believed me and took me seriously surprised me, although it really shouldn't have. For so long I'd lived around people who belittled or scoffed at my opinions and observations—I hadn't realized until then how much it had beaten me down.

My aunt got on the phone at one point to listen in, then my grandma spoke. "We'll set this right, Lacey," she said, that old familiar note of steel in her voice. "Keep us updated if you find anything else, but I'll figure out what to do if I have to come down there myself."

Relief flowed through me, and I sagged in the truck seat. "Let me know if you need anything," I said, letting my head fall back over the bench seat.

"Now, your aunt and your cousins want to talk to you, but don't sign off without saying good-bye to me."

An hour later, I finally got off the phone with my family. My eyes were puffy but dry, and I couldn't help but think I'd finally done something right. The conversation with my grandmother and aunt had been long but, I hoped, worthwhile. I'd told them everything I knew, even gave them the contact info from the security guard and Davy's teacher, and they'd said they would take care of everything.

I prayed that was the case.

I had a family again, people who cared about me. I'd always had them, and it killed me to think about how much time I'd lost buying into my grandmother's lies. They'd even asked me if I wanted to move home with them, and I couldn't deny the offer was tempting.

It puzzled me why I didn't take them up on the offer then and there, but that was something to contemplate another day. I was alternately thrilled and beat by the whole ordeal, and starting my truck, I left the lot and headed home.

chapter twenty-two ❧

It was almost dark when I finally arrived back at Cherise's property. The bartender's truck was there, but I didn't see any lights on inside. I needed to change clothes before I went and knocked on any doors, so I headed toward the pale yellow trailer that was my new home.

"Gotcha."

I'd barely got the beginnings of a scream out when a thick hand clamped over my mouth. Arms dragged me backward into the darkness as I struggled to free myself, pulse racing. The hand over my face covered both my mouth and nose, whether by design or accident, making breathing difficult.

"I've been wondering where you got off to," Macon murmured, laughing as I tried to butt his head with mine. "You can fight all you want, but you're coming with me."

Maneuvering my head around, I bit down around flesh and heard him howl. He hit me in the temple with the heels of his hand before I could get any sound out, and then continued dragging me back.

"You got away last time, but there's nobody to help you out tonight." He kissed my neck, sending chills up my body. "You need to be taught a lesson, Lacey, and I'm more than up for the challenge."

"That's where you're wrong, asshole."

A shot went off from somewhere nearby, the unexpected clap almost deafening. Macon fumbled his grip on me, and I snatched myself away, landing heavily on my back. In the low light I saw Macon's head dart frantically all around, trying to figure out who was shooting.

Another shot rang out, and there was the pop and hiss of a tire. Macon seemed to forget momentarily that someone was trying to kill him when he saw the damage to his truck. Two more booms sounded, hitting another large tire on his beloved truck and taking out the front lights.

"Who's out there?" he shouted, circling around. "Who the *fuck* is shooting at my truck?!"

I stayed on the ground, figuring it was safer than standing upright. Scooting backward on the red clay, I put distance between myself and Macon, who didn't seem to notice my presence anymore. "Show yourself!" he screamed into the air when nobody answered, sounding more like a child throwing a tantrum than anyone formidable.

"Gladly."

I'd recognized Cherise's voice when first she spoke, but the woman looked somehow different, holding the long shotgun on a suddenly terrified Macon. She had on long pants and boots, as if she'd been out hunting in the wiry forest behind her property. The darkness wrapped around her like a cape, lending shadows to her expression that made it downright sinister. She looked as comfortable with that shotgun in her hands as she would be wearing a hat. Her eyes were fixed on Macon, lip curled ever so slightly in distaste.

"I wasn't . . . She . . ." Macon moaned, and then gave a small, "Oh shit," as Cherise levered the weapon up under his chin. I sat frozen on the ground, as shocked by the sudden turn as Macon.

"Boys like you think you're so sneaky, don't you? Thought you could come onto my property with that big truck and nobody'd notice." Cherise's eyes flickered to me. "He hurt you any, babe?"

I shook my head, scrambling to my feet. "Honest," Macon said in a pleading voice, "I just wanted to talk to her. I wouldn't have hurt her, I swear."

"You know, I once believed the same story from a boy like you. Handsome boy, talked real sweet. He was my first kiss, but decided he wanted to go a little further than I did. " Cherise gave a tight smile, her voice almost conversational. "Want to know what happened to him?"

Macon shook his head, eyes wide, but Cherise didn't seem interested in listening. "Come on, let's go for a walk and I'll show you myself."

"Cherise." The other woman turned to look at me, and I shook my head. I couldn't tell if she was being serious or bluffing, but either way I wanted him gone. "Let him go."

She squinted at me, frowning. "You sure?"

I shrugged. "No, but you've already scared the piss out of him." I gestured toward his crotch. "Literally."

Macon hunched over as a smile spread over Cherise's face. "Well, look at that!"

"I'm going to bring the law down on your heads so hard,"

Macon promised, his voice high and shrill. "You'll rot in prison, I swear to you."

"You realize you're trespassing on someone else's property in rural Mississippi, don't you?" She cocked the shotgun again, and then looked at me. "What did you say his name was again?"

"Macon Gautier."

Her mouth twisted. "Meh. Never liked that name." She swung the gun down a little until it pointed toward the ground. It went off, spraying the clay at Macon's feet, and he squealed.

I had to admit, it was a satisfying sound.

"If I ever find you on this property again, you'll disappear. I know places to dump a body where you'll *never* be found. If I hear that one hair on this girl's head's been touched, you'll be the first person I'll come after. Now, you got five seconds before I start aiming a little higher. One."

Macon turned toward his truck, but stopped short when a spray of shotgun pellets peppered the expensive grille in front of him. Steam immediately rose out from around the hood. "Nope, that stays here as evidence. Two."

He bolted down the driveway, meandering in a zigzag pattern. Cherise made a small approving sound. "He's done this before." Reaching behind her, she pulled another gun from her back waistband and called out, "Four!" Before I could say anything, she got off three shots.

"Don't!" I cried as I heard Macon howl. He continued to run, albeit with an unsteady gait, back toward the main road.

Cherise held the weapon up to me. "Air gun, just shoots salt pellets. Doesn't do too much damage at that distance, but they hurt like hell." She rolled her eyes at my incredulous look. "Hey, if I can't use real bullets, at least this way I still get to shoot the bastard."

I watched Macon disappear, and a slow smile stretched across my lips. "Think you can teach me how to use that?" I asked, and Cherise laughed.

"Find me sometime tomorrow, and I'll teach you. Now, let's go inside and have some of that gumbo I've got cooking."

"Has anyone told you that you're just a bit crazy?"

"Heh, all the time, but you're the first today."

It was a Tuesday when my mother showed up at the trailer.

I was helping Cherise do some weeding around her vegetable garden, so I didn't hear the car pull up the long gravel driveway. It felt good to be helpful, seeing as how Cherise had been so good to me, but it also relieved some of the boredom. Living this far out in the country was often a lonely affair, so I appreciated her company.

Even now, nearly two weeks after I'd left the mansion, to think about Everett made my heart hurt. The worst part was that he never once tried to contact me, never texted or called. Maybe I could have held on to my anger if he'd been trying to force his way back into my life, but the silence told me so much more.

I missed him something terrible, but I couldn't go back, not with what I knew.

"Lacey?"

The familiar voice startled me, and I turned around to see my mother standing behind me. Her hands were clasped in front of her, and I saw the way she twisted her fingers nervously, playing with the old wedding ring still on her hand. I was speechless with surprise, unable to think of what to say to her.

"Can I help you?" Cherise asked when nobody said anything.

That seemed to startle my mother out of her silence. She stepped forward, extending her hand. "I'm Gretchen St. James, Lacey's mother."

"Ah."

The simple word spoke volumes, and Cherise slanted a look over to me. I still wasn't sure how to react myself, but stood up and took my gloves off. My mother was watching me, and I could see the nervousness in her eyes. She looked unsure about my reception, clearly expecting me to lash out, and that gave me a profound sense of sadness. Whatever she'd been the last four years, I still remembered the happy woman who had raised me, even if those memories seemed further and further away.

"Can I talk to my mom alone?" I asked, looking down at Cherise, who nodded.

"Let me take these veggies inside and I'll meet you there, sound good?" She hefted the basket of cucumbers, green beans, and tomatoes. "Holler if you need me."

I watched her walk toward the main house, then looked back at my mother. Now that we were alone, the silence was more awkward. I had no idea what to say to her, no clue how to start a conversation. Too much had happened since the last time we'd had a heart-to-heart, and I wasn't even sure why she was here.

Gretchen took a shaky breath before speaking. "Your brother's gone to Oregon. His aunt picked him up yesterday."

"What?" A million questions danced through my head. "When did that happen? Why did you give him up?"

"Because I . . ." She looked away, clearing her throat. "Because he deserves more than this. And I'm moving out of your grandmother's trailer."

"Did she kick you out, too?" I said, surprised at the bitterness in my words.

She gave a humorless laugh. "As a matter of fact, yes."

I stared at her in shock as she continued. "Your grandma Jean managed to get my number, I guess from you. She told me about what happened with Davy in the store, said she could get signed witness accounts from both the clerk and the security guard, as well as Davy's teacher at school. It didn't matter though; my mother had already told me about it, hadn't bothered to deny anything at all about what happened.

"Grandma Jean gave me an ultimatum: either I send him to live over there for a time, or they'd sic Child Services on me." She closed her eyes. "I hate myself for how easy that choice was for me."

"And Grandma didn't like your choice," I said in a soft voice. I saw the strain on my mother's face—the decision hadn't been an easy one. But a part of me hated her for waiting so long to grow a backbone.

"I didn't tell her until after Davy was gone." She wrapped her arms around her body as if suddenly chilled. "Your aunt Jeanine was the one who took Davy, and the looks she gave me . . . We used to be close, she and I, but when your stepfather died, everything changed."

"Father," I corrected her. "He was my father."

She stared at me, and then slowly nodded. "He was, he really was."

"I needed you, Mama." The words were ripped from me, and I saw her flinch. Tears streamed down my face as I continued. "You have no idea how much I needed your help, your support. You threw me to the wolves and watched as they chewed me to pieces every single day without raising a hand to stop it. *Why?*"

She wouldn't look at me, but I could tell from her shaking shoulders that she was crying as well. "I was lost after your father died. I didn't know what to do with myself, let alone a teenager and a baby. Your father . . ." She swallowed. "He pulled me out of my own private hell, gave me a good life and a good family. When he died, I felt like I'd lost everything. I came here believing there was no other option, back into the same situation I'd run from so many years before." When she finally raised her eyes, they were red with tears. "I was selfish, couldn't see past my own pain, and I will live with those consequences every day of my life."

I took a deep, shuddering breath. "What happened when Diana found out?"

"We had a falling out, to put it mildly." She snorted. "Called me a turncoat and a traitor, said I was turning against family by taking her baby away. Caused a big enough fight that the neighbors called the police, but I'd already left by then."

"Where are you staying?"

"At your uncle Jake's place, just for the time being. I'm moving into an apartment in Bay St. Louis the day after tomorrow. Found out today my application was approved for the place. Oh, and speaking of paperwork . . ." She reached around and pulled something from her back pocket, then handed it to me. "These came for you while you were away. They were what I managed to save from your grandmother, at least. She destroyed the rest of your letters."

I took the small stack of mail from her hands, staring at the one on the top. "My GED results," I said hoarsely, suddenly uncertain.

"You going to open it?"

I looked at her, then down at the letter. With shaky hands, I slid my finger under the flap and tore it open, pulling out the letter. Relief coursed through my body as I read the results. "I passed."

"I'm proud of you."

It occurred to me that, in our whole conversation, I'd never once heard her apologize to me. A part of me wanted to hate her, wanted to tell her to leave and never come back into my life. Her apathy the last four years had made my life a living hell; waiting for her to rise to my defense like a good mama bear was an exercise in futility. She'd lost every ounce of my respect, yet looking at her now, I began to understand why she'd done it. She was just too weak to stand up and fight for herself. I wasn't sure if I'd ever forgive her completely, but what I saw now made me only pity her. She'd suffered in the same life I had, albeit in a different way.

When nobody said anything, she cleared her throat. "Anyway, I thought I'd bring by your mail," she said, stepping back.

"Mama?"

Gretchen St. James looked back at me, hope in her eyes. That look made it harder to say what I needed. "Was Diana the only one hurting my baby brother?"

My mother hunched in on herself, face going pale, and I had my answer. A cold spot settled in my soul as I stared down at her, watching as she tried to find the right words to justify herself. The mother of my childhood was a different person; the woman standing before me was pathetic. "Never mind," I said harshly, but she still wouldn't meet my eyes.

"See you around, baby."

I didn't answer, just watched as my mother walked away, a hunched figure moving up the gravel driveway. Only when she'd disappeared did I look down at the letter in my hands. Slowly, a wan smile moved across my lips, and I turned back toward the trailer, moving inside to sit at the small kitchen table. Setting the paper down, I laid my head on the back of the chair and stared up at the ceiling, reminiscing about my life.

Before this summer, I'd been a mess, partly of my own making. Now, I had a place of my own, a kickass job doing something I loved, and a decent paycheck each week. No more having to worry about my grandmother's smothering rules or whether my little brother was getting the love and attention he deserved.

It was more than even that, though. The notion that family was blood had been drilled into me since moving in with my grandmother, and believing that had made my life miserable. Benjamin St. James had raised me from before I could remember, been a real father to me, and to forget that the last four years was an insult. I closed my eyes and could still hear the loud sounds of his machine shop, watching in awe as he created incredible things from a block of metal.

He was my father, and I owed it to his memory to never forget that fact.

Everett's face flashed through my mind again, and I closed my eyes. None of this would have been possible if he hadn't been there for me in my darkest moments. Despite everything I knew, despite all he had done in the past, I missed him fiercely. It felt as though something was missing in my heart. More than once, I'd started to text him about something wonderful, only to have reality come crashing down on me. I wanted so badly to forgive him, to call and ask to get back together, but I couldn't let myself do it.

Pulling my cell phone out of my pocket, I keyed in digits I knew I'd be calling very often, and settled the phone against my ear. "Hi, Grandma Jean? Yeah, I'm doing fine. Can I . . . Can I please talk to Davy?"

chapter twenty-three ❧

"Wow."

"Yeah."

Clare was quiet for a moment and then twisted in her chair to look at me. "She really . . . ?"

"Yup."

We were lounging outside the trailer, staring out at the pine forest that made up most of Cherise's property. I'd just finished telling her about Macon's visit, and Clare couldn't seem to grasp that my landlady had offered to deal permanently with my ex. "And you're sure she wasn't . . ."

"Joking? Didn't sound like that."

"Huh." A smug smile tipped her lips. "Wish I could have seen his face."

"Trust me, it was epic."

Clare gave a sigh and tilted her head toward me. "Now that you've got your GED, any plans on how to use it?"

I shrugged. "I'd like to take a few college classes."

"And Everett?"

I didn't answer, just stared out at the forest. Hearing his name made my heart hurt. There had been no word from him, and I knew he was due to leave for New York soon. I should have been happy to see him go, but the thought of him not being around anymore still made me want to cry.

"I saw him a few days ago at the club, you know."

"You did?" I said quickly, annoyed at the eagerness in my voice. "How'd he look?"

"Unhappy." She eyed me. "You really won't tell me why you two broke up?"

I shook my head but stayed silent. I wasn't sure why I hadn't told her the truth about Everett. Maybe it was because I knew what it was like to have a secret you were trying to get away from.

Then again, my secret hadn't killed a person.

"He was having lunch with his friends at the club," she continued, "and I swear he kept looking at that piano as if hoping you'd magically appear."

"Clare . . ."

"I just don't get it. You two were so *happy*, and between one moment and the next it was over. What did he do to you that made you run like that?"

"He didn't do anything to me." Even now, two weeks later, I still didn't know how many details to share with Clare. She still had a good opinion of Everett, and for whatever reason I didn't want her to feel otherwise. That she might tell others wasn't the issue, but I'd had time to think about it. There had been so much pain in Everett's eyes when he'd spoken about the whole situation; I couldn't get the image out of my head. The defeat I'd seen on his face as I fled, the complete radio silence since our fight, spoke volumes. He didn't think he deserved forgiveness, but the more I thought about it, the more I desperately wanted to give it to him. It killed me to even think that way when a girl was dead because of his actions, but I wanted so badly to forgive him.

"So he hurt someone else? Come on, you've gotta tell me something. Should I hate him?"

The answer to that question should have been easy, but I couldn't speak against him. "He was always good to me," I said firmly, knowing that wasn't really an answer to Clare's question.

Clare made a frustrated groan. "Lacey . . ."

"Excuse me."

We both turned around at the new voice to see Skye standing behind us. "Hey," I said, surprised by her sudden appearance.

She gave a small wave, glancing between Clare and me. "Can we speak alone for a second?" she asked.

"Um, sure." I looked at Clare, who was watching the other girl with some interest. "Would you mind getting us more tea?"

"Not at all." Clare stood, taking the tall glasses off the small table. "Do you want some?" she asked Skye.

"No, thank you."

I eyed the other girl as Clare moved away. She looked even thinner than before, her skin a sickly white, but was still overdressed for my current surroundings. I couldn't imagine walking up the lumpy driveway in those heels, but she'd managed to do it quietly enough to surprise me. "I thought you'd be back in New York by now."

"I was, but I came back for my brother. He's leaving for home today."

I bit my lip and looked away. Her words made my chest squeeze painfully. "So he *is* leaving," I said softly.

"I . . ." Skye paused, then moved forward and sat in Clare's seat. "You're wrong about my brother. So very, very wrong."

I frowned. "How am I wrong?"

She looked away, her brow furrowing, then took a deep breath. "My brother didn't spread those pictures of Emily. I did."

Her words were like a sucker punch to the gut. "What?" I whispered, my mind reeling.

Skye swallowed. "I was young and stupid and . . . No, that's not it, either. My brother was all I had in the world, or at least that's how it felt at the time. I was jealous for his attention but knew none of the other girls held his attention. At least, until Emily came around.

"I thought, when they first got together, he was playing some kind of game—two people couldn't be less alike. He changed, became this alien creature who was totally into this nice girl. It only got deeper, and he spent more time with her than with me.

"I tried to sabotage their relationship, made it sound like he was just using her for laughs. It was pure spite and jealousy on my part, but I didn't care. People told them I was spreading the rumors, though, and that just made my relationship with my brother worse. Then one night, I overheard a conversation he was having with his friend Bryson about pictures he took of them together. Naked pictures."

My fingernails dug into the hard plastic of the chair as she continued, her voice suddenly strained. "All I could think about was breaking them apart and getting my brother back. I'd never do anything to hurt him, but I didn't care about her at all. Bryson asked to see the pictures, but even though Everett said no, it planted the idea in my head. That night, I snuck into my brother's room, took his phone, and sent those pictures to every single contact on his list."

I recoiled and Skye looked away, shame written on her face. "By the time he woke up the next morning, the damage was done. Everyone at the school had the pictures, and in a heartbeat everything changed. We'd always been popular, mainly because we were rich, but after that it was different. Nobody believed him when he said he didn't send the pictures, least of all Emily. She'd been in the school on a scholarship, and when the dean was shown the images he revoked it, citing indecency.

"My brother had always had a reputation as a player, but it was worse after Emily left. Boys thought he was cool and came to him for advice, girls avoided him as much as possible, and Everett, well, he pulled away from everyone and everything. He blamed himself for being careless with his phone and telling his friend about the pictures. He felt like he set the whole thing in motion. Everything happened just before finals, and even though he failed most of them, it didn't stop him from graduating. Less than a month later, we all found out Emily had committed suicide."

I was shaking, my stomach roiling like I was going to be sick, but I had to know everything. "Everett mentioned a lawsuit," I whispered when Skye was silent for a while.

She nodded. "Emily's parents tried to sue Everett for wrongful death, but New York anti-bully laws hadn't gone into effect yet. Everett said he'd be willing to plead guilty, but my parents wouldn't have it. He was shipped off to college while my parents put the lawyers on the case and managed to get it thrown out of court."

"Did you own up to your mistake?" I asked, not caring about the harshness of my words.

"I tried to, but no one believed me. They all thought I was covering for my brother and that it was sweet. Even my parents didn't believe Everett was innocent, and I think that was the last straw."

Your pictures killed that poor girl, didn't they? My words to him echoed through my mind, as did the memory of his stricken expression. "Oh God," I moaned, covering my mouth with one hand. My insides were roiling from panic and regret, and my heart threatened to burst free of my chest. I'd asked Everett all the wrong questions and made a terrible mistake. "Oh my God, I'm going to be sick."

"Hey, what happened?" Clare came running from the house and knelt at my side, glaring at Skye. "What did you say to her?"

"I have to go," I said before Skye could answer, and lurched to my feet. My mind kept replaying my last angry words to Everett, and tears streamed down my face. "You said he's leaving today?"

Skye nodded and that was all I needed. I raced to my Bronco and jumped inside, firing her up as quickly as possible. Clare hurried after me, the sweet teas in her hands sloshing around. "What's going on?" she said.

"I have to go get Everett."

"But I thought you said—"

"I made a mistake. I'll tell you everything later, but I've got to go." I didn't wait for her to step back, jamming it into reverse. Gravel flew as I backed up, then peeled out of the driveway. My hands dug into the steering wheel as I turned onto the narrow road leading toward civilization. Maybe I should have asked Skye for more information, but all I could think about was getting to him before he left forever.

I just prayed it wasn't too late.

chapter twenty-four ❧

Everett

"I really can't change your mind about leaving?"

"No, but I appreciate the fact that you're trying."

Trent's brow was furrowed, his hands stuffed in his pockets. "You going to at least come and visit?"

Everett didn't answer, just continued packing his suitcase, and Trent groaned. "Why can't you just call her?" he muttered for what felt like the millionth time. "Tell her exactly what happened, how it wasn't your fault. She'll listen, she loves you."

"But it *was* my fault."

"No, it *wasn't*." Trent threw his hands in the air. "Goddammit, I let you have your pity party, thinking you'd kick yourself out of it eventually, but now I see what you need is a swift kick in the ass."

The argument was the same one they'd had for weeks now, and Everett didn't bother participating anymore. "You don't have to go," Trent said quietly as Everett zipped up his suitcase. "You have a place here, you have a job here, you have friends . . ." Trent cut himself off. "You're not even listening to me anymore, are you?"

"Hm?"

Trent snorted and shook his head. "You're still an idiot," he said, then clapped a hand on Everett's shoulder. "I'll meet you downstairs."

Everett sat down on the bed after his friend left and stared at the wall. With Lacey gone, everything good in his life had left with her, leaving him drained and broken. Everything reminded him of her, even work. The house wasn't the same—gone were the memories of his childhood; now everything reminded him of Lacey, the new memories made in that one summer.

None of this he could share with Trent, but he had a feeling his friend knew anyway. Everett's eyes shifted to the piece of paper on the edge of the bed. His parents had sent him an e-mail two days ago saying it was once again "safe" for him to come back to New York City. The Hunt family had accepted a deal that would end the "court nonsense," as they put it.

He wondered sometimes if they realized just how selfish they sounded.

There was a commotion downstairs but Everett didn't pay it any mind. Feet pounded on the steps leading upstairs, and Everett barely got the chance to stand when the door burst open and Lacey launched herself into his arms. "You can't go!"

Her momentum sent Everett sailing backward onto the bed, with Lacey's soft body landing on top of him. Shock stiffened his arms for a moment. He could barely believe his senses, then he grabbed her in a hug all his own. "Lacey?"

She let him go and lifted up, straddling his stomach. "What is *wrong* with you?" she hissed, glaring down at him.

The sudden change in attitude confused him. All he wanted was to keep holding her, not have a conversation, but clearly she had something else in mind. "You lied to me!"

Her annoyed tone got his attention, and he stared up at her. "Your sister told me what happened," she continued, swatting his shoulder unexpectedly. "What the hell, Everett?"

In no world was this conversation making any sense to him. "Huh?"

Her answer was a kiss, and words flew out of his mind. He pulled Lacey down against him, hands roving over her body as if to be sure it was really her. She moaned against his mouth, and in one smooth motion he rolled her over on the bed so that she was beneath him.

She broke off the kiss and glared up at him. "We're not done talking."

"We are for now," he murmured, lowering his lips to hers. This time she didn't protest, snaking her arms around his neck as he pushed his hands up inside her shirt.

"I'm, uh, gonna close the door now."

Everett lifted his head to look at Trent, standing in the doorway. Lacey hid her face in Everett's shoulder as Everett chuckled, and then gave a small wave. "Thanks."

Lacey pulled him back down to her and for a long moment there was nothing but her touch, the feel of her soft body beneath him. Everett was hard as a rock, confused still but wanting more. When his hands hit her pants, however, she covered them with one of hers and he stilled.

"Why didn't you tell me the truth?"

Her words and soft expression drained everything out of Everett. He collapsed sideways and Lacey followed, resting her chin on his chest. "Why did you let me believe you'd done those horrible things?" she continued, her eyes tinged with hurt.

He flinched and looked away. "Because I was the one who took those pictures that set everything in motion. Ultimately, it was my fault."

"Horseshit."

"It's the truth, and you know it."

She stared down at him for a moment, then leaned over and kissed him. Everett cupped her face with his hands, wanting to hold her there permanently. She broke away after several delicious moments, tucking her head under his chin. "Why did you let me believe those horrible things about you?" she repeated, and Everett realized she wasn't going to let it go.

"Because . . ." He trailed off, gathering her in his arms, loving the feel of her resting atop him. "If I hadn't taken those pictures, none of it would've happened."

"Well, why did you take the pictures?"

"Because I was young and stupid, and she was so damned beautiful lying there in bed." He stroked Lacey's hair, lost in thought. "I loved her, or at least could have. Those pictures were our first night together, her first time, and . . ." Pain choked Everett's words. "She died thinking I'd betrayed her, and I can't forgive myself for that."

Lacey tightened her arms around him, tilting her head to kiss his neck. "I'm so sorry, Everett," she whispered, her voice thick.

He let out a shaky breath and pulled her close. Holding her like this made his life seem a little better, but the memories were still brutal. "My parents sent word yesterday that they'd reached an agreement with Emily's family for compensation. Nothing will ever be enough to fix this, though, nothing. I have to live with this hanging over my head the rest of my life, and you deserve so much more than that."

"Don't you start telling me what I deserve," Lacey muttered, and Everett hugged her close. "You didn't do it. I know that, and so does everyone who loves you." She rolled over to look up at him. "Did you mean what you said when we fought, that you loved me?"

He stroked her beautiful cheek, the skin soft under his thumb. "With all my heart."

She swallowed hard, biting her lip and staring at him with wide eyes, and then tapped his nose with her fingertip before snuggling down beside him again. "Good."

Good? When she didn't say anything else, Everett's eyebrows rose. "So you're going to leave a guy hanging?" he said, a slow smile creeping across his face.

"What, you said it first. You love me, I totally get it."

Everett chuckled, the action making Lacey bob atop his chest. "I do," he murmured, stroking her arms. "I really do." They lay there for a minute, just cuddling, before she spoke up again.

"Are you still leaving for New York?"

There was reluctance in her voice, as if she was afraid of his answer. "I don't know," he replied, picking up her hand and twining their fingers together. "Trent's dad offered me a full-time job instead of just the summer position, so there's that. I think I have a good reason to stay here anyway, right?"

Lacey relaxed against him, breathing a small sigh of relief

against his neck. "Good, I was worried I'd have to buy a ticket to New York."

Everett laughed at that, then wrapped his arms around her once more. "I love you," he said again, not sure if he could ever say it enough.

"Well, I like you a whole lot, too."

"Tease."

"Drama queen."

He didn't bother to deny the last accusation, stroking her arm contentedly. A thought that had been in the back of his mind since she'd arrived nagged at him, and Everett frowned. "You said Skye told you all this?"

"She found me about an hour ago and told me everything."

His frown deepened. "What's she doing here?"

"I figured she was going to accompany you home." Lacey looked up at him. "Are you going to forgive her?"

Everett tried for the right words but nothing came. "I'm not sure if I should," he said finally, the words making his heart hurt. "There was a time when she was my only family, but now when I look at her all I see is the pain she caused."

Lacey sighed. "If it's any consolation, I don't think she'll forgive herself, either. It'll follow her around for the rest of her life, which may not be much longer because of the cancer." She paused for a moment, and then said in a quieter voice, "She could probably use her big brother."

Everett's chest squeezed painfully. Even now, the thought of losing his sister tugged at his soul. "We talked a little bit before, back at the house," he said slowly. "Things still aren't good between us, but they're better." He stroked Lacey's hair, still finding it hard to believe she was in his arms. "Maybe even better, now." His sister had given him back Lacey; maybe he could try one more time to repair things.

"So, what should we do now?"

Her leg shifted up his, knee pressing softly against his cock. It stirred, along with his libido, and Everett smirked when Lacey rose up to straddle his hips. "Well," he drawled, moving his hands up her sides, "Trent did shut the door for us. He must have thought we'd be getting up to all sorts of naughty things."

"Shall we prove him right?" Lacey said, bending down and pressing a feather-light kiss on Everett's lips. With a growl, he rolled them over until she was beneath him again, still straddling his hips. He rocked himself against her, and grinned when she gave a small sigh.

"God, yes."

epilogue ❧

S o you got the new job?"

"Yes!" Clare beamed at me. "I'll be working alongside Allen, the club's main photographer, at the wedding this weekend."

"Sweet, I'm playing for them, too!"

The towel beneath me kept the hot beach sand off my skin, but the blazing sun made the water look so appetizing. "Where are the guys anyway?" I wondered aloud, scanning the highway and parking area behind us.

"Andrew said they'd be here by now. Where could they have gone?"

"Oh, I'm sure they're on their way," I said, grinning. Clare's boyfriend was like a fish out of water with the rowdy group of construction workers, but they were determined to make a "real" Southern boy out of him. "Oh, hey, I have a favor to ask."

"What's up?"

"Cole is trying to get his band an online presence, and he was wondering if you could take some pictures of them in action at an upcoming rock concert?"

"That wouldn't be a problem. Where's he playing?"

"Actually, they've been chosen as one of the local opening bands for the Blue Jokers. They're going to be playing in Biloxi next month." I shielded my eyes and scanned the nearby parking lot, looking for the familiar signs of my Bronco, which I'd let the boys borrow. *They'd better not put any more scratches on my baby!*

"Is that Wade Jax's band?"

"Sure is. According to Cole, getting Twisted Melody into the concert was a serious coup and could help them break out into mainstream."

When Clare didn't answer me, I looked over to see her staring out at the water, expression inscrutable. "Earth to Clare," I said, waving my hand in her face. "You in there?"

She turned her head sharply toward me as if I'd surprised her, and then a rueful smile crossed her face. "Sorry, got lost in thought for a minute. They're really opening for Jax?"

"I know you've heard of them. I saw his poster in your room that night I brought you home."

"Yeah," she said slowly, "you could say I've been a fan of his for a while."

The dull roar of an old Ford reached my ears, and I grinned. "They're here." Bounding onto my feet, I hurried across the pale sand toward the parked Bronco. Boys scrambled out of every opening, but I only had eyes for one. I knew the minute that Everett saw me because a smile spread over his face, and I hurried my pace. "Took you guys long enough," I said, moving into his arms.

He gave me a light kiss. "Miss me?"

"Hell no." I gave my truck a few pats. "I was worried that you'd damage my baby."

That got a laugh out of him, and beside me even Cole grinned. "If you ever want to dump this loser," the rocker said, sticking his thumb out toward Everett, "I'll take a girl like you any day."

"Sorry," I murmured, twining my arms around Everett's neck, "I'm officially off the market."

"You'd better be," Everett growled against my lips before taking me up into a searing kiss, and I sighed into his mouth. I loved his kisses, the feeling of his body against mine. From the little poke in my belly, I could tell he felt the same way.

"My parents texted me about Skye while we were out."

I squinted up at him, confused. "Your *parents?*"

"They've been calling me more often lately, although a text message is unusual for either of them." He lifted a shoulder. "I usually let it roll over to voice mail, but they've kept me updated on her condition."

I contemplated that for a while. "Maybe you should try talking to them," I said softly. "At least yours are trying."

His arms tightened around me as my thoughts turned melancholy. I hadn't heard a single peep from my mother since she'd visited me, and that hurt more than I'd thought. She had my number and knew my address, it wouldn't take much for her to reach out, but it was radio silence. On the other hand, I was in almost daily contact with my Oregon family and talked with Davy any chance I could.

My aunt Jeanine had suggested I move there and live with her and my brother, but I'd turned her down. It was an offer that, only a couple short months prior, I would have been leaping to take, but things had changed so much for me in a short time. I still rented the trailer from Cherise, and Everett was still in his parents' house. Despite the fact that I spent more nights in that grand mansion than the little trailer, I was enjoying my freedom too much to give it up just yet.

"They wanted to let me know that my sister's trying a new experimental treatment and actually seems to be responding this time. It's too early to know anything for sure, but they're hopeful."

"Have you tried calling her yet?"

He nodded his head but didn't elaborate, and I didn't press any further. I knew if someone asked me to call my grandmother Diana, I'd tell them to fuck off. I tried not to push him on it but was glad he'd made some contact. "Well, summer's been officially over for a few weeks, but it's still hotter than Hades around here," I said, and twined my arm through his. "Should we go enjoy this beach?"

Down on the sand the guys were setting up a volleyball net, and the cooler Andrew and Cole had carried down was already wide open. Several more people were walking down the beach toward them, and something told me this would be a much larger beach party than I'd thought.

"You sure you don't want to head home for a little while?" Everett murmured in my ear. "You know, before we get sand into unmentionable places."

The idea was tempting, but I leaned up and kissed his cheek. "I'll make up for it later," I whispered, then tugged at his hand as we headed down toward our friends.

author's note

In late 2005, I traveled down to the Mississippi Gulf Coast to help with the cleanup after Hurricane Katrina. The devastation was incredible; you see pictures, and hear people describe these scenes as war zones, but the reality is that it's so much worse than that. Yet the strength I witnessed there of residents, many of whom had lived their whole lives down there, humbled me. Instead of complaining or crying about the unfairness of it all, they rolled back their sleeves and started over, cleaning up their streets and helping their neighbors. The character of many people I met down there, defiance in the face of adversity, stuck with me. I fell in love with the area, and although I'm too wimpy to live down there (the humidity, the bugs *shudder*), it'll always hold a special place in my heart.